LEGACY & DESTINY

LEGACY&
DESTINY 9/6/00

Von —
You have a great matter.
I am looking forward to
the project.
Best wishes,
Mik Reidie

J. MICHAEL REIDENBACH

DANA K. DRENKOWSKI

CORINTHIAN
BOOKS

Mt. Pleasant, S. C.

Publishers Cataloging-in-Publication Data
(Provided by Quality Books)

Reidenbach, J. Michael
   Legacy & destiny : a novel / by J. Michael
Reidenbach & Dana K. Drenkowski -- 1st ed.
   p. cm.
   ISBN: 1-929175-06-X

   1. Women presidents — United States — Fiction.
I. Drenkowski, Dana K. II. Title

PS3568.E4785L44 1999   813'.54
                QBI99-893

Corinthian Books
an imprint of
The Côté Literary Group
P. O. Box 1898
Mt. Pleasant, S. C. 29465-1898
(843) 881-0232
http://www.corinthianbooks.com

In Appreciation

In addition to those many friends, colleagues, and family members whose encouragement meant so much to us, we would like to give special thanks to Richard N. Côté, editor-in-chief of Corinthian Books, and to Duncan Greene, Alicia Lutz, Karen Mitura, and Dr. Elizabeth Burnett for their valuable assistance.

1

COMMAND DECISIONS

A BOLT OF LIGHTNING flashed from one storm-swollen thunderhead to another, cracking around the tiny high-powered turboprop. The fuselage shuddered. Elizabeth lurched awake.

The plane suddenly had taken on a life of its own, a wild animal, convulsing as if it sensed mortal danger. It slammed into an air pocket and plummeted so swiftly that the seat beneath Elizabeth dropped, leaving her momentarily suspended in air. Only the strong webbed seat belt prevented her from being smashed against the curved cabin ceiling.

She cinched the belt tighter, low on her hips, and looked into the open cockpit, seeking the form of her husband for reassurance. She could see that his attention was riveted on the instrument panel, but she understood Peter well enough to know that part of his mental energy was focused on her. She wanted to reassure him that she was okay. She started to whistle the song from *The King and I:* "Whenever I feel afraid. . . ."

Drowned out by the noise of the storm and the whine of the engines, the melody might register only subliminally, but she was sure he'd hear her message, be reassured, and turn his full attention to the situation at hand. She took heart, reminding herself that their pilot, Bud, had successfully dodged anti-aircraft missiles over Hanoi. Lightning and air pockets were a lesser challenge, reasoned Elizabeth — lightning doesn't take aim at you.

She watched the degree of concentration both men exerted
as they made decision after decision. She could sense the hair
raised on the back of their necks. A shock of tension ran through
her as jolting and violent as if one of the bolts of electricity had
struck her heart. If Senator Peter Armstrong and Colonel Bud
Hawley were reacting with fear, the situation was serious.

Elizabeth Armstrong was not skittish. The former governor
of New Hampshire was always in full control of herself. A te-
nacious learner throughout her life, the strength and powers
she had mastered by the time she reached forty were considerable. Now closing in on fifty, she was nothing short of formidable. In the face of the unknown danger that now confronted
her, she told herself that the woman who had taken the helm of
New Hampshire as governor could not let herself be daunted
by a little air turbulence.

Unable to deceive herself by downplaying the situation, she
whistled louder. An experienced flyer, she normally rode out
turbulence with little notice. This storm, however, was like nothing she had known. The tight anxiety in her lips turned the
tune shrill. She remembered the endless hours she and Peter
had flown when they had first become involved.

It had been insanely difficult to maintain a relationship while
traveling between New Hampshire, his office in Washington,
and his home state of Texas. During that difficult period, she
did volumes of state business in flight. She could treat the Merlin, or even a scrunched-in economy seat, as if it were her private office. She jokingly referred to their three-pointed travel
plan as the Bermuda Triangle, because so much of their time
vanished into it. In all those flight hours she had never encoun-
tered treacherous turbulence like this.

Seeking an antidote for her fear, she concentrated on the superb abilities of the two men on the flight deck. Despite a grueling schedule, Peter had used their commutes between Washington and Texas to log in enough flight time to stay sharp.
Even an ace like Bud respected his skill. As the plane was cata-
pulted again by a sudden updraft, Bud was damned glad he
had Peter's expert assistance in the second seat.

Peter was known to his constituents as Pistol Pete because
he shot down questions from the press as fast as they could
throw them at him. He had the kind of innate confidence

that took charge in any emergency. His self-possession was backed by skill and the sort of fierce determination that had made the citizens of the Lone Star State proud to send him to Capitol Hill three times. Folks in the state thought he was as tough as a boot — a high compliment indeed in his neck of the woods.

At six feet, four inches, his height alone made him dominate any crowd. His deep blue eyes communicated openness and had an ability to make anyone he focused them on feel like the most important person on earth. Add to that a smile, wit, and humor that rivaled that of John F. Kennedy, and the power brokers were only too happy to use slogans like "the New Hope of Our Nation" to describe him.

As the twin-engined plane rode out a wind shear, Elizabeth reminded herself that Peter always came out on top. Even his marriage to a liberated Yankee like her hadn't detracted significantly from his popularity. That was saying something, since Texans didn't cotton much to anyone from north of the Mason-Dixon Line.

Elizabeth remembered how she had been the perfect target for the Republican opposition seventeen years ago. The disparaging phone calls and word-of-mouth campaigns accusing Peter of immorality started the first time she spent a night at the Double V, Venidero Ventura, his sprawling ranch in the hill country near Fredricksburg, where LBJ had lived.

Although Venidero Ventura means "future luck" in Spanish, her introduction to the local citizens seemed ill-fated. Peter wanted to spend every minute he could with her that weekend. But as a man who believed in commitments, he needed to keep to his scheduled series of campaign stops. Having come to the conclusion that she was an important part of his future, he chose to take Elizabeth with him.

She should have gone shopping in Dallas with the wives and oohed and aahed at one trifle or another at Nieman Marcus. Instead, there she was next to him on his ranch, with a rod in her hands on the banks of a pond stocked with bass. She baited the hook herself without a hint of squeamishness. The guests from the Alamo Preservation Society, accustomed to only men at these events, were not charmed. They liked it even less when Peter stuck to the official schedule instead of lingering with them to tell jokes and swap long rambling stories as he usually did.

This offense was minor compared to her presence in the hunting blind with the macho Confederate Hero's Day Committee and the delegation of men from the various organizations supporting the celebrations held on San Jacinto Day. They just didn't want a woman there. It didn't matter that New Hampshire was a hunting state and she could target a deer as well as the best of them. In fact, it made matters worse. She was damned if she did, damned if she didn't.

"Texas—It's like a whole other country," was a slogan that was ironically true for her then. She was an unwanted stranger in an alien land.

Elizabeth, however, had her own charms. One of them was her dedication to her community, regardless of where she resided. She had never been able to turn her back away from those in need. Once she finished her term as governor and was able to move into Venidero Ventura as Peter's bride, she applied her phenomenal administrative abilities to helping community organizations. The Texas women went from hating her for her brunette, hazel-eyed beauty to valuing her help with their charitable efforts. As the years passed they even shifted the blame from her to their husbands when they caught their spouses admiring her ample curves too directly.

When these men were on board the Merlin, they tended to treat Elizabeth Armstrong as if she were a flight attendant. Although she did not mind playing the role of hostess—as long as Peter performed equivalent services as host—former Governor Elizabeth Chambers chaffed under their condescension.

On one of these flights things went a step too far, and Elizabeth's reaction became a Texas political legend. A blowhard who was disliked by the in-crowd for swindling ranchers snapped his fingers at her. "Bring me a bourbon and branch. And some coffees for my friends."

Elizabeth let his rudeness pass by her without ruffling her feathers. She returned with a tray bearing the coffee cups and his drink and balanced a coffee pot in the other hand. Then he made the mistake of continuing, "You are the cutest stew on this flight."

As he reached out to take his glass, staring at her breasts instead of looking at what he was doing, Elizabeth adroitly turned the coffeepot, pressing the handle into his grasping hand.

"Thank you," she replied with her sweetest smile. "And you are the cutest steward." She put the tray down in his lap and turned sharply on her heel, retreating to the only closed space on the plane: the lavatory.

From there, she heard the other men laughing. They harassed him into serving them the coffee. Reportedly, retired Brigadier General Robert C. Sanford had even pinched his bottom. She never picked up a tray on board the Merlin again.

Elizabeth regretted her thoughts had returned to the plane. The tense scene in the cockpit had not changed during her reverie. On this night, she would have happily served a full ten course dinner, if the cabin would only steady enough to make it possible to get out of her seat safely.

She forced her eyes away from the cockpit, seeking company that wasn't there, surveying the custom-designed cabin's swivel seats. Only one other was occupied. The emptiness left her with an eerie feeling, as if ghosts suddenly had materialized and sat there.

The last of the leather chairs cradled Peter's top aide, William Barton. Despite the pummeling the plane was taking, Will was sound asleep. Regardless of her desperate need for company, Elizabeth would not let herself succumb to the temptation to wake him. She reasoned that it would do no good to alert him to a danger that held them both captive. He deserved the peace of his dreams. He was a tried and true friend who worked feverishly out of personal loyalty to the Armstrongs and devotion to a charmingly idealistic belief that participatory democracy could actually create a better world.

When the plane again pitched and rolled furiously, Elizabeth reached for the airplane telephone. She selected "#1 – place calls," glad that she could skip even the seconds required to run a calling card through it, as she would have had to do on a commercial flight. She punched in the sequence of numbers she desperately hoped would connect her to her daughter.

Amy was begrudgingly staying with a friend in the D.C. area for the weekend, annoyed that she was not going to the ranch, which she loved. Elizabeth was grateful that she had made it standard practice to memorize the number where Amy was visiting. In this relentless turbulence, she could not reach her laptop computer to access her phone data. There were often moments when she needed to reach Amy immediately or lose the chance, and she was accustomed to seizing them. She would not submit herself to the self-torture of how final this particular opportunity might be.

During the seemingly interminable interval while the phone rang on the other end, she prayed that God would one day cause Amy to want to reach her. She had become so distant lately. They needed to be able to talk to each other.

The ringing stopped. The voice of Amy's friend's father answered, "Hello."

"Hi, Jerry," she said, rushing the words out in one hard, quick breath. "I'm sorry to call so late, but I really need to talk with Amy." As he was calling Amy to the phone, Elizabeth steadied herself. She had to sound normal.

Even under ordinary circumstances, her next conversation with Amy was unlikely to go smoothly. Peter usually put aside his duties and fixed a special pancake breakfast for Amy on Saturdays. This week's special father-daughter time had been canceled because of this trip back to the Double V. Amy assumed that it was her mother's idea and resented it.

Elizabeth felt simultaneously guilty and more than justified in her decision to leave Amy at home. She hadn't had a full day with Peter alone, nor a single night without Amy right down the hall in months. Amy had developed an uncanny way of knocking on their door at the most inconvenient moments. Elizabeth needed this weekend. More than that, their marriage demanded it. She hadn't managed more than a few words to Peter recently without Amy or the phone interrupting.

Her attention shifted as Jerry came back on the line. "Just a minute, Elizabeth. The girls are kickin' up such a ruckus that they can't hear me." She heard the soft click as he put the phone on hold.

The plane took the worst jolt yet. Elizabeth felt as if her stomach had been smashed up against her heart. She focussed on calming her breathing, not wanting Amy to hear the small gasps of panic that were threatening to take over.

As the deadly silence of being on hold was broken by another click, Elizabeth gratefully anticipated hearing her daughter's voice.

"Lizzy?" It was Jerry again.

"Yes," she choked.

"Amy says she'll call you back when they finish listenin' to their CD."

These words were a blow to her solar plexus more violent than the slam the turbulence had just caused. "I have to talk to her right now," Elizabeth insisted. Immediately appalled at her loss of control, she apologized. "I'm sorry, Jerry. This is an emergency. But I don't want Amy to know. Get her now."

Stunned by her urgency, Jerry knew not to ask questions. Her last words were spoken calmly and precisely like an order from a commander. He'd never before heard her skip saying "please."

"Right," he acknowledged. He did not pause to hit the hold button this time.

Good, thought Elizabeth, realizing the line was open. She had hated the blank silence on the other end of the line. She was thrilled to hear a explosion of music, even though it was a rebellious act by Amy. Although she could be forced to come to the phone, she was not about to concede to leaving the music.

Her attitude made itself known long before she reached the phone, as she added her voice to the music from Meatloaf's *Bat Out of Hell II.* She belted out the lyrics in acid condemnation of her mother: "'I know that I will never be politically correct/ I don't give a damn about your social etiquette/ As far as I'm concerned/ the world could still be flat."

Elizabeth moved the receiver away from her ear as Amy continued to blast away: "And if the thrill is gone — then it's time to take it back.'" She paused a moment and then with impatience spat out, "Yes?"

Elizabeth swallowed tensely. "Amy, it's me, Mom."

"HEL-L-O-O . . . like, I know tha-a-t. Who e-else would drag me away from my friends and to the phone?" Her whining could drive a saint to homicide.

Christ, thought Elizabeth, *the last thing I want is a fight.* She searched frantically for something that would be safe to say. "I'm sorry," she nearly whispered.

Amy was stopped cold by this softness, having anticipated

a reprimand for her rudeness. "Well, you should be," she snapped back.

Elizabeth, who had written and delivered the most stunning State of the State address in the history of New Hampshire, was at a total loss for words. Finally she faintly uttered, "I love you."

It had been a long time since she had said that, Amy having made it totally clear she didn't want to hear it. In a few more years she would be off to college and gone. *Please, God,* prayed Elizabeth, *let me survive to have the chance to cope with that.*

Elizabeth's heart widened as Amy, caught off guard by some undertow in her mother's voice, responded reflexively, "I love you, too." Then realizing with her mind what she had said from the heart, Amy renewed her declaration of war with a chilling, "I really love the way you screw up my life."

Afraid Amy would hang up on her, Elizabeth talked fast. "Call me anytime. I— "

The sharp click on the other end terminated the exchange.

Elizabeth winced, cradling the handset. One of her friends, who had raised four children, commented that each had gone through a period at a different age of entering a black hole when they were inaccessible and sullen. Amy was clearly in her black hole phase. Knowing that it ought to pass was scant consolation.

Elizabeth felt all the more lonely. She considered calling her parents or Peter's. Political artisan though she was, she was not a good enough actress to contact them without letting on that something was extraordinarily wrong. She reluctantly clicked the phone back in position, aching from the loss of contact.

Will was still sleeping the sleep of the innocent. He was one of a handful of senior staffers on the Hill who could honestly present himself as guiltless of even a petty breach of ethics. This thought prompted Elizabeth to indulge in a moment of theorizing. She had often quoted Lord Acton's dictum, "Power tends to corrupt. Absolute power corrupts absolutely." Dividing up the power, Elizabeth mused, didn't eliminate the corruption: it just fractioned it, weakened it, but distributed it further.

Politics was power, Elizabeth observed to herself. You

couldn't be active politically without getting at least a flirtatious sense of the thrill that power and its sources provided. Peter lusted after power. That was why he loved the thrust of the turbine engines, why he wanted Elizabeth as his wife, and most of all why he was laying the groundwork for a presidential bid.

Elizabeth turned her attention back to Peter. He held one finger pressed to his earpiece to help him hear Air Traffic Control more clearly. She clenched. She knew every inch of his body. The tension it conveyed to her now was a disciplined reaction to danger. Sensing the pheromones released by fear, Elizabeth unexpectedly found herself becoming aroused.

Death suddenly unleashed its aphrodisiac effect, evoking the memory of her first coupling with Peter. A tremor of sexual desire surged through her, momentarily giving her a respite from her fears.

She might have lost most of the feminist support if they knew how willingly and shamelessly she subjugated herself to him for his pleasure. The deeper truth was that he also let himself be completely vanquished by her. They were mutually aroused by power and that included the joy of taking sexual control of each other, each leaving the other helpless with pleasure. Losing power to Elizabeth in bed was the only defeat in life Peter suffered willingly.

The plane lurched again and Elizabeth shuddered. She felt trapped, but knew enough not to leave her seat in such treacherous turbulence. Every nerve in her body was alert. Something about the sound of the engines had changed. Elizabeth could not exactly describe the shift, but her stomach turned over in response. Her instincts knew it meant trouble.

Bud gave a shout as the port engine stalled with a sputtering cough. "Shit! We lost both engines!"

He was not much louder than before, but now her hearing had become ultra sensitive. Looking out the window over the wing, she watched in horror as the prop spun slowly in the air, powerless, then came to a stop, frozen in time.

"Emergency restart checklist," Bud commanded Peter, his words firmly measured.

Peter tabbed immediately to the correct procedures and tore the yellow page out of the manual, holding it closer to the cockpit light and reading with an exacting precision. "Airspeed — less than 180 knots indicated!"

"Check." Bud's voice was tight.

"Fire handle!" Peter directed.

"In."

"Throttle!"

"One inch above flight idle."

"Fuel boost pump!"

"On."

"Fuel enrichment switch!"

"On."

"Propeller governor control switch!"

"On."

"Feather valve and NTS check switch!"

"Set at Valve."

"Engine generator switch!"

"On."

"Engine bleed air valve switch!"

"Open."

Bud made the lethal pronouncement, "No ignition."

Elizabeth shouted across the cabin to her sleeping friend. "Will!" Elizabeth was no longer fighting fear. She couldn't sit there and hide within herself. She knew it was time to prepare to survive.

"Will! William! Barton, wake up!" Her voice had the barking quality of a general leading troops into battle. Once awake, it took Will only moments to understand the situation. Sweat beaded on his forehead.

Bud double-checked the gauges. The readings they gave were impossible. "The tanks register half full. Shit! It looks like a blocked line. Maybe a vapor lock or a rupture."

Peter couldn't believe it either. "Hell, not both engines!"

Bud flicked on the emergency transponder that would automatically send out a radio signal to mark their position. Air traffic controllers would scramble to reroute other planes and clear the air of other flights that might complicate their descent.

Bud gave the order no captain ever wants to have pass his lips. "Send out a Mayday. Give our position."

Peter did as he was told while Bud struggled to keep the plane in a controlled glide.

"Roger," responded Peter. "Mayday, Mayday, Mayday. Merlin three-two-two, twin engine failure. Descending through flight level two-four-zero. Two-three-five degree radial at six-five miles off channel niner-five."

He moved on to the next item on the checklist: cabin preparation. Automatically turning to flash one quick look at his wife and his best friend, he simultaneously ordered them to prepare for an emergency descent.

There was no time for anything else. The look that passed between Peter and Elizabeth in that instant conveyed all the variations of love that had passed between them over the years, along with the pain, battles, and reconciliations.

Peter turned immediately back to the controls, totally confident that Elizabeth knew what to do. She had helped him prepare for the Senate investigations into airline cabin safety. She knew only too well the significance of what he had broadcast.

As Peter's voice echoed in her ears, Elizabeth swiveled her seat into an aft-facing position and locked it firmly into place, calling to Will to do the same. Passengers in aft-facing seats had a better chance of survival.

Her stomach clenched as it responded to her knowledge of the corollary to that: you can't land a plane facing backwards. The cockpit crew was highly vulnerable. She fought the reflexive urge to empty her bowels.

A weaker, less realistic person might have thought it would be good to die with Peter. But Elizabeth just did not think like that. She had to survive — Amy needed her. If Peter didn't make it, Amy'd need her even more.

If it were humanly possible to get this plane on the ground in one piece, Bud and Peter would do it. She surveyed the cabin, looking for any items that had not been stowed and might hit them. A crash landing would multiply things by their G-force. If anything were loose in the cabin, something like a camera case would become an airborne missile with a possible impact of 50 to 100 pounds.

Elizabeth almost wished she knew less than she did at the moment. That was not, however, a choice she would have made in reality. Her knowledge of the grisly details increased her odds of survival.

The return message to the Mayday had been radioed from

the ground. The words were a matter of procedure. No air traffic controller was fool enough to ad lib an exchange that could mean life or death. The next question was meant to let the rescue services know how many people they needed to find after a crash. Without the checklist, someone might word it, "How many bodies on board?"

The prescribed statement was kinder. The tower radioed, "Roger, Merlin three-two-two. Say souls on board and state intentions."

The Merlin was equipped with all the amenities of a major airliner, including the capability of broadcasting the radio transmissions through the passenger entertainment system. Knowing that Elizabeth would want to know everything, but that she should not have on a headset during a crash, Peter flipped the switch putting it on the cabin speakers. He was sure Will, although less versed than Elizabeth about aviation, would not want to duck the reality of the situation either. Not knowing what was going on would only heighten their anxiety.

Peter simultaneously responded again to ground control. "Four souls on board. I cannot restart the engines. Will seek landing immediately. Request vectors to nearest field."

A metallic voice on the radio responded, "Copy four souls on board, Merlin three-two-two. Where do you want to go?"

"Johnson City looks closest. Give us a vector."

"Roger, Merlin three-two-two. Turn right to zero-one-zero degrees. Say altitude."

"Passing flight level two-two-zero at this time."

In the darkened cabin, Will turned to Elizabeth. "Where are we?" he asked plaintively, having lost track of the flight's progress while he was sleeping.

"Somewhere over eastern Tennessee." Elizabeth didn't emphasize what Will would realize if he thought about it. They were still over the Appalachian mountains in a steep unplanned descent in pouring rain and pitch darkness that was only broken by lightning.

Elizabeth watched Will shifting from side to side, rocking himself to quell his anxiety. His hands clenched and unclenched, as if they were readying to grab something — anything.

"Hang tough, Willy. They'll get us down okay." Elizabeth flashed him a reassuring smile and reached across the aisle to pat his hand. Will did what she had anticipated, seizing her hand. She was doubly glad she had offered it, needing something to hold onto herself.

Unseen by them in their aft-facing position, Peter had already opened his chart case to look for a better alternate landing site. "Johnson City is close enough and it has a lighted field," Peter said over the cabin speaker. Peter studied the charts, while Bud kept an eagle eye on the instruments, quickly making adjustments as needed.

Bud switched off the cabin speaker. Facing reality was one thing — extinguishing hope was another. "Peter, we're not going to make Johnson City. There are mountains all around it and our glide path will take us right through them."

"Where, then?"

"I don't know. Keep looking."

Elizabeth felt Will's hand loosen. She studied him for a moment. He didn't notice her as he mentally detached from what was happening. He was still functioning, but only mechanically. She observed his blank stare directed towards the galley bulkhead facing them. She realized that if she didn't get him out of this, he'd be likely to go into a negative panic, freezing in his seat, unable to escape once they were on the ground.

She jiggled his hand. "Hey, Willy-boy, how about this one? 'Things are more like they are now than they have ever been.'"

Will smiled despite himself. Identifying famous political misstatements was a game they often played with Peter on the campaign trail when they needed some good cheer. "Gerald Ford," he responded.

"Good," she exclaimed, in much the same way she had when Amy was only nine and had given the right response during her multiplication drills. She fed him an easy one, "Hawaii has always been a very pivotal role in the Pacific. It is in the Pacific. It is a part of the United States that is an island that is right here."

"Cinch. Dan Quayle."

On the flight deck, Bud appeared at a loss for the first time. He and Peter searched the darkness welling up in front of them for some idea, some hope, some salvation.

In the darkness of the passenger cabin, Elizabeth's heart was pounding as the plane pitched into a steeper descent.

She mentally scanned her list of favorite gaffes in an effort to calm herself. The next one on the list, she didn't say out loud. "This is a great day for France!" had run through her mind. It was not the quotation that was the problem, but the circumstance in which it was delivered. Nixon said it when representing the United States at Charles De Gaulle's funeral. Elizabeth determined that this would not be a night leading to anyone's burial.

She needed to give Will something else to think about and fast. She thought of another quote. Elizabeth pronounced each word with calm authority. "I am in control here. As of now, I am in control here in the White House."

She knew he'd get it. "Alexander Haig."

"When and why?" coaxed Elizabeth, again sounding like an encouraging mother.

"Well, my dear, let me tell you." Will affected a Ronald Reagan-like whisper, only too glad to mentally tune out of their current plight. "When I was shot, little Alex forgot that as Secretary of State, he was fourth in the line of succession and was not the one in control. Dan Quayle was — theoretically." He smiled at his swipe at Quayle.

Then a shout came from the cockpit that required no amplification.

"Lights!" Peter pointed.

"Yes, in a row! It must be a road. Something flat."

"It looks straight," agreed Peter.

"We better go for it."

Peter turned on the cabin speaker again. Bud yanked the plane to the right, then stood by with the gear and flap handles as he began talking to air traffic control. "ATC, this is Merlin three-two-two. We have what looks like a road in sight."

His decisiveness gave them all new hope.

Peter radioed the vectors of their anticipated landing site, then turned off the cabin speaker for the last time. Will and Elizabeth could not hear the tower's last words to them. "Roger, Merlin three-two-two. We're going to lose radar and radio contact as soon as you drop below the mountains. We have your location for rescue assistance. Good luck and God bless."

2

FIRES IN THE NIGHT

As THE MERLIN made its steep descent, it was so black outside that it was impossible to know what was in front of them. Bud wrestled with the controls, trying to line up on the lights. Elizabeth could tell they were now below some mountains. The "road" appeared to be some kind of track through a long valley. *Better than nothing*, she thought.

"Gear, now!" Bud ordered.

"Rog."

"Give me 50 percent flaps," Bud ordered.

"Flaps coming down, 25 percent, 40 percent, 50 percent. . . Now."

"Okay, girl," Bud half whispered, half prayed. "Do your stuff."

The plane's descent slowed along with its speed.

As Peter watched the indicators, Bud saw something coming at them in the dark.

"Oh, shit!! Here we goooo!!"

Something brushed against the wings, softly at first, then ripping like the talons of a predator through the Merlin's fuselage. *Tree tops*, Elizabeth thought.

She felt a hard blow from below the plane which seemed to bounce it back up in the air. Another impact echoed sickeningly through the passenger cabin.

Elizabeth couldn't see anything. She was smart enough and disciplined enough to keep her head down. She bent over at the waist, pressed her face into a folded blanket, and clasped her arms tightly around her legs. She remained braced for the shattering force of the impact that was almost sure to follow.

The wrenching sound of tearing, twisting metal flooded her consciousness. She had no way of knowing that the right wing had just been sheared off by a tree, the separate pieces coming to rest more than the length of a football field away.

The plane rolled hard to the right in response to the upward pressure from the left, jerking Elizabeth out of her bracing position. On the edge of her consciousness, she saw Will's arms and legs flailing around as if he were a rag doll in the mouth of an angry Doberman. She suddenly realized the latch on her seat had let go and that she was spinning into a forward-facing position.

Bud slammed his left foot hard into the rudder, locking his knee, while turning the control yoke as hard as he could to counter the plane's right roll. Within half a second, the plane flipped on its back.

Will screamed, a high pitched wailing of pain and terror. Bud yelled, "Shit!"

A long grinding sound obliterated everything else. What little Elizabeth could see vanished into endless blackness.

The void transformed itself slowly into blurred images. Elizabeth dimly wondered why she had her arms above her head.

It was still dark, but she could see a bit by the light of flickering fires. Where was she? Were those lights fireflies? Campfires? Christmas lights? *I must be dreaming*, she thought, unable to make sense of the changing patterns of light and shadow shifting before her eyes.

She struggled valiantly to keep her eyes open and figure out what was happening to her. She lost the battle, descending into unconsciousness.

An eternity later, her eyes slipped blearily open. Small fires burned again, providing a little light. She saw Peter. He had his arms up in the air up as if he were being held up by a robber.

Thank God! He was alive! She rejoiced inside. He could not hold up his arms like that for so long if he were seriously hurt, she reasoned. Before she could wonder why he had his arms up like that she fell into a deeper darkness.

When she woke again, she heard moans somewhere. It was too dark to see now. Was it Peter? Was he hurt worse than she had thought? If it wasn't him it must be Will or Bud. She remembered Will's body being jerked around by the force of the crash.

She felt dizzy and exhausted, as if she had some fatal illness. She tried to bring her arms down to her sides. One didn't seem to work. She just could not make it move. The effort to do so brought a sudden flash of pain and with it a peculiar clarity. Her body told her the arm was badly damaged — probably broken.

The numbness she had been frozen in vanished, washed away by burning agony. She wanted to fall asleep. But the searing torment that now controlled her body would not let her.

Lights danced on the horizon, growing larger as they seemed to approach her. They stopped and were joined by smaller beams that swept the area.

She saw a man's silhouette in the darkness. Her first thought was that it was Peter. Then she realized it was more likely to be the rescue team. She tried to call to them. She was shocked to hear the pathetic little moan her shout became. She could not form a word.

Peter. They had to find Peter. And Bud. And Will. But most of all Peter. Please God, let him still be alive.

As if in answer to her prayer, one of the sweeping flashlight beams illuminated Peter's face. She breathed a small sigh of relief, then sucked it sharply in as the undeniable truth the visage before her told her. Peter's face was white, sagging, oddly contorted. His eyes were open but vacant. The bright yellow T-shirt he'd changed into on the plane with "World's Best Dad" was now red around the waist, soaked with blood.

This must be a dream, she thought. A very bad dream. He couldn't sit up like that dead. It made no sense. It was as if she were trapped in some hellish theater showing a midnight zombie movie. The undead did things a normal dead body could not. Peter's arms were still over his head. So were hers.

She suddenly realized the plane was upside down. They were still strapped in their seats, inverted. Elizabeth could not stop herself from looking, despite what she knew she was likely to see. The lower half of Peter's body was gone.

Her gagging was louder than her attempted shout had been.

A man's voice shouted, "Hey, I think there's another one alive over there!"

"Jesus Christ! She's alive! Get her down fast!"

Elizabeth was relieved to feel strong hands lifting her from the seat that was dangling from the torn fuselage.

"Be careful. That thing could let go any minute," one of the men cried.

Elizabeth saw a chunk of the dismembered cabin hanging in her face as they lifted her down. The tangle of wires seemed like a mass of writhing snakes threatening her.

They accidentally touched the badly injured arm and she screamed with pain. Her legs were numb — were they still there?

"Get a splint kit and a back board over here now!"

The next thing Elizabeth knew, she was lying on a stretcher on the ground, one blanket over her, and another under her. Despite the insulation they offered, she was freezing. She could not move her head and slowly realized they had put her in a neck brace.

She felt a large needle go into her arm, surprised that it did not seem to hurt. Almost immediately, she started to feel warm and comfortable. She drifted into a daze.

Men in farmer's overalls and khaki uniforms were crouching over another figure. It looked like Bud. One saw her move and came back to her.

She faintly perceived the workers pulling a blanket over an inert form. Will?

"Don't worry, Governor Armstrong." A uniformed man at her side placed his hand tenderly and carefully on her forehead. It was the only place he thought it was safe to touch her, given that they did not know the full extent of her injuries.

He continued gently. "A medical chopper is on the way. We'll get you to the hospital. It'll only be a few minutes."

Her eyes rolled up and closed. His voice grew louder. He was almost shouting, but she could barely hear him. "Stick with us, Governor. Don't lose it now. You're almost outta here. You made it through so far — you can make it through anything."

His voice was so kind and reassuring that she was able to comprehend and find strength in it. The other sounds and images around her were a jumble. She thought she saw men in army combat uniforms. The ground torn open by the belly of the plane was like a battlefield.

Her mind distorted by pain, she fell into troubled dreams. She saw herself on the backboard, lying on the floor in Peter's office. His files had been dumped, the folders strewn around her. A vortex of wind spun the white papers stamped "Top Secret" into a snowstorm.

She heard a flapping noise and was struck by debris scattered by the helicopter. Several uniformed men hovered around her to shield her from the turbulence as the chopper landed.

The rescue team quickly lifted her on board. Just before they strapped her in place, she heard the same kind voice that had told her to hang in there. This time it sounded cool and professional.

"There was no fire — nothing major anyway," he said to someone nearby. "Strangest thing I ever saw."

3

A Holy Alliance

THE DISTINCTIVE SOUND of squealing breaks was followed by the deafening crash of two cars slamming together. Jack Bradshaw counted, "One, two, three — "

BAM! Right on cue, another squeal. Then a third car slammed into the first two.

Simultaneously a dozen hands in surrounding cars reached for cell phones at the same time Jack did. While he hoped nobody was hurt in the accident, this was par for the course for the daily L.A. commute. All you could reasonably do was call it in.

"Shit," he breathed under his breath, realizing that now traffic would be even worse — if that were possible.

On this smoggy November morning he had been trapped in freeway traffic for a solid hour. The drive should have taken twenty minutes. He sniffed the oppressive air. There was nary a hint of California orange blossoms these days. They ought to bottle the smog as "Eau de Los Angeles," he thought.

As he inched along, he wondered why he endured this ever-worsening daily ritual. He fidgeted in the bucket seat of his Pontiac Grand Am, reacting to a familiar, unwanted twinge in his lower back. It was almost 10 A.M., well past the peak commute hour. Was there no escaping this insanity?

He began fiddling with the FM push buttons on the car

radio. Not finding any music he liked, he switched to AM and hit the seek button, listening for something better. He only paid partial attention as he wondered how he was going to make today's deadline. For two cents, he'd quit his job as a *Los Angeles Times* political correspondent, focus on his book on American foreign policy, and maybe take a crack at that novel he'd had in mind for years.

Most of the stations were airing news accounts of yesterday's election. Commentators were trying to explain the Democrats' stunning defeat. Two years earlier the story had been the same. The fact that Jack had favored the losing Democratic candidate, Robert O'Reilly, did not help his mood any. Why couldn't the Democrats produce another Franklin Roosevelt or John Kennedy? The latest humiliating defeat was certainly not due to anything Republicans had done to gain the win. Despite their well-financed campaign, Democrats had earned their loss.

At long last he pulled into his reserved space in the multi-level parking garage and walked the short block to the *Los Angeles Times* building. It was a cold morning, at least by L.A. standards. *It must be in the low 50s*, he thought, adjusting his coat. He had been lucky to find it before heading off to work. He rarely needed it. The only real weather concern in Southern California was how high the pollution index would go.

He remembered how hot it had been just a few weeks before. A fire had swept through the canyons. As he thought of it, he got even more pissed off at the world — and at his profession. Those who lived in the canyons were wealthy Angelenos who could afford to escape the pollution and hazards of life in the city. Yet the loss of expensive homes owned by the privileged got extensive news coverage. That, in turn, generated intense pressure in the legislature to push through a financial relief package for rebuilding in the fire-stricken area.

Jack kicked impatiently at the curb while waiting for the light to change, reflecting on the contrast between the swiftness of relief in that situation and the lack of it in the poor communities. Parts of the neighborhoods burned in the 1992 Rodney King riots remained charred, like open wounds. Even some of the downtown area of Watts burned in the '60's was still scarred, boarded up, and covered in graffiti.

Jack imagined the plight of a manager of a McDonald's or

a Burger King who had been burned out, bankrupting the poor guy forever. *What had anyone in the legislature ever done for the Watts victims?* He asked himself rhetorically, knowing the formula. Rich plus white equaled priority political action. Poor plus black equaled speeches about budget cuts and boot-straps.

He was contemplating this injustice as he headed through the main floor of the newsroom to his office. Although it was not much more than a cubbyhole, Jack appreciated the luxury of his private little space. The open-bay newsroom was often boisterous when editors and staff mustered together, all try-ing to put in their late changes before the day's deadline.

In the far corner of the newsroom across from his office, some of the staff were chomping down on donuts and sandwiches, carrying on their endless debates. *No doubt about it,* Jack chuck-led to himself as he salivated at the sight of a French cruller. *Writers are as oral as hell. That's why we love words so much.*

A couple of reporters were watching a television monitor suspended above their heads. Jack angled in that direction. He was surprised to see former Governor Elizabeth Armstrong being questioned about the disastrous election results for the Democrats the night before. *For a politician, she's an extremely attractive woman,* he thought. He knew she was six years older than he, but she looked younger.

He watched her interview intently. In about twenty-four hours, he would be meeting her in person. The program came from the Democratic Party's campaign headquarters in the Park Plaza Hotel in Boston. The line of questioning being pursued by Sam Kates, the moderator of *Capitol Landscape,* both inter-ested and irritated Jack.

"Governor Armstrong, considering the fact that there are sig-nificantly more Democrats registered in this country than Re-publicans, how do you account for what happened last night?"

"Sam, I fully support our party, but we failed to put forward candidates who reach out to mainstream America."

Kates turned a fraction of an inch to redirect his chiseled pro-file to the camera. "Do you think that explains the number of losses the Democrats have suffered in recent presidential elec-tions?"

She paused and chose her words carefully. "As a party,

we'd be more successful if our presidential candidates were more conservative on some national issues, like spending. Two years ago, Senator O'Reilly was painted by the opposition as a 'big spender' senator from Massachusetts, a 'limousine liberal.' That image just doesn't play well in middle America, where the folks who pay most taxes come from."

"Limousine liberal, my ass," muttered Jack, still rallying around his man.

"You actively supported Senator Platt in the primaries. He was a conservative and a protégé of your late husband, Senator Peter Armstrong. Do you think he could have won?"

"I supported him because he represents a mainstream philosophy that I believe would have carried the election. He's a Democrat with both a social conscience and a clear awareness of how much money is being taken from the taxpayers."

Elizabeth turned squarely into the camera, talking now more to the audience than to Kates. She knew she could only get away with that about once in an interview. Air time on national TV was a precious commodity. She wanted to make this count, to push the issues she felt should be in the forefront next time around.

She spoke straight to the heartland. "Some people in our party still do not understand that money for all these programs does not come straight from the printing press. It comes from taxpayers, who do not deserve the excessive tax burden they are now forced to carry."

She suddenly realized she sounded as if she were running. The thought made her inwardly chuckle. *Make 'em sweat,* she thought, but quickly added, "Senator Platt is a man who knows the sweat Americans put into earning those tax dollars. Platt values them and their labors."

She turned back to Kates with a winsome smile. Jack actually laughed aloud. He knew that smile really said, "I got in my pitch straight to the audience and there is not a damned thing you can do about it."

Jack respected her acumen. Now he was really looking forward to interviewing her. Anyone who could get the camera to pull in on her on Kates' show was a master. Kates was such a prima donna he was probably writing a poison pen letter to his camera crew right now.

As Jack licked the last of the sugar glaze from his fingers, a younger man called out to him. He was a newly hired reporter who delighted in getting under Jack's skin. "Hey, Jack, your boy sure took it in the shorts. I wish I'd taken that bet."

Jack was not amused. "Shut up, Larry," he responded, not bothering to mask his frustration.

As he entered his cluttered work space, he realized that Mike Farnum, his editor, had followed him. "I've got to make some assignments, Jack. What have you got on your platter for the rest of the week?"

"I'm just finishing up the story on the election and have that piece on Bangladesh that we discussed. I'm taking the red-eye out tonight to Boston to interview Elizabeth Armstrong."

"I don't remember assigning you something about Armstrong," Farnum observed.

Jack had been hoping that this fact would escape Farnum's attention. "You didn't. It's for my book on foreign policy. Her husband was a key player in our policies towards Afghanistan."

"Jack, you're our resident expert on the national political scene. I want more coverage on the aftermath of the election."

Hoping he could escape the rest of the lecture, Jack offered a solution. "Let Larry do it. Even a cub could write this one. Shit, Mike, all he needs to do is cut and paste it from the wire services. There's nothing new here."

"If I were you, Jack, I'd be a little more concerned about him stealing your job."

Jack snorted and even Farnum couldn't help smiling. The threat was hollow. They both knew Larry was a lightweight.

Farnum launched into the lecture as if on autopilot. "We both know you want to write books, to do in-depth investigative reporting. The problem is we've got to get a newspaper out every day and we have daily deadlines to meet. You've got to carry your share of the day-to-day stuff."

Jack knew arguing would be a waste of time. The best strategy was to agree and then find a reason to do what he wanted anyway. "I understand that. Have I ever missed a deadline? This interview was not easy to get. I had to set it up weeks in advance."

"Just hustle back here when you're done."

Jack sighed with relief. He realized that this interview with Governor Armstrong was one he wanted more than he had anticipated. That smile of Elizabeth's had definitely reached straight out into the audience—he was not immune.

Twenty-four hours later, Jack's plane descended into Logan International Airport. He washed and shaved as best he could in the cramped lavatory space, but the tiny airplane soap refused to make a lather. The shave turned out uneven and not as close as it could have been. As he combed his hair and examined himself in the mirror, he reassured himself that he wasn't there to win any beauty contests. *Good thing*, he thought.

The plane taxied interminably, finally pulling up to the gate. He stood up stiffly and stretched, trying to shake out the kinks from his wrinkled slacks. He started to pull his folded coat out of the overhead bin, only to find that another passenger had left a flight bag on it for the whole flight. The coat looked worse than the pants.

He found a cab and arrived at the Park Plaza downtown in about thirty-five minutes. He went straight to a courtesy phone and called Elizabeth's room, noting he was a full half hour early. She answered the phone herself and cut off his apologies. "I'll be right down," she informed him.

He walked to the elevator lobby and surveyed the people getting out. He started to head towards a brunette in a tailored business suit when Elizabeth's rich voice sounded behind him. "Mr. Bradshaw?"

Jack turned. The first thing he saw was her smile. She already had her hand extended, with a politician's instinct to press the flesh.

Her handshake was that of a confident professional. Her perfume was nothing like "Eau de L.A.," however. The scent of crushed roses touched with orange blossoms caught Jack off guard.

"Yes," he said awkwardly, looking for something to say other than, "Jeez, you smell good."

"How did you recognize me?" he asked.

She indicated the wall of mirrors across from them. "You look like a reporter."

Jack laughed ruefully and took off his rumpled coat, folding it over one arm. "Excuse my appearance. I just got off the red-eye from the West Coast."

"That's okay. I know you reporters have more important things on your minds than fashion."

He caught her noticing the pens he had clipped in his shirt pocket.

"Audio Visual squad or Physics Club?" she asked.

He squirmed just a bit realizing that she had him pegged. "You don't look like a politician," he countered. He was afraid he sounded a little too personal. However, it was obvious that he was referring to the fact that she was wearing a jogging suit.

"I know," she agreed, "A politician should look like that brunette you were about to follow."

Jack laughed in admission that she was right. Damn, she was observant as hell. More than that, he thought, she'd knocked him off center.

"I was just going to go for a run along the Charles, since I wasn't expecting you for a while. I'm still working on strengthening my legs, but it hurts like hell. I thought you could join me." She looked down at his scuffed shoes. "Don't worry. I don't expect you to run in those. I'll make it a brisk walk instead."

"I'll make you a deal," Jack offered. "Give me a place to change and I'll run with you. As long as we can work in the interview."

"Don't worry. I'm good at doing more than one thing at once. Although you may have to employ your memory instead of your note pad."

She gestured toward the elevators. The elevator ride gave him a moment to study her. Even in jogging shoes, she was taller than he expected, reaching almost to his shoulder. Her shoulder-length brown hair was pulled back into a ponytail like a young girl's. Her face was framed with soft curls shining with strands of grey which she chose not to camouflage.

Neither did she hide the fact that she was also assessing him. A unique intensity emanated from her hazel eyes. They were penetrating, but twinkled a bit, as if entertained by what they saw. Jack wondered if she found him amusing or whether amusement was her reaction to life in general.

She ushered him into her room and indicated the bathroom. As soon as he opened his carry-on bag, he realized his mistake. He had his jogging clothes with him all right — nylon shorts and a mesh shirt. Hardly suitable for Boston in November. Hell, he thought, so he'd get pneumonia. He wasn't going to back down. The informality of the interview would give him a chance to really get to know her.

He emerged from the bathroom and was again disarmed by the frankness of her laughter when she saw how he was dressed.

"Here," she said tossing him an extra-large men's sweatsuit. "You can borrow this."

Noting the arch of his brow and recalling that anything he picked up on might appear in his column, she confessed the truth. "It was my husband's. I sleep in it."

She turned away from him, but not before he saw the flicker of pain in her eyes.

"Thank you," Jack said softly. A politician without guile was not something you see everyday. Then again, she wasn't trying to get elected. Too bad, mused Jack, we could use someone with her skills and charm. He abruptly became businesslike.

"Thank you for agreeing to talk to me about your husband for my book. He was a key figure in U.S. foreign policy."

"Yes, his work left a significant legacy." A chill seemed to have crept into her voice.

"And you see yourself as the steward of that heritage?"

Elizabeth admonished him lightly. "Please, Mr. Bradshaw, why don't you get dressed before you start the interview."

Jack suddenly felt naked and aware that he had not been working out anywhere near as much as he'd promised himself. He silently swore he would skip the fried clams he'd been craving. The hours a reporter spent sitting at a computer had taken their toll. He clutched the jogging suit over his genitals as if she had just ripped away his fig leaf, quickly ducked back into the bathroom, and dressed.

As they walked down Arlington Street heading towards Boston Common, Elizabeth brought the conversation back to the purpose of their meeting.

"Your book sounds like an interesting project. But to be honest, when you called I wasn't sure I wanted you writing about my husband." Her cool tone took him by surprise. "Neither of us — neither I nor Senator Armstrong — appreciated a number of things you wrote about him. You wrote one article regarding American actions in Afghanistan that infuriated him."

She had pushed Jack off balance in a different way this

time. He found himself wanting to defend his positions, something he had stopped doing long ago. "I disagreed with him over the years on domestic and foreign policy issues. To me, he often sounded more like a Republican than a Democrat." He kept his voice neutral, but Elizabeth bridled nonetheless.

He explained, "When I was younger I enjoyed putting burrs under saddles more than I do now. Now I'm more interested in finding the truth."

Knowing that she tended to be overly sensitive about even an implied criticism of Peter, Elizabeth shrugged. "Politics is supposed to give you a thick skin. Guess it didn't work with me."

"I'll tell you what, since you aren't entirely comfortable with this, let's make this discussion off the record. Then we can make a decision later as to whether I can use any of the information."

"Reporters usually have a hard time going off the record."

"Hey," Jack smiled and patted the spot where the pens had been clipped to his shirt. "I don't even have a pen with me."

"Okay," Elizabeth said, sprinting for the park. "If you can keep up with me."

"Fair enough," shouted Jack, pouring it on to catch up with her. He was sure, based on how hard she was running, that Elizabeth Armstrong had never let anyone win against her without a fight. He liked that.

She grimaced against the pain and Jack recalled that her injuries in the accident had been extensive. "What would you like to know?" she asked.

"First, let me recap what I have so that I'll be sure I've got it straight."

"That would be refreshing. A reporter who not only did his homework but cared about accuracy."

Jack ignored her attack on his profession — especially since he agreed with her.

"As I understand it, you were first a state representative from New Hampshire and then became governor at an extraordinarily young age."

"Right. I was put on the ticket for lieutenant governor. They wanted a woman to pull in those demographics."

"And when the governor died unexpectedly, you filled his shoes," Jack added.

Elizabeth nodded. "Both to my surprise and that of New

Hampshire. But the voters seemed to like me, and I was elected on my own. Then I met Peter and married him, moving to Texas. After our daughter, Amy, was born, I decided not to run for any office again. I turned to supporting Peter's career and raising Amy."

"So, you were being the self-sacrificing wife and mother?"

"I was being the political realist. I knew from the day I met him that Peter had a crack at the presidency. A prominent wife from New England could put him over the top."

Jack was clearly getting winded. She took pity on him and slowed to a walk. Once he could breathe, he plunged ahead. "As the senior senator from Texas, Peter became the vice chair of the Intelligence Committee and was also highly influential on the Judiciary Committee. That's heavy duty stuff."

"He was a heavy duty kind of guy." Her continuing love for Peter was evident. "He was proud of his work on the Intelligence Committee. He wanted to make a stronger and more efficient intelligence organization for the United States. At the time of his death he was working on an investigation regarding America's role in the uprising in Afghanistan against the Soviets."

"The focus of my book is the connections between our international policy and drug smuggling."

"I didn't know much about it because a lot of it required a security clearance. We were both scrupulous about that kind of thing. I do know he felt that the committee's work on international drug trafficking and drug interdiction was important to our society."

She stopped walking and turned her face to Jack in much the same way she had directed herself to the camera in the TV interview. "He was also a very compassionate man."

Her accusatory tone triggered his memory. "Now I remember what I wrote. I said something about him being to the right of the principles of the twentieth-century Democratic Party."

"You said, and I quote, 'Senator Armstrong's policies in regard to welfare cuts would have an effect that Hitler would have admired.'"

Jack's mouth felt dry. "I write three columns a week. That one must have run something like at least three years ago. Not an excuse — an explanation for why I didn't remember."

Here he was, walking through the park wearing the senator's jogging suit. It was a wonder she was talking to him at all, he thought. "I'm sorry." The words slipped out. *The first rule of journalism,* Jack reminded himself, *never apologize for what you write.*

There was no mistaking the edge to her voice. "In our opinion, your thinking is to the left of mainstream Democrats today. You're entitled to your opinion, of course, but as a columnist you are shaping perceptions and influencing the philosophy of those who have control of the party. You may well have played a role in forming the perceptions that led to O'Reilly's nomination and consequently to our stunning defeat."

"I'd hate for that to be true. O'Reilly was just what the country needed — even if they didn't know it."

It was her turn to be pushed a bit off balance. There was not a trace of arrogance in his voice.

Jack noted the "in our opinion." Part of him was a bit put off by it; another part found her enduring loyalty endearing.

He tried to smooth things over. "Obviously, we have a difference of opinion. Regardless of that, there was no question that your husband was a leading party nominee for the presidency. Do you think he would have made it?"

"We had a family saying: don't count your chickens before the hen's been laid. Nothing is certain in politics. Despite which, I haven't a single doubt about it — he would have won. If," she continued haltingly, "he had lived."

She walked over to a drinking fountain and slowly sipped the water. Jack knew she was trying to regain her composure.

When she turned back to him, she was perfectly composed. "The power vacuum was filled once again by the liberal wing of the Democratic party, which makes a habit of putting up losing candidates for presidential office."

He was surprised by how forcefully she expressed herself. Since her return to public life after Peter's death, she had become a powerhouse, working for presidential commissions, often in close liaison with the United Nations. The Secretary General himself joked that he had often wished he could do more by having himself cloned, and that his wish had come true when Elizabeth Armstrong appeared on the scene. He conceded that she was a new and improved model of himself.

"Let's shift gears. Why did you get involved in international affairs after you recovered from the plane crash that killed your husband?"

The strain in her face evidenced pain. She took a sharp breath.

He cursed his mistake. "I'm not going to ask you about the details of the accident. It must be very painful to recall."

"It was a terrible tragedy. For a moment I was considering what might have been. The accident affected both my family and the direction of politics in this country, and yes, it changed my focus."

Jack knew he could win her cooperation by hooking into her pride over Peter's work. "I understand what you mean. From what I've been able to put together about the connection between Afghanistan and drug smuggling, if he had been able to complete his work, thousands of tons of drugs would have been kept off the street."

"Yes. And drugs not only cost dollars for law enforcement and medical care, they destroy our people too. The Afghanistan connection was an important part of the investigation. Peter was constantly studying documents and making notes." Elizabeth thought for a moment, as if making a decision. "I just received some of those documents."

Jack approached this carefully, deciding it was best to hint at what he wanted and let Elizabeth take the lead. "I've tracked the rumors that flourished then about the investigation reaching into intelligence agencies. But so far I don't have anything but speculation."

"Proving that there was drug trafficking and then stopping the smugglers would have been a major accomplishment. It may not be too late. If it could be done, it would be a tribute to Peter. I don't have the time to make the kind of systematic review of the details it would take to piece things together."

"I happen to know an investigative reporter that would be extremely thorough and efficient. And he comes cheap." Jack hoped his pitch wasn't too obvious.

Elizabeth let his comment drop with an apparent thud. He couldn't guess what she was thinking. She went on as if he had not said anything. "I have a meeting on the Hill tomorrow afternoon to review how our flood relief plan for Bangladesh is working. The representatives from South Africa checking on the political prisoner situation come in two days later. If I'm going to be up to speed, I'll have my hands full reviewing background material. After that. . . ."

As she rattled off one trouble spot after another from around the globe, Jack was impressed anew by the level of her participation internationally, despite her refusal to fly. She rivaled Jimmy Carter in working as diplomat without portfolio. Clearly Elizabeth was not just a goody-two-shoes bandage roller. The aftermath of the crash had left her with a terror of flying, but her diplomatic skills were so great that the mountain was quite happy to come to Mohammed.

The Republican President Taylor had invited her to Camp David to negotiate the delicate trade agreement between Turkey and India. Her skill was so great, foreign nations began to request her as the American representative. However Taylor felt about her politically, he was pleased to have her assistance. She always made him come out looking good.

Jack realized he had lost the thread of the conversation. After a moment, Elizabeth picked up the ball she had intentionally dropped. "Let me review Peter's papers to see if there are any security implications. If there aren't, I'll let you review them on condition that you clear that portion of your book through me." She silenced Jack by lifting her hand as he started to reply. "I know that's never done. But it's the only way you'll get the information."

Jack extended his hand to shake hers. "You drive a hard bargain. But it's a good one. Deal."

"Mr. Bradshaw, my guess is that this matter is of greater consequence than a chapter in a book. I consider myself a good judge of character, and you seem to have integrity. I'm relying on that."

"I've never revealed a source or broken a confidentiality agreement."

"I know. I checked on you before deciding to give you an appointment. It turns out you have interviewed a number of my colleagues. I'm here because I felt you could make the most of the information I found."

"You can rely on me."

"I will." Her words carried significant gravity. "You and I disagree on the method of getting there, but we share the ideal of creating things the way they ought to be. Before the accident, Peter was becoming suspicious, even of people he knew, based on something he didn't tell me about. I hope the information is in the documents."

"What kind of documents are they?"

"Sorry, but you'll have to see for yourself. The National Security boys went through everything while I was still in the hospital. They left only the things which weren't secret and it wasn't that much. You know, they always have a tendency to err on the side of too much rather than too little secrecy."

Jack gave her a sheepish grin. "I guess it was a bit naive to think that you had the Pentagon Papers in your possession."

"Or that I'd admit it if I did," Elizabeth acknowledged with a matching smile. "But then the Pentagon Papers did surface. The papers I have show dates, events, and topics of committee hearings. I don't know myself what they add up to. If I did, frankly, I wouldn't need you."

"It sounds like we've reached an alliance."

"Remember Thomas Jefferson's take on foreign relations, Jack — 'peace, commerce, and honest friendship with all nations, entangling alliances with none.' Let's just say for now we have a working agreement."

"When can we meet again?"

"I commute between Boston and Washington — my daughter attends Millbrook Academy here. Washington would be a better place to meet. Tell you what: Since you're from L.A., we'll do this Hollywood style. I'll have my people call your people."

4

LEGACY

SNOW SWIRLED AROUND Jack's plane as it touched down at Dulles International Airport three weeks later. He surveyed the pattern of snow mounds and drifts that snowplows had left at regular intervals along the taxiway.

When Jack gave his driver directions to the Marriott in Crystal City, he noted with surprise the man's articulation and his identity card on the back of the seat indicated that he was a native-born American. He actually spoke English.

Jack casually remarked, "Crummy weather, huh?"

The Virginia countryside appeared more developed every time Jack came to Washington. Fast food restaurants and strip malls dotted the rolling hills.

The cab pulled up in the driveway of the Marriott, slaloming between the snow drifts. Jack paid his fare, then stepped out into the bitter wind. It cut through his clothes, reminding him that the rains and mud slides at home weren't such a bad alternative.

As soon as he checked in, he called his number at *The Times*, expecting to reach his answering machine. He was surprised when Larry picked up. "Moving right in, are you?" asked Jack.

"Mike said I could use your office while you're gone," Larry happily informed him.

"Enjoy it while you've got it, cause you're not gonna have

it for long." Jack paused to let this sink in. "What did you find on that material I asked you to check?"

"Not much. It reconfirmed what you had. One thing was kind of curious though. If anybody'd know everything about Afghanistan, it was the senator. He and the last administration worked hand-in-hand on that. He was intimately involved in that administration's clandestine efforts that became the catalyst for the turning point in the war. I can't imagine what the senator could have been investigating that he didn't already know about. Why don't you ask Governor Armstrong for some of the details about that?"

"Okay, sure." Jack bridled at Larry telling him what to do. He'd been asking questions long enough to know how to do it.

Larry could hardly keep the glee out of his voice. "Farnum wants to talk to you too."

"Oh, shit. Tell him I've got to leave, will ya? Can you get rid of him somehow?"

"That would be a little hard to do, Jack. He's standing here listening on the speaker phone."

Jack forced a measure of good cheer into his voice. "Hi, Mike. What can I do for you?"

"Yeah, right, Jack. I know how glad you are to hear from me. Hope you're having fun at the paper's expense. What are you doing for me while you're there?"

"I'm going to keep up your profile. When the hottest political book since *All the President's Men* hits the best-seller list, you'll be cashing in on having me on your editorial page."

"All right, but you might try to interview the California Congresspeople while you're there. If you plan to keep working for a California newspaper, that is."

Early the next morning, as Jack left the hotel, the day was cold but clear. Without the wind, he felt much more comfortable. It reminded him of the winters he'd spent in Colorado as a kid, and the warm pancakes and hot chocolate his mother had waiting for him when he came in from sledding down the iced-over slope in front of his house. In a nostalgic glow, he walked to the corner to flag down a cab and gave the cabbie the address of the American Red Cross.

The cabbie's response sounded like Turkish. "What did you say?" he asked the driver.

"Oh, I am begging your pardon, sir. I am still working on English."

Jack repeated the address again slowly and deliberately.

"Oh, yes, effendi. Right away!" the driver replied, with a flash of ivory teeth rimmed with gold.

Jack noted several statues of military leaders on horseback on the route. He started to explain to the driver that if the leader had died in battle, the horse was rearing with two legs off the ground. Then he decided it would be too hard to communicate.

Once at the large Red Cross building, Jack navigated the narrow corridors looking for Elizabeth's office. He had made a point of getting a decent shave. His haircut wasn't too old, and he'd even sent out his clothes for valet service so they wouldn't be wrinkled. Prior to stepping into the slush in front of the building, his shoes had glowed. Only the supply of pens in his pocket gave him away as a reporter.

Outside the entrance to her suite, he paused a minute to gather his thoughts. He had looked forward to seeing her again, but he hadn't expected to feel quite so unnerved, as if he were a cub again. A secretary directed him toward the right door.

When Elizabeth opened it, he immediately caught the faint warm fragrance of orange and roses. After the cold, gray day outside, it was like inhaling the first summer morning when he was ten and free of school for a while.

He tried not to stare. The form-fitting dress she wore was a far cry from the baggy sweats she had on for their run. She had great legs.

"Nice to see you, Governor Armstrong."

"Elizabeth," she offered. "It's been seventeen years since I was governor. I wish the title hadn't become glued to me."

As if testing himself with the name, he said, "Elizabeth, the weather's a bit different than when we met in Boston."

"Everybody says that this winter Washington is colder than a witch's you-know-what."

"I always thought they were referring to its lack of soul, not its weather," Jack said.

"At times like this, it's both."

"Thanks for taking the time to see me again so soon. I know the refugees in the Balkans have been taking a lot of your time."

"It's a horrific situation and, as usual, it's the children who suffer the most. Slobotkin isn't ready to talk seriously about them yet, but he may come to the U.S. next week." She looked at Jack with narrowed eyes. "You look like you're still freezing. Why don't we get you a cup of coffee."

"Thanks." Jack thought it interesting that Elizabeth could carry off using the royal "we" without sounding pretentious.

As she escorted him down the hall, signalling "no calls" to her secretary, he launched into business. "I found the senator's work on the Intelligence Committee intriguing. I understand the United States worked hard to get weapons to the Afghan resistance movement."

"It was one of the brighter examples of bipartisanship on the Hill. A strongly Democratic congress worked closely with a Republican president."

She showed him into the employees' lunch room, tossed some quarters from her pocket into the collection cup and poured Jack a steaming hot cup of coffee. After he added two sugars and a shot of fresh milk, they settled in at a relatively private table near a large window.

"Hope you don't mind the setting," she said. "I don't like to talk about sensitive issues in my office."

"Oh?"

She shrugged. "Just mild paranoia, I guess."

Jack wrapped his hands around the warm mug. "I haven't figured out why that out-of-the-way country got so much attention, have you?" When she didn't answer, he continued. "Senate Intelligence Committee, high-powered generals—"

"I don't know what you're getting at. Peter worked like hell to forge a coalition and come up with policies that supported the freedom fighters."

"Freedom fighters? NIRM? The National Islamic Resistance Movement never had freedom on their agenda—at least not the kind of freedom we care about." Her silence indicated agreement. "Why did Peter travel there at the height of the conflict?"

"Peter and several others went on a fact-finding mission that was ostensibly to Pakistan. Later, it became common knowledge that they went into Afghanistan, where they met directly with several of the resistance leaders."

He raised an eyebrow. Politicians didn't usually risk their hides. "Some people would call that foolhardy."

"It was a calculated risk that took real bravery. If the KGB found out where they were, they would have spared nothing to capture or kill an American Senator to create embarrassment for the United States."

"But he didn't have the blessing or the protection of the administration. He did it on his own."

She drew back, coloring slightly. "What are you implying?"

"Nothing, I'm just curious. Aren't you?"

"Yes." That short syllable held a conflict of emotions. So she, too, thought things weren't exactly what they seemed. But did she trust him yet? Would she tell him everything she knew? He took a swig of the coffee and wrinkled his face in distaste.

Elizabeth laughed. "I'm sorry, Jack, the Red Cross isn't noted for its cappuccino."

She continued to fill him in as he took smaller sips. "Peter brought back hard evidence of the atrocious conditions in Afghanistan under Soviet rule. They documented the use of poison gases and evidence of torture and mass murder."

"I remember the Soviet's use of explosive toys that maimed children."

"Peter's personal testimony on issues like that won over the right people on Capitol Hill. It created a public clamoring for aid to the Afghans. Peter was then able to sell the idea of funding additional supplies to NIRM, setting up supply routes and medical facilities, and advocating the shipment of far more sophisticated weapons. That weaponry turned the tide of the war."

Elizabeth qualified what she had said. "I don't want to sound as if Peter gets sole credit for what happened. Many others were involved. What was special about Peter was that he helped the people solve some of their key problems through diplomacy. He worked closely with General Frank Shotwell."

"The head of the National Security Council? I interviewed him. He was the man most active there in assisting the Afghan resistance groups."

"Exactly. Frank ran operations from Pakistan. His work there put his career on the fast track. Captain Don Larkin was his chief aide. He's now a lieutenant colonel working as one of General Shotwell's closest advisors in the National Security Council. Frank and Don are both good friends of mine. They gave me a great deal of help after Peter's death. They even made sure that our pilot, Bud Hawley, was taken care of after the crash. I was in no condition then to do much."

Jack followed her unconscious gaze down to her legs. He was so struck by their shapeliness before, that from a distance he hadn't noticed the scarring that was clearly visible through her opaque stockings. It was undoubtedly why she had not chosen to wear sheer ones.

She caught his glance and blushed slightly. Jack jumped back to the subject. "How did Shotwell come to work in Pakistan for the resistance groups, if he was in the U.S. Army at the time?"

"It was one of those deals the military has with the intelligence agencies during clandestine operations. I don't know if he reported to the CIA or the army or what. All I know is that he was there."

Elizabeth abruptly slipped her fingers into her upswept hair and let it down. She absently played with the hair elastic as she continued. Jack watched her, fascinated.

"Frank assisted the guerilla groups. One of the big problems he and Peter worked on was the diversity of groups and the lack of logistical support they had. They made sure the medical aid arrived at some remote guerilla hospital instead of on the black market in Islamabad and saw that the Stinger ground-to-air missiles and TOW anti-tank missiles went to men trained in their use instead of to some local warlord who wanted them as status symbols."

As Elizabeth matter-of-factly pulled her hair back up and fastened it, Jack found himself absorbed by how that motion shifted her body and exposed the curve of her neck. He decided he'd better focus more before he totally lost track of what they were discussing.

"I thought I had a pretty good start on the research," he said. "But you're way ahead of me. I want to demonstrate how the expense and the drain on morale led to the collapse of the Soviet Empire. How long did the Senator and General Shotwell work together?"

"Three years. Peter and Frank were in constant communication. I'd have to check the documents at my apartment for the exact dates. I know Peter would have turned them into a book. I'm hoping you'll do what he would have done."

"I'm eager to go through your material."

Elizabeth smiled. "No time like the present."

5

THE PAPER TRAIL

JACK KNEW HE WAS in real trouble now. From the instant he stepped into Elizabeth's Watergate apartment, he was overwhelmed. The spacious and elegant — almost professionally impersonal setting was full of a womanly scent that belied that image.

A brick fireplace was the focal point of the room. It was lined with bookcases filled with art objects that Jack was sure did not come from Wal-Mart. A picture popped into his mind of the fireplace lit, him sitting on the cream-colored carpet in front of it, Elizabeth next to him. He reminded himself that he was a professional with a job to do.

He looked at the fragile glass coffeetable, searching for something neutral to say. "My sister's kids would destroy this room in five seconds."

"No kids of your own then?" Elizabeth asked as she hung their coats.

"No," Jack answered. "It just didn't work out that way."

"Do I detect the bitter aftertaste of a divorce?"

Jack smiled to make what he was about to say a closed door rather than a slammed one. "You got that right. But I'm the investigative reporter, remember."

"In which case, let me show you Peter's study," she said, motioning to the right and escorting him past several doors. He glanced into what looked like a teen-aged girl's bedroom done up in yellow with a bed full of stuffed animals.

"Amy?" he asked.

"Yes, but she thinks it's too juvenile for her now." Elizabeth sighed. "The school in Massachusetts is so much better for her than anything around here. Still, it's hard to be an absentee mother."

He volunteered, "My mother's still alive, lives in Colorado. I have a sister near me who has a house full of kids."

She led him into a small den crammed with bookshelves. The files and clutter made Jack feel right at home. Elizabeth knelt down in front of a concealed wall safe. Blocking his view of the combination, she opened it.

"This is where you should start," she said, pulling out a huge expandable file folder stuffed with loose sheets of paper.

Jack gave a low whistle at the size of the folder. "How did the National Security boys miss this?"

"Peter left it with his parents and had his father conceal it. He was concerned that it could fall into the wrong hands."

"You didn't mention that before."

"I trust you more now than I did then. We know each other a little better."

He looked over the papers, considering the importance of anything a Senator would conceal from the NSC. "Christ, do you realize what that means? He thought the NSC might have moles."

Elizabeth nodded. "That's why I had to check you out so thoroughly. Of everyone who knew something about you, Frank was the only one who seemed taken aback when I told him about your book. But then he went on to say what a good idea it was to have Peter's book completed. Everyone seems to think you're a very competent writer."

"I don't know if I could tolerate much higher praise than that from Shotwell." Elizabeth frowned.

Jack hastened to explain. "I've done some off-the-record background interviews with Shotwell about drug interdiction and crime. I couldn't name him or anyone else he mentioned. He has some pretty extreme ideas about law enforcement."

"I suppose you'd compare him to Hitler too?" The conversation had moved exactly where he didn't want it to go. Then Elizabeth backed off. "I have to admit some of his views are extreme."

Glad to drop that issue, Jack began to rummage through the material to get an overview.

"I'm going to check my messages and make some phone calls while you work. Would you like something to drink? There's a full bar."

"Coffee'd be great. If it's no problem."

"None whatsoever. I can even guarantee it will be better than the last one you had with me."

Once alone, Jack turned to the folder. Wondering what the NSC involvement was, he remembered hearing that Peter's accident was a lucky event for someone, unnamed. He couldn't run down who it was. The official report made it clear that no foul play was involved in the crash.

Becoming engrossed in the file, Jack lost track of the time. When Elizabeth returned with the coffee, he was sitting on the floor surrounded by organized sets of papers, concentrating so hard that he startled when she approached him.

"Cinnamon," he noted as the scent steamed up to him. "Nice. You got it right, too."

Elizabeth smiled. "Two sugars, lots of milk. It's easy for me to remember. That's how Peter took his."

Jack was glad for the moment that this was a professional relationship. The next man who took Elizabeth on would find Peter's ghost hard to escape.

He stood to stretch his legs while he drank and noticed a photograph on the wall. In it the Senator was wearing a rough woven robe and turban. He was unshaven and dirty, but grinning like he was having the time of his life. Frank Shotwell and Don Larkin flanked him. Another similarly dressed man was in the background. The terrain was arid and rugged, like the San Gabriel Mountains not far from where Jack lived. The shot was probably in Afghanistan.

"That was taken during his first trip in from Pakistan. Neither a Senator nor any U.S. Army officers were supposedly in Afghanistan while the Russians were fighting the war. Peter knew he shouldn't have kept the photo, but it was taken by a twelve-year-old kid who had his legs blown off by a Soviet booby trap. Peter gave him his camera. He kept the picture under wraps for a long time. As you know, it caused quite a ruckus when the trip was uncovered. That other photo at the

Capitol was taken the day they got the relief support approved."

In the second picture, Frank and Don were in uniform. Jack studied the photo. A man in the background was slightly out of focus and cut off by the edge of the picture, as if he had tried to step out of frame.

Jack pointed to his image. "Who's this?"

"I don't know. I never noticed him before."

"What about him?" Jack indicated the unknown man in the Afghanistan photo.

"I don't know."

"Do you have a magnifying glass?"

Elizabeth thought a moment. "I think so. Let me check. I got one for Amy when I was trying to interest her in stamp collecting." She turned to leave, sadness deepening her voice. "I thought it would help her connect with me when we traveled. That was before the accident."

A moment later, she returned with the magnifying glass. Jack studied both pictures and handed it back. "Look for yourself."

"Whoever he is, it's the same man. He has a large mole on the right side of his chin. And from this you conclude — what?"

"Absolutely nothing." Jack smiled. "I'm just in the gathering in phase. All I'd say for sure is that he was part of the action there and has some kind of connection to Shotwell or Larkin."

"I don't know how I could have gotten through without Frank. I was a wreck, physically and emotionally. I went through more than a year of physical therapy. Frank was there to take care of everything. He made sure I got top doctors and the right treatment. He even took care of Peter's funeral arrangements."

"It was a national ceremony, wasn't it? The longest funeral queue since Bobby Kennedy."

Elizabeth nodded. She continued, "Frank arranged for Peter's family to take care of Amy while I was in the hospital. Most of all, he was a comfort to her. She suffered so over losing her father. Frank even made a couple of special trips to the Double V and took her along with his wife and grandkids to Six Flags Over Texas."

"Shotwell riding spinning sombreros? I'd have liked to have seen that! I'm sure Peter would have appreciated all that he did. Are you still close to the general?"

"Unfortunately, I haven't seen much of Frank lately because

we're both so busy."

Jack continued to study the picture. "How did he become a general?"

"I'm sure his efforts in Afghanistan had a great deal to do with it. He got a lot of recognition in the army and in intelligence circles. After his work there, he rose very quickly and was assigned to the National Security Council. He brought Don with him. Don is, as I understand it, Frank's eyes and ears."

The ringing of the phone cut through her words. Elizabeth moved reluctantly to answer it. "That's our private number."

After a few moments of listening to the voice on the other end, she looked as though she'd been sandbagged.

Jack couldn't help but hear as she raised her voice. "What do you mean you're in jail?"

6

GUILT EDGED

"ARE YOU ALL RIGHT? What can I do?"

The silences following Elizabeth's questions were brief but voluminous. "How much money do you need?"

Jack was nearly ashamed of himself for listening. But he was a reporter, after all. Poking into other people's business was his job.

Elizabeth continued. "I'm not sure if I have that much right now. Let me see what I can pull together. It won't be easy at this time of night. Are you sure you're all right, Amykins?"

The bewilderment in Elizabeth's voice almost broke Jack's heart. He had been down this road himself with his wife. He could guess most of the answers Elizabeth was hearing.

"If the judge said a rehab stay is required, we'll have to do that. Did they make any recommendations or suggestions? I'll be there as fast as I can. I love you." She put down the phone.

"Amy?" Jack asked tentatively.

Staring off into space, her face ashen, her nod answered the question. "Oh, God. . . I've had my suspicions, but didn't want to believe that it might be true."

She looked quickly at him, her eyes suddenly widening, realizing that he had heard everything.

"What —?" He knew that any question would make him sound like a reporter and shifted his tone. "Maybe I can help."

45

"I'm afraid not." She was striving for control.

"You're trembling. What is it?"

"We're off the record on everything right?" To his surprise, she added plaintively, "Please."

Somehow, it hurt him to see her so vulnerable. "I guarantee it." His reassurance came from his heart.

Having decided to trust him with her husband's legacy, Elizabeth decided to allow him one step further into her life. "Amy's just been arrested for drug possession. I need to arrange bail and get her into rehab. I don't understand why —"

"Is there anybody I can call for you?

She shook her head.

"Listen, I've been through a similar situation with a close member of my family as well. Let me help."

When Elizabeth didn't answer, he decided to have as much faith in her as she'd had in him.

"My former wife, Joanne, nearly died of an overdose a number of years ago. It's a long story."

"That could happen to Amy." The blood had drained from her face.

"It won't. We can get a good rehab facility for her. Together we'll come up with the best for her."

"It's my fault. If I hadn't insisted on that trip with Peter, he'd still be alive."

"That's nonsense. And even if it were true, you aren't the one popping the pills in her mouth. She is. Let her catch a whiff of guilt from you about this and she'll hold it over you forever. Drug addicts are master manipulators. It will be difficult for both of you, but if she wants to get out of this cycle, it will be the best thing for her."

"I'll do anything for her."

"Where is she? Where did she call from?"

"Boston. I've got to get up there to help her. I feel so awful. She blames me for so many things."

He led her back into the living room. For some reason he did not fully understand, he was intent on helping her and Amy. He knew it would take time and effort, but he wanted to do it.

He sat across the coffee table from her and listened intently as Elizabeth unraveled the past. "I was in a wheelchair at the funeral. They brought me there in an ambulance and took me right back to the hospital afterwards. I was so out of it on pain killers that I couldn't respond to Amy's grief. She thought I was unfeeling. . . ."

Tears pooled in Elizabeth's eyes. Jack reached over and took her hand, letting her relive the memory. "I couldn't do anything. Amy started crying uncontrollably. Between sobs she let out a high-pitched laugh that was like some unearthly scream. She threw herself at the coffin, trying to pull up the lid."

Jack knew from the news that the casket was closed because the body was so mutilated. He put his other hand under Elizabeth's, steadying her as she relived the horror.

"Frank and Don tried to pull her back. Two guerilla fighters were no match for one small, grief-driven little girl. She flung herself on the coffin, but she couldn't get it open. She never saw her father for that one last time. She hasn't been the same since."

"Stop blaming yourself. Believe me, I know from my own experience that sometimes events are beyond your control. You sacrificed a lot for Amy. You gave up your career for her."

"No, I didn't. I just traded in mine for Peter's. Politics ran our lives. She never had a home like I had when I was a child."

"That doesn't mean what she had was bad. You did your best. You're being unfair to yourself and that won't do you or her any good. What we need to do now is get some help for Amy."

Elizabeth wasn't listening. "Maybe I should have let her live on the ranch in Texas — but I couldn't bear to live there without Peter — I insisted she go to a New England school like I did —" She buried her face in her hands.

Jack summoned all the strength he had to keep from putting his arms around her. "You'd better pack, Elizabeth," he said, his voice husky. "We can still catch a train to Boston tonight."

7

ON THE HILL

A PROFUSION OF PINK cherry blossoms framed the Lincoln Memorial as it came into view through the car window. Elizabeth's spirit matched the day. She couldn't remember how long it had been since she had felt this happy. She always found the sense of rebirth that came with spring and the Easter season. This year was particularly joyous to her because Amy's situation was very hopeful.

She had been in rehab for months now and was doing well, thanks largely to Jack. He had found her one of the best criminal attorneys Boston had to offer. Still a juvenile, Amy would have no blight on her record. She was placed in an outstanding treatment facility in Boston. Elizabeth wanted to believe that she and Amy were communicating a little better. The estrangement was still there, but perhaps they would grow closer over time.

Her thoughts turned to Jack. She felt an enormous sense of gratitude to him and a touch of guilt for sidetracking his project by leaning on him so strongly. She had let him take Peter's records to Boston with them. By the time he had left — a long forty-eight hours later — she trusted him enough to turn all the paperwork over to him.

She had not seen him since then, but they often talked on the phone. At first he called to ask after Amy or she called to ask how the research was going. Gradually, they started sharing more confidences. She told him of the thousand petty cruelties she and Amy had unwittingly inflicted on each other. He told her the anguish he had felt in having to give up on his wife and get a divorce.

He reminded her of Peter, though they looked nothing alike. Peter was far more polished, but they were both big men and she liked the presence that created. Both were sensitive — Jack more so because he was not so driven by his career.

It occurred to her as odd that it had been male acquaintances, not women or family, who stepped in to help her in crises. First there was Frank Shotwell, now Jack. She wondered who she could have called on if Jack had not been there. Frank was a possibility, but she had not seen him for almost a year now. Otherwise, she drew a blank. She had no living brothers or sisters and no close women friends. She had many acquaintances and friends in political circles, but nobody she would call on in a personal crisis. She was accustomed to giving help, not receiving it.

Through the vision of cherry blossoms and banks of crocus and grape hyacinth, she tried to visualize Peter. An image of Jack came into her mind.

"Here we are, Governor," said her driver.

"What did you do, Freddie, take a short cut?"

"No, ma'am. Went the long way so you could enjoy the flowers."

"Thanks, Freddie. See you tomorrow."

As Elizabeth climbed the white marble steps of the Capitol and passed through the metal detectors, she realized that her heart was racing. It wasn't the thought of testifying before a Senate subcommittee. It was the knowledge that Jack would be there before the hearing was over.

Elizabeth was already seated at the witness table when she caught a glimpse of Jack as he slipped in and took a seat near the back of the sparsely populated chamber. She went on autopilot for the swearing in and preliminary questions, finding herself looking forward to seeing Jack more than she wanted to admit. She was pleased that he had made it in time to see her testify.

The questions were becoming more detailed now and she forced herself to focus on them. A senator tried to reshape her answer with another question. "Are you then saying that the private relief agencies are not doing a sufficient job?"

"No, I'm not saying that at all. There is a fundamental difference between the approaches of governmental agencies and
the private sector. Most private charities have their own agen-
das in addition to providing aid. Many are church oriented."

Another panelist challenged her. "Governor Armstrong, how
do you view the role of government in terms of international
relief?"

"I'll take Somalia as an example. There is an old Chinese
proverb that if you give a man a fish, you have fed him for a
day. If you teach him to fish, you've fed him for a lifetime. In
Somalia we kept trying to give the people fish. We never taught
them how to fish. The relief agencies went in during the emergency situation and provided food, clothing, and shelter as
we're supposed to do. The problem was when the government
came in, they continued doing the same thing. They created a
nation of dependents, bankrupting what few farmers Somalia
still had because local farmers could not compete against free
grain."

"What are you advocating as our foreign policy when it
comes to aid and relief?"

"The government must stop giving untargeted aid and instead start channeling financial resources into long-term solu-
tions. Third World nations are well known for putting money
into megaprojects, like dams that they do not have the where-
withal to keep up. Aid should be directed to the poorest of the
poor. The aid money we give should come with strings attached.
The average American thinks it is a handout of food to starv-
ing masses. They don't know that most aid goes to the countries in which the U.S. has a massive military presence — such
as the Philippines. They don't realize that how that money is
used is up to the government receiving it. As it is now, it seldom goes to the people."

Elizabeth wanted to make the most of this opportunity. Amy
had just been learning to walk at thirteen months when Elizabeth had watched a film of a five-year-old who was also just
learning to toddle. His body was so debilitated by inadequate
nutrition that he was years behind American youngsters in
development. That image and the knowledge that things didn't
have to be like that had stayed with her.

Feeling that child's needs and knowing that there were

thousands like him, she continued her explanation. "In Somalia, for example, we could have sent seed grains and farm tools instead of just food. We could have spent our time and effort building roads to bring food from field to market. Remember that the food crisis there was artificially imposed by a combination of drought and military regimes which deliberately kept food from the people. Our foreign aid efforts only made the situation worse by destroying the agricultural infrastructure of that country. You don't make a man a fisherman by giving him fish."

The inevitable question resounded from the Senator's microphone. "If these people survive, won't all of us run out of food and other resources?"

"Senator, it has been well documented that populations stabilize when the death rate among children drops. When parents know most of their children will die as infants or young children, they have more children to ensure that someone will survive to take care of them. They have no pensions, no social security. They need hands to scrounge firewood and haul water for miles just to cook some simple grains. The best way to defuse the population explosion is to assist child survival. When people know their children will live, they are willing to have fewer children. Populations stabilize with an increase in wealth and education too. Female literacy is the number-one factor in child survival and, ultimately, population control."

She was starting to add some details when the senator cut her off abruptly. "Ridiculous. Cut the birth rate by helping children survive? It flies in the face of common sense."

Elizabeth steeled herself and answered with a calm smile, "Unfortunately, common sense is not always right. Among others, UNICEF, the World Health Organization, and OXFAM — all highly esteemed international organizations — agree that once people believe their children will survive, they then are willing to have fewer children."

Before he could respond, she pulled a dozen bound reports out of her briefcase and stacked them one by one on the table next to her microphone so that it picked up the slap of each large report. They mounted up: "State of World's Children Report 1990. State of World's Children Report 1991." One by one she enumerated a decade's worth of documentation.

As the Senator backed off, Jack again marveled at Elizabeth's strength and skill.

She wrapped up her testimony, hoping it had made a difference. Jack was waiting for her in the doorway. She greeted him warmly, rising on tiptoe to kiss him on the cheek. As her lips touched his freshly shaven cheek, she felt an excitement she thought had died along with Peter.

"Why don't we take a walk on the mall and find a hot dog somewhere before the Senate Intelligence Committee hearings start?" she asked.

"Sounds like a good plan," said Jack.

They walked slowly down the Capitol mall along the reflecting pool toward the buildings of the Smithsonian Institution. Jack slung his sports jacket over his shoulder.

"Weather's a little warmer than the last time I was here."

"Well, some things haven't changed," said Elizabeth, playfully patting the collection of pens in his shirt pocket.

He laughed lightly. "Think of it as a trademark. How's Amy?"

"The last couple of weeks have been better." Elizabeth shifted the conversation, feeling a need to stay on more neutral topics. She pointed. "There's a hot dog stand."

Jack bought them a couple of sodas and hot dogs, slathering his with mustard. They picked a shady table and sat down. With his first bite, the mustard oozed out onto his tie.

"Hell, why does this always happen to me?"

"Here, let me help you." Moving closer to him, Elizabeth used a wet napkin to undo the damage as best she could. She looked up at him, catching a twinkle in his eye. She felt a flush and slowly moved back, continuing to smile as her eyes returned to the tie. *He's a very cute klutz*, she thought.

"You should get this cleaned as soon as you can," she said.

Jack looked as if he might lean forward and kiss her. Elizabeth wasn't sure she was ready for that. "Eat the rest of your hot dog, then we'd better start back," she said.

Within minutes they entered the hearing room for the Senate Intelligence Committee. It was already crowded. The commotion was silenced when the gavel was pounded. Everyone quickly took a seat. The chair called for order.

"The purpose of these hearings is to take testimony on the subject of international drug trafficking. We are going to call as our first witness General Mike Teufer. General Teufer started his career with the U.S. Army in World War II as a member of the Office of Special Services, which preceded the CIA. He parachuted into occupied France and worked with the resistance there, then did the same thing in China."

The chairman looked up from his notes and into the C-Span cameras. "During the Korean War, he was loaned out to the Central Intelligence Agency and organized large resistance bands behind North Korean lines. Throughout his career he exposed himself to danger on behalf of this country. He was commander of all Special Operations Forces in Vietnam, a position he held for almost five years. This was phenomenal, since most commanders in Vietnam were given only one-year tours. He retired as a major general and has been involved in civilian activities in support of U.S. government policies and in aid of refugees around the world. This committee thinks highly of his work and is pleased to have him appear before us voluntarily to give information and testimony. I would now ask General Teufer to please be sworn in."

After some preliminary questioning, the senator got to the point that interested Jack. "General, we are looking into international drug trafficking by resistance groups, especially those that the United States supported. It is my understanding that you have some information on this subject."

"Yes, Senator. I hasten to point out that it was never the United States' policy to support drug trafficking, or to use drug trafficking in any way to support resistance movements. However, sometimes when you have to go around established government networks to get supplies to opposing forces, you have to use smugglers. Sometimes smugglers do not limit themselves to the tasks that you give them and do something illegal. They are just continuing doing what made you hire them in the first place — only with drugs instead of guns and medical supplies. When that happens, the intelligence networks must decide whether to provide information to law enforcement and expose their own routes, or remain silent and shift their work to other people."

"Why has this been such a significant problem?

"There's big money involved in the drug smuggling business around the world. It's highly tempting to people in clandestine efforts. Sometimes government officials become corrupted by that money."

"Can you give us any specific examples where this has occurred recently?"

"Yes. The activities that went on in Afghanistan. We were supporting Afghan guerrillas behind the scenes, but could not officially be recognized as doing so for fear of upsetting our relations with the Soviet Union. That meant we had to work with existing clandestine networks. Unfortunately, some U.S. money ended up in the hands of narco-terrorists and narcotics dealers around the world."

"Are you at liberty to identify any specific groups that fall into this category?"

"This is a touchy subject, Senator. We're dealing with allegations here. I will say that one group, NIRM, appeared more interested in smuggling opium than it was in fighting the war. In other resistance groups, sometimes there were one or two corrupt people who had to be purged. No one was ever eliminated from the National Islamic Resistance Movement when we complained. I was quite concerned that the United States kept supporting this group in spite of my personal reports and recommendations."

"Who did you report to?"

"I reported a number of my findings to the chief of the U.S. military mission who was the liaison between the U.S. and NIRM. Some years later I provided further information at Senator Armstrong's request. I assumed he shared it with this committee, but I didn't hear anything more about it. Then, of course, he was killed."

"I am not aware of any information given to this committee. You can give it to us now."

"Unfortunately, I turned over everything to the Senator. I didn't retain any of it."

Jack and Elizabeth looked at each other, a mutual question in their eyes. A movement behind Jack made him turn. He saw a man halfway out the door. Something about the way the door frame cut the view of him reminded Jack of the half-figure of the unknown man in the picture in Elizabeth's den, the man with the mole on his chin.

Whoa, Jack, he thought, *don't let your imagination run away with you.* Despite his reality-check, something made him sense it was not fantasy. His investigative instinct kicked into high gear. He smelled danger.

8

Trespass and Sweet Offerings

A DECIDEDLY SEXUAL THRILL ran through Elizabeth as Jack held her coat for her. As the satin lining slipped over her bare arms, she shivered a little.

They were back in her apartment after an elegant meal at Tiberios accompanied by a bottle of Mumm champagne. Dropping her coat into his hands, she stepped away and turned to look at him, savoring the changes in her aroused body. It had been a long time.

He looked her up and down more obviously now than he had in the restaurant, encouraged by the subtle shift in her behavior — her widened eyes, her softening lips. Her black silk crepe dress clung to her. Below its scalloped neckline the soft creamy flesh of her breasts was enticingly revealed.

She had chosen that dress after considering a black dress with a lace bodice that had been Peter's favorite. Purchased for a long-ago embassy dinner party, the dress reminded her of an especially passionate evening with Peter. He had loved her in it. She felt guilty when she caught herself thinking that it would have the same effect on Jack.

Deep in her soul she knew that Peter would not want her to be alone now. He would want her to have love and companionship. Despite that knowledge, wearing that particular dress brought back too many memories. She put away her guilt along with the dress as she placed it back on the rack. She wanted no ghosts with her this evening.

Now she stood looking at Jack in that split second between feeling their desire was mutual and the decision to touch. She felt more exposed now than she had this afternoon, lying naked in her tub. As she readied herself for their date, the late afternoon sun had poured through the stained glass window, casting its warm colors over her smooth white flesh, turning her breasts crimson, as though coloring them with passion.

When she opened the drawer containing her lingerie, she saw in the back, never worn, a black satin and lace set. She put it on. As she pulled the silky stockings over her legs and slipped on her high-heeled black strap shoes she felt a sense of pleasure in her reawakened sexuality.

Now, looking into his attentive eyes, she thought of how Jack would feel at the sight of her in the french cut briefs and shimmering bra. She breathed deeply, sensing her breasts rise, knowing that he noticed.

She reached out and with two poised fingers lifted the tip of Jack's tie. "You changed it," she teased.

Jack flooded with desire. He started to move closer to kiss her, but she abruptly pulled away and looked beyond him down the hall. Something about the angle of the door to the den drew her attention.

"What's wrong?" he asked, alarmed.

"Someone's been here," she mouthed.

Jack followed her stealthily down the hall, his heart pounding. The den looked the same as it had earlier. Papers were stacked on shelves and in cubbyholes. Nothing struck him as unusual.

Elizabeth opened the safe. This time she did not bother to conceal the combination. She pulled out a file folder and looked through it. In it were the papers too sensitive for Jack to take back to Los Angeles. He had read them so many times on the flight to Boston that he had practically memorized them.

"Look at this," she said, handing him the file. "They're out of order."

Jack studied the folder a minute. "You're right. Did you go through them on your own?"

"I haven't touched them since I went through the sequencing with you in Boston except to put them in the safe. Jack, I'm frightened. I know someone's been here."

Jack felt the hair prickle on his neck. Could the intruder still be here? "We'd better look around," he said, keeping his voice low.

They inspected the door and windows for signs of tampering. There were none. They searched the other rooms in the apartment. Nothing. There were no obvious clues that the apartment had been broken into, but there was no doubt in either of their minds that someone had gone through those papers.

"The only other person with keys to the apartment is Amy, and she's in the rehab center," Elizabeth said thoughtfully.

"Would she have given them to anyone else? One of her druggie friends? I know kids who have had their friends burglarize their parents for drug money."

"The facility still has all of her possessions locked up. She's not allowed anything of her own. With the exception of a picture of Peter."

Jack noted that she had not said "a picture of Peter and me." Evidently, despite her hopes of reconciliation, Amy was still cutting Elizabeth out of her life.

"Do you have a maid? Could she have moved them?"

"Yes, but she has no access to the office area. It has a separate lock on the door and I always keep it shut when she's here. Peter set up that system for security because he was on the Intelligence Committee."

"Who would want those documents?" Jack mused. "I think we need to consider the possibility that the forces Peter was ready to expose are organized, dangerous, and still have an interest in you. We have to assume that someone noticed that you were at that hearing this afternoon and decided to find out what information you had."

"I hate to admit it, but you may be right." Elizabeth bit her lip. "Nothing else makes sense. As far as I know, Peter's father is the only other one who knows the combination, and he's in Texas. Peter even made him memorize it instead of writing it down. Whoever got in here was professional. "

"I agree." Jack looked suspiciously at the pictures of Shotwell, Larkin, and the unknown man. He wasn't ready to share his hunch with Elizabeth, however.

"Jack, do you think we should call the police?"

"What are we going to tell them? That we found some papers out of order? Nothing is missing and there's no evidence of a break-in. I don't think we can do much more than worry right now. But I'd like to start investigating this."

"You have been."

"I've been researching a book. Now I'm looking at something that could be a danger to you."

Elizabeth reached for his hand, touched by his concern for her. The spark that had been set aside earlier rekindled. Now a touch of fear breathed it into a flame of different intensity.

It would not be easy to regain the sweet relaxation that had filled her earlier in the evening, but she was determined to try.

"We can't do anything else about this tonight. I feel like having some wine. Would you like some?"

"Sounds great. Got any Napa Valley wines?"

"I don't know. Let me see." She disappeared and returned momentarily, bottle in hand. "I have some Chateau Lafite, 1955."

"Chateau Lafite doesn't sound like California to me."

She laughed, lightening the mood. "Actually, it's a nice California Chardonnay, Chateau St. Jean. It was recommended to me," she paused to emphasize what she would say next, "by a very dear friend."

"Sounds appealing." He was speaking more of her than of the wine. He knew that he had mentioned the Chateau St. Jean in a conversation they'd had two months ago. He was pleased she remembered.

"I'll get the wine bucket and chill it. Why don't you come keep me company?"

He was only too glad to leave behind the implied menace they had found in the study and lock the door on it.

Elizabeth set up the ice bucket on a stand and picked two beautifully fluted glasses of Waterford crystal from an antique cabinet. She gave one to him. His eyes scarcely left her face as he reached out for the glass.

As they held the delicate stem of the glass, her eyes rested on his hands. They were strong yet smooth. She remembered that snowy day she had met Jack at her office. She was extremely attracted by his hands as they held the coffee mug. Now she was swept away by the thought of his hands caressing her. When they had touched earlier, an excitement, a shock wave of desire, had penetrated her loneliness.

Stirred by her excitement, Jack sat down awkwardly, knocking over the wine bucket stand and spilling ice on the table. They both reached to grab the falling stand and their hands seized it, one on top of the other, in the same place. She didn't take hers away.

"You really are all thumbs." Her voice was warm and thick.

They froze for a moment, his body poised over hers. She turned her face up to his and they kissed, coming together simultaneously.

As though too moved by the intensity of her feelings, she turned playful, grabbing an ice cube from the table and rubbing it on his neck.

He gently took the ice from her hand and drew just the barest tip of it down her throat to her breast, following it's chill with the warmth of his lips.

She gasped and they embraced each other, seized by a passion that had been building through their late night phone conversations.

He stroked her shoulders and they kissed more deeply, opening themselves each to the other as neither had done in a very long time.

His heart pounded as they awakened each other's desires. She pressed her body to his and felt her breasts against his chest. He could feel her heat. Holding her with his arms and his eyes, he slowly escorted her to the bedroom.

She felt the zipper go down her back and her dress open. He lowered her dress off her shoulders, kissing her gently on the neck and then on each shoulder. He dropped to his knees before her and breathed in her fragrance, allowing it to intoxicate him, something he had wanted to do for a very long time.

9

SONOMA

JACK FLINCHED, DUCKING a switchblade that was being wielded at him. He pulled back into himself in fear, and then realized that the gleam he had taken for the honed edge of a knife was actually a pair of mirrored sunglasses being flashed by a street vendor in the warm spring sunshine.

He hated to admit to the prejudice that his reaction portrayed. Perhaps that was what John Sonoma, candidate for mayor, wanted him to learn when he had suggested they take this walk while Jack interviewed him.

Jack had now been caught off-guard twice on this assignment; once by the sunglasses, and once by his lack of preparation. He had spent too long with Elizabeth on the last trip back East and hadn't done his homework on this one. He'd have to watch and listen this time around.

They continued on down Alameda Street with Jack feeling they had entered a different world. This was Latino Los Angeles, less than five blocks from city hall.

Sonoma gestured broadly, smiling. "Look at it! It's alive, vibrant and pulsing with activity."

The wide street was packed with small shops, all bearing signs in Spanish. The sidewalks in front of them were crowded with people who were shopping or just sauntering along to see and be seen. Many recognized Sonoma and waved or stopped to shake his hand.

"Here is where many Latino Americans come to work, play, and share in the American dream. Look how the little shops spring up everywhere. There are no government handouts here. These are people trying to make it themselves. All they want from their government is to be protected from criminals and otherwise left alone."

Several shopkeepers called out to Sonoma as the two of them passed by their open stalls offering food, clothing, and jewelry. He returned their banter, sometimes in English, sometimes in Spanish.

"They all know this is a great city," he said, beaming. Jack could see his pride.

"*Alto! Alto!*" The shout interrupted them. They turned to see a young Latino running from a market. He was wearing a Raiders football jacket, baggy pants, and Reeboks. He was sprinting, easily outrunning his overweight pursuer.

As he passed nearby, Sonoma suddenly shouted in a harsh, authoritarian voice, "Stop right there! José! *Alto, alto*, José!"

The youth slowed and Sonoma shouted decisively, "*Ahora!* Now!" The youth skidded to a stop a few feet away.

Sonoma walked over to him, grabbing him firmly by the arm, like an angry father with a misbehaving child. "José Martinez, I know you. I used to live on your street."

When José didn't answer, Sonoma continued. "What are you doing?" The inquiry was more an angry demand than a question.

"*Nada*, Señor Sonoma," the youth mumbled, averting his dark eyes from Sonoma's piercing stare.

The proprietor caught up with them, panting from the exertion, his face red. A small crowd began gathering around them. The proprietor spoke in Spanish to Sonoma, and Jack couldn't tell what he was saying. The boy looked around nervously.

Sonoma turned to the boy. "Empty your jacket pockets."

The boy produced several packs of cigarettes and a candy bar.

"José, I am ashamed. Ashamed of you!" José winced and stared at his shoes.

"I know your father. He is working at his second job right now, trying to earn enough money to send you to college. If you get arrested, you won't go to college. Is this the way to thank your father?"

José said nothing.

"*Digame!* Tell me," Sonoma said in a tone that demanded an answer.

"No, Señor Sonoma."

"Return the items immediately."

The youth complied. He kept his head down, not allowing his eyes to meet the proprietor's. Sonoma turned to the man.

"I notice that your store has been recently tagged with graffiti. Would you like some help to clean it up?"

When the proprietor nodded yes, Sonoma turned back to the youth. "You will spend the afternoon cleaning that wall."

"But —"

Sonoma cut him off. "You have only one choice. You do it, or I turn you over to the police. And then we will tell your father."

"Yes, Señor Sonoma, I will do it."

Jack noticed with curiosity how Sonoma's accent and speech pattern had changed to reflect that of the Latino crowd around him.

Turning to the proprietor, he asked, "Will that satisfy you?"

Again, the proprietor nodded. Once he did so, the crowd's energy seemed to dissipate.

A police car stopped nearby. Two officers got out of the car on opposite sides, each slipping an L-shaped billy club into a ring on their belts. They approached the crowd.

"Then I turn him to your care," Sonoma said, escorting the youth to the proprietor. Sonoma handed the man a business card. "Call me once he has finished, or if he goes back on his word."

"I know who you are, Señor Sonoma. I would be honored if you would stop by my store sometime soon. *Muchas gracias.*"

"*De nada, señor. Mucho gusto.*"

As the crowd broke up, Sonoma approached the ranking officer and spoke to him briefly. The officer smiled and shook Sonoma's hand. Then Sonoma turned to Jack. "Let's continue. There is more I want you to see. There is another neighborhood I am not so proud of."

Jack admired the way Sonoma had handled the incident. "Why didn't you have the boy arrested?"

"We try hard in our community to teach a sense of right and wrong and deal with problems. Community is like family. The police understand that and appreciate it. They have enough other serious problems to handle." He added ominously, "Street justice is surer, quicker, and fairer than that of our modern judicial system."

They walked farther south. The neighborhood began to change. Store fronts were boarded up, homeless people wandered on the streets or sat by the buildings. There was litter everywhere — on the streets, the sidewalks, in empty lots. Graffiti was on every building, much of it crude.

"Nearly everyone you see here — black, white, Latino, Native American — is on some form of government assistance," Sonoma said. "That means those people whose shops you just left, those happy people on the street you saw, their taxes are paying for programs that keep people like this on the street."

"Are you saying we should stop welfare and aid to the homeless? That sounds pretty radical."

"I am saying we are doing something wrong. We did not create programs which told these people to get up and do something for themselves. We said in effect, if you do nothing, we will support you. Period. Government should be there to protect and to provide assistance in times of need. It should not provide a guarantee that keeps anyone from taking responsibility for themselves and their families. Once you guarantee basic living conditions, you take away the responsibility of the family."

"So, how does this philosophy play into your plans for Los Angeles if you are elected mayor?"

"It is my belief that unless we provide programs that strengthen the family, unless we make people once again responsible for their actions, we have nowhere to go in this society but down. We need to look to government for support, but not to do the job for us. We need to scale back government and reorient programs to shift initiative to the community. This philosophy has worked well in my council district."

"You think this would work for all of L.A.?"

"We've made great strides in my district since I was elected. There are more viable businesses, less crime, cleaner streets. My district contains people of many ethnic origins, not just Latino. You know, it is interesting that the Latino community has always been underrepresented in L.A. politics. Only a few of us have ever made it to the city council. We have always had to reach beyond our ethnic boundaries to get elected. I believe that my philosophy will have broad appeal and that I will be elected mayor."

"How do you intend to deal with the worst crime areas?"

"I have a plan I call Project Second Chance. We bring law enforcement more heavily into those areas."

"I've heard about that. It involves street sweeps, right?"

"Yes. It's an effective way to clean up the worst crime. It gets treatment for street people by placing them in shelters, treatment programs, or even jail, depending on their circumstances. We need to make these areas safe. It gives both the neighborhood and the people a second chance."

They were getting close to city hall again. "Let me ask you one last question. You were way out front with that kid back there. I don't think you did anything because of me. Are you concerned about what I'll write?"

"Not really, as long as you report it accurately. I did what I believe in. If the voters agree with me and my accomplishments to date, I'll win."

They shook hands and Jack turned in the direction of the *Times* building. He was mulling over how he would construct the article. He could see that the old political beliefs he had grown up with were changing. The electorate was moving back toward the center.

He realized he had actually forgotten about Elizabeth for a couple of hours. The parallels that existed between what Sonoma said and some of the philosophical arguments he had with Elizabeth occurred to him. As he continued to walk, the deadline for the special election insert loomed larger.

Jack's impatience with the deadline transmuted itself into a general sense of anxiety. He dealt with deadlines all the time — they were a routine part of his professional life — so he wondered why he was feeling so uneasy.

He glanced back over his shoulder. The street was empty except for a man at a distance, walking in the same direction. Jack returned to mentally writing the article, but could not shake his uneasy feeling. He looked over his shoulder again and saw the same man still behind him. He'd made several turns, and it seemed odd to him that someone would be on the same route. This was, after all, L.A. Nobody walked.

Jack turned into a convenience store. He walked aimlessly through the aisles and thumbed through a copy of *Life*, killing time. When he left the store, he looked around, knowing that if the same man were there, it would not be a coincidence.

And then what?

10

AMY

"YOU'RE FUCKING HIM." Amy snarled. She mimicked her mother. "'A very special friend.' That's code, right? For 'He's fucking me.'"

Elizabeth knew reprimanding Amy for her language would be a waste of effort. Amy was trying to bait and shock her. Elizabeth did not want to play into her hands, even though she knew her words had carried down the halls. What other people thought about them was not important.

Jack should be arriving any minute to meet Amy for the first time. He had stayed behind the scenes on the trip to bail Amy out of jail. Elizabeth thought it was time they got together.

This trip had been worked out for weeks. Amy seemed resigned to it, if less than enthusiastic. So why was she having a fit now, minutes before Jack's arrival? Elizabeth wondered. Then she realized, that was the reason: his arrival. Amy knew she could play her hand to the hilt.

Elizabeth focused on her breathing to calm herself and studied Amy in careful silence. Amy was dressed in jeans and running shoes which made her several inches shorter than her mother. Her sweater accentuated her full, graceful figure and made it clear that despite her petite stature, she was no longer a child.

Her lovely young face was surrounded by long, naturally curly blond hair. The Aphrodite-like picture was distorted by

66

piercing eyes and a hostile expression.

Elizabeth should have known that if she left a silence this long, Amy would fill it. "So, Mother," she practically spit the words, "how many men did you fuck when Daddy was still alive?"

Elizabeth drew back and slapped her in the face. Blood trickled down Amy's rapidly swelling lip. Amy knew her mother had drawn psychological blood as well.

Elizabeth used every ounce of restraint she had. She leveled her voice and lowered it. "I loved your father with all my heart, Amy. I was incapable of being unfaithful to him."

Elizabeth held Amy's eyes with hers by a force of will, refusing to allow her to interrupt. "When he died, part of me died. But I've stopped mourning. I won't bury myself alive anymore. I know that you think I was the cause of his death. I wasn't. I won't let you put that on me anymore."

She reached out for Amy's hand, knowing that she would pull away. She couldn't control what Amy did, but she would continue to offer her love, support, and warmth. She also knew that she was a good mother now and that she always had been. She would not let Amy manipulate her with the archaic images of Betty Crocker or June Cleaver.

"Amy, I know I wasn't an advertising icon or a sitcom Mom. I'm real. And if I'd made myself less than I am and not done the work that I'm good at, you'd hate me for that too. I love you profoundly. Maybe someday you'll see that and see me for what I am."

"I know what you are, you bitch. You're the reason my father is dead." Amy burst into tears. "You're the reason I-I hurt so much. I —"

Elizabeth spread her arms out to Amy, offering to embrace her, but not approaching her, allowing her the freedom to refuse.

She lowered her arms as Amy turned away from her and tried to work affection into her voice. "You're right about one thing, Amy. Jack is my lover. You may be able to cut yourself off from human affection, but I can't."

11

A Change of Season

Elizabeth buried herself in her passion for Jack. To her hunger for him was added the aching need to hold Amy in her arms. Instead, she enveloped Jack and drew him into herself in every way she could imagine.

She had met Jack at the front entrance to the clinic, her eyes streaming with the tears she would not allow to fall in front of Amy. She explained that Amy was not ready for her to have a relationship with another man, and since Amy had refused to join them, she wanted nothing more than to get out of there.

As they drove south, the wide highway became lined with trees. The variety of greens created an irregular patchwork design.

As soon as they came to a roadside inn, Elizabeth dropped her plans of driving and taking in the spring wildflowers. She asked Jack if he'd like to stop. The quaint building was constructed of irregular bricks and inset stones. A magnificent brick arch and a massive chimney dominated the front facade. Elizabeth wasn't paying much attention to the charms of the inn.

The instant the door to their room was closed, Elizabeth engulfed him. She felt a surge of warmth pass through her body as she responded to his mouth. She ran her fingers through his hair and arched her back, offering him her breasts. He fondled them and pulled up her sweater, kissing them tenderly and then gently lowering her to the bed.

Her deep kisses demanded his whole being. Jack wasn't sure he had that much in himself to give. His body responded, but he felt a part of him pulling back, wanting to save something for himself. Elizabeth's need was all-consuming.

Exhausted, they both fell asleep. In a few hours, she awoke, pleased to see that they had not missed the sunset. The thick stands of trees had turned black with the approach of evening. A brilliant band of yellow hung just above the treetops, surrounded by a layer of pink. A few thin, gray clouds gave texture to the vivid sky.

Elizabeth rolled over and looked at Jack asleep. Content and satisfied, she simply watched. He had given her the gift of losing herself in his lovemaking. A warmth filled her as she thought of all he had done for her and Amy. She reached for him, running her hand through the hair on his chest. Jack opened his eyes.

"I'm sorry," she whispered. "I didn't mean to wake you."

"That's okay. I guess I went out like a light."

"Indeed you did."

"It's been a long time."

"It was wonderful, Jack."

He smiled as he caressed her face. They snuggled in each other's arms and despite, or perhaps because of, the totality of the passion they had just shared, she embraced him again, kissing him deeply, and sliding her hand up one thigh and down the other.

Jack felt himself harden again. He took her hand in his and kissed her fingertips gently. "Why don't we get dressed and find a restaurant."

Elizabeth moaned, kissing him again and slipping her body on top of his. He gently moved to one side and kissed her quickly with simple affection. "I'm hungry. We really need to get something to eat. We skipped lunch."

Elizabeth wanted to say, *Ah, but we ate each other*, when the shift in his tone grew clear. She struggled to take it at face value, but could not. Hurt, she vowed to keep her feelings to herself and tried to make the silence that had fallen between them a comfortable one.

Jack was lost in thought. There were too many questions about their relationship. Neither of them could pull much time out of their careers. A simple Saturday night date cost them nearly a thousand dollars and the whole weekend. Yet, despite the short time they'd had together, it felt as if they had known each other for years.

Jack put his hand on Elizabeth's back, rubbing it in smooth circles over her sacrum. The base of her spine still troubled her even after all the physical therapy that she had. At least she was no longer self-conscious with him about the scars on her legs. He moved over and cupped Elizabeth's foot in his hand, kissing his way up from her ankle to her calf, as he had the first time they were together.

He wanted her to know that he was not rejecting her by not making love with her right now. He had been so overwhelmed by the intensity of her passion for him that he did not know how to handle it. His body responded, but he feared some measure of his soul was not quite a match for hers.

He got out of bed and pulled on a rumpled pair of jeans. Words spilled from him like water down an opened sluice. "I divorced my wife six years ago, after she nearly died of a drug and alcohol overdose. She'd had breast cancer two years before. She had a double mastectomy and then chemo. All the follow-up tests were fine. I couldn't convince her that the scars didn't bother me."

He handed Elizabeth her skirt. Then he knelt and lifted her leg and kissed again along the same line from ankle to calf. "My wife's scars didn't matter at all, Elizabeth. Neither do yours."

He kissed each knee playfully, then rose and pulled on a blue denim shirt, buttoning it as though doing so was a way to focus on what he was saying. "You are beautiful. So was she. She and I both had taken pleasure in her breasts. But there was more to her than that. And more to my love for her. She couldn't believe that. I couldn't stand her not believing it. Sometimes I felt I should have done more, but I didn't know what. The divorce was ugly and painful. Losing her hit me hard, even though it was my decision to call it quits. After that, I hid in my career. I haven't been serious about anybody since."

Elizabeth knew that what had been unsaid was, "Until now." She left it unsaid. They both knew it was true.

"She — your wife — must have suffered without you." They were both silent for a while, then Elizabeth forced cheer into her voice. "Let's go straight to the dining room. The food's great. I've been here before."

The restaurant, modeled on an old English pub, was paneled in dark wood. A young woman led them down a narrow passageway to a candle-lit table in the back of the dining room. For some reason she assumed they were on a honeymoon. Elizabeth smiled and laughed it off, sensing that Jack's retreat made this a less than auspicious moment to bring up thoughts of a wedding.

As they settled in for a leisurely dinner, Jack asked, "Where are we, Elizabeth?"

For an instant, she thought he meant with the relationship. She paused, debating what to say.

Fortunately, before she could say that she thought they were at the point of making a commitment, he added, "Are we near Durham?"

"Yes," she breathed, thanking God she had been spared a disastrous turn in the conversation. "Connecticut. My mother grew up near here. I thought I'd show you a few of the places from my childhood."

She watched him carefully for his response. She had intended that this trip be more than a vacation. Her childhood was only part of what she wanted to share with him. She did not want to hit him with her plans too bluntly. She anxiously gauged his initial reaction.

"Sounds fine to me," Jack said.

She felt relieved. That night when she curled up next to him in bed, he put his arm around her. Feeling his warmth and gentleness, she decided she'd wait for him to initiate their next round of lovemaking.

12

MEMORIES OF THE FUTURE

THE NEXT MORNING brought a glorious new day. The sunlight woke them both early. They quickly got ready and hit the open road.

"What a breathtaking setting," declared Jack.

"I'm glad you like it." Elizabeth was hoping that he would not withdraw from her like he did last night.

Trailing arbutus and wild violets bloomed along the highway. Jack pointed out a grassy field with a small pond surrounded by maples just leafing out. The sunlight rippling through the pale green leaves in one stand of beeches created an effervescent effect, like champagne bubbles rising and sparkling in a flute.

"Some of this reminds me a bit of the area west of Fort Collins. L.A. sure isn't like this."

It was Elizabeth's turn to grow pensive. They drove for several miles in pleasantly companionable silence. Finally Jack said, "A penny for your thoughts."

"I was just feeling good about being here with you. Sometimes I wish I were still living here. This part of the country brings back a lot of memories. Did I tell you how my parents met? Mom went to Boston University as an undergrad. Dad was there in law school. He heard about this attractive woman from Durham and decided to seek her out since he came from there too. Turns out she was from Durham, Connecticut, not

Durham, New Hampshire. They fell in love and married, settling in New Hampshire. That's where I grew up."

"That's a wonderful story," Jack said a little nervously. He wondered why Elizabeth wanted to tell him about her parent's courtship.

"I used to go to Connecticut all the time to stay with Grandma. I was hoping we could drive by her house." Jack relaxed, thinking she must just be reminiscing about her childhood.

As they drove along the two-lane highway, they passed a yard containing a number of rickety old white tables, each covered with May baskets. A small grove of cherry trees was aflame with pink blossoms.

"Look at that!" Jack was delighted.

"Wait 'til you see how some of the old houses are done up. The older the better is the attitude here."

In a few minutes, she pulled over. The front porch of the house across the road was decorated with pewter figures. A colonial flag fluttered from the porch and wooden baskets of flowers lined the steps.

Jack's enjoyment thrilled Elizabeth. She had been hoping he would find New England appealing, perhaps even more so than Los Angeles.

Within minutes they entered the center of town. The town square consisted of a long grass field sparsely covered with old trees and a couple of huge, conical evergreens. She bought a mixed bouquet of violets and pansies from a street vendor, exchanging pleasantries with the old man.

"That's the town hall over there. Originally, it was built as a church. When the steeple fell down in a storm, the congregation took it as an omen and never occupied it. Eventually, it was taken over for the town offices."

They drove up to the white colonial-style building. Elizabeth parked and led the way down a road along side of it. They passed through two columns built of stone dug out of the hard New England earth and entered Durham Cemetery.

Elizabeth inclined her head towards a solitary evergreen. "That's where Mom's buried. She said she wanted to come back home." Elizabeth knelt and pulled some weeds from around the base of the stone. "Mom was a wonderful woman. Always there for me and my brother. Wasn't into politics like

Dad. Never worked outside the home. She always had something baked for us when we came home from school. She was a great cook. We had wonderful Sunday dinners."

Jack noted that back on her home ground, Elizabeth had reverted to some of the clipped speech patterns of her terse New England forbearers.

"I lost both Mom and Dad while I was governor. We lost Mom to cancer and that just seemed to take away Dad's will to live. He died about a year later of a heart attack. I always thought it was a broken heart. My brother's death aged them both."

Jack knelt and helped her with the weeds by her mother's stone. "I didn't realize you had a brother."

"I should bring grass clippers next time." Elizabeth swallowed. "They take good care of things here, but they never cut close enough to the stones. Randy was killed in Vietnam."

Jack felt the darkness of the thought close in on Elizabeth. "I'm sorry," was the best he could offer.

She moved over and started clearing a stone with her grandmother's name on it. "I miss her. And I miss New England so. I've maintained my legal residence in New Hampshire, even though I live most of the time in D.C. I'm seriously thinking about coming back here to live full time."

"You mean now? Seems like a pretty radical idea, what with your career and all."

"There's too much cynicism inside the beltway. A lot of Peter's money went to foundations, but he left me well off. It's no trouble to maintain two residences. This would be a good place to live."

"You mean you would give up your international troubleshooting and relief work?"

Elizabeth placed the flowers she had bought on the graves and stood to leave. "I don't know for sure. Remember how you said you might like to buy a farm someday because you were so frustrated with life in the city? I feel a lot like that now that politics is behind me. Sort of at sea without any sails."

"With everything you've been facing, maybe you just need to retreat for a while."

"I've really been thinking about something more permanent. If I were living in New Hampshire and not working, I'm sure they'd release Amy to me. I could make a home for her."

"A home isn't a building, Elizabeth. It's what people build

together with how they treat each other. Have you talked to Amy about this?"

"Not yet. I don't want to get her excited until I'm sure I want to give up the job and our unit at the Watergate."

"This might be a good time for you to live somewhere a little more out of the way," Jack agreed. "Living in a small town could be safer, but it seems like the kind of place where everyone knows everyone else's business."

Elizabeth became defensive, thinking that Jack might prefer the anonymity of a big city like Los Angeles. "It's not that bad."

"I was thinking it might be good to get away for awhile." Jack paused, weighing what he was about to say. "I've gone over and over the files and read everything I can get my hands on. Nothing is out of place that I can find. But I'm convinced there's something wrong."

Elizabeth frowned. "I thought we decided that we were worrying too much."

Jack took both of her hands and held them gently. "I decided you were worrying too much and didn't need anything else on your pretty shoulders. If you're thinking of retiring, I think you should take this situation into consideration."

Elizabeth pulled her hands from his and brushed dandelion fluff from his hair. "It's not like you to act like an alarmist, Jack."

"You're right. It isn't." He told her about the man who had tailed him after the interview with Sonoma. "When I came out, he was standing in a phone booth talking. He clearly had the door of the convenience store I was in within his sight."

"That still could have been coincidence, Jack."

"Maybe. I was in the store a good twenty minutes. I'd bet if it had been all day, he still would have been there when I came out."

"Why would someone be tailing you?"

"That's what I want to know." Jack frowned.

Elizabeth considered what he said, as they walked back towards the car. "Then you think New Hampshire would be a good place for me? You'd still visit me there?"

"I'd take New Hampshire over D.C. any day. As a sage woman once said, D.C. is colder than a witch's tit."

Elizabeth laughed. "Didn't say tit. I didn't know you that well then."

Elizabeth turned when they reached the front entrance to

the town hall. "Let's go inside. Somebody works here who I'd like you to meet."

Toward the rear of the building, in a small open office, they found a tiny elderly woman hunched over her desk as she sorted through papers. Her simple gold earrings, unadorned gold-framed eyeglasses, and short gray hair conveyed a no-nonsense New England attitude.

She looked up with a start. "Lizzy, is that you?"

She got up and hugged Elizabeth enthusiastically. Her round face sparkled.

Elizabeth squeezed her hand. "Dorothy, this is my friend Jack Bradshaw. He's with the *L.A. Times*. Jack, this is Dorothy Hutchinson. She's Durham's tax collector. More importantly, she and Mom were best friends."

"So, you're Lizzy's fellow. You'd better make her happy, young man. She deserves it."

Jack felt as if he were an awkward sixteen and picking Elizabeth up for a prom date. Elizabeth hooked her arm through his in a proprietary way and filled in the silence. "He makes me very happy."

For over an hour Jack sat patiently, listening vaguely to their memories. As Elizabeth laughed and chatted with Dorothy, it was as though part of her had grown young again. He could see the light-hearted girl she once was. Jack found her charming and wished that he could weave a magic spell to let her stay in this protected moment.

He was intuitive enough to sense that Dorothy was a stand-in for Elizabeth's mother. The trip to the cemetery and this visit were as close as Elizabeth could come to bringing him home to meet her parents. Jack was certain that he loved Elizabeth and he knew that they suited each other as lovers. Regardless of that, marriage was something he just wasn't ready to consider. He tuned back into what Dorothy was saying.

"I miss your mom so. It was hard for me when she met your father and moved away. But we kept in close contact. I used to cherish those long stays at your house. I've kept all of her letters. I'll give them to you someday."

"Mom was such a bundle of energy. She never could sit still. Seemed like the only time she relaxed was in the bathtub at night."

"I remember once when she fell asleep and dropped a book

she was reading into the water."

"Oh, she did that all the time. The library staff kidded her for that. It was such a happy time. Mom kept the house so nice. There was always a bustle of activity with lots of people around and great meals. I respected Dad so much for what he accomplished professionally. I loved Mom and the home she made."

"Your mother accomplished more than you give her credit for. In many ways, she made your father a success. She supported him in every way. Prepared all those special meals whenever he wanted to entertain his political friends. She ran the house and took care of all the finances. Your mom's inheritance allowed your dad the freedom to follow his political ambitions. Your dad was a lucky man."

"I remember Dad as the intellectual and Mom as the happy, carefree soul."

"I think it was a little more of a combination for both of them than you realize. Your mom was an extremely smart woman. I think her willingness to accept a supportive role tended to camouflage her intelligence. And it was almost impossible for her to speak in public. But she would lead the charge when an issue involved one of her passions. Remember some of the historic preservation battles she fought? Your mother was also the one who spearheaded the fundraising drive to add the Sunday School wing at the Congregational Church in New Hampshire."

"Yes, but —"

"But she wasn't a governor? Lizzy, your parents lived in a different era. Women started families young and took second place to their husbands. Your family life was happy, not because of your parents' roles, but because your parents were happy. They were very much in love and thoroughly enjoyed each other. Happiness can exist in different settings. Times have changed."

At last Elizabeth bade farewell to Dorothy. She turned to Jack as they got to the car. "Now I want to show you Grandma's house."

They drove for about a mile and turned off to the left. The quiet road led around a bend. Elizabeth pulled to the side.

A handsome, two-story, white colonial clapboard house stood in front of them with an American flag flying over the porch roof. It was set back from the road, surrounded by enormous rity. The huge trunks of the oaks, with their outstretched branches, bespoke familial and community roots that went deep.

Elizabeth's voice was full of honeyed contentment and the desire for something more. "This was my grandma's house — where Mom grew up. During the holidays all the fireplaces were lit. Grandma cooked Christmas dinner on the hearth. I'd sit and watch the snow storming outside and listen to the turkey juices popping as they dripped from the spit to the flames. The smell of warm cinnamon and allspice in her pies would mix with the pine from the Christmas tree."

Jack admired the house and then became silent. It was a cool, collected silence that turned inward, not the shared warmth she had hoped. Elizabeth wanted to connect the love she had felt as a child to the love she felt for Jack. This wasn't the reaction she expected.

As they headed north toward Springfield, she tried to remember when he started to withdraw. She traced his coolness back to when they had made love at the inn. He had enthusiastically responded to her at first and then — and then what? Elizabeth couldn't figure out what had changed.

About forty minutes later they passed a sign for South Hadley, Massachusetts, and entered the town. "You don't mind if we make another stop, do you?"

Jack assented, but sounded non-committal. "That's fine. I need to stretch my legs."

Elizabeth pulled through a massive brick gate marked by two sets of twin pillars, explaining, "This is Mount Holyoke. I went to college here." She parked and began walking him around the stately old campus.

"This is really a beautiful place. These trees are spectacular," said Jack as he noticed the mix of old buildings with leaded glass dating back to 1837, and spare squared-off new ones. As they walked past a vine-covered, red brick building with a chimney and gables, he felt as if he should be carrying Elizabeth's books for her.

Elizabeth still had the determined stride of a young coed. "I used to sit for hours under that tree on the edge of the lake and study."

"Somehow, I'd picture you over there by that building. It looks like a castle."

"That's the Science Tower." Elizabeth laughed. "As you might guess, I was not one to play the damsel in distress." She paused, realizing again how much strength and help he had given her with Amy. "Although you've done an excellent job of chasing away some of the dragons in my life lately."

Elizabeth took Jack's hand and hooked her arm through his. She was aware that although he held her hand when she reached for it, he seldom took hers. "I came to school here because of Dad. After Randy died he focused on me as a replacement. He wanted me to follow him into politics. He thought women developed more self-confidence at an all-female school, so he pushed me in that direction."

"I'm surprised that you didn't find that patronizing. It implies women can't function in a man's world."

"In a way that's true. Women can't perform to their fullest in a world in which less is expected of them. I really sensed a difference in the science classes. The profs were there for me. I got the kind of attention that makes you believe that you're just as good as anybody else. It prepared me to face a world that would see me as less than a man."

"They must have done something right. You're certainly capable of holding your own with any man."

The sound of water hitting stone in the brook echoed as it dashed down a spill-over. Something inside Elizabeth froze. Was this why he had pulled back from her?

She stopped and waited while he turned to face her inquiringly. "Are you bothered by that, Jack?"

"You are a strong woman, Elizabeth."

But, Elizabeth thought, *not quite strong enough to ask what that means.* The shadows seemed to lengthen and darken the Quad. If she pointed out that he hadn't answered her question, and if he hadn't answered on purpose, she'd be cornering him. If he were a political opponent in a debate, she'd have quashed his evasion. This wasn't an adversarial relationship, however. She knew full well she could be overwhelming.

Thinking it over, Elizabeth changed her plans. Between Amy's hateful reaction and Jack's pulling into himself, this was not the time to ask him to quit his job and come live with her. There was no way she would bring up that subject now.

They circled back to the car in silence. Looking over the maps, with Elizabeth pointing out the alternatives, they decided to head north and turn east on Highway 2. That way, Jack could see some different countryside.

She tried to keep a conversation going. "Dad was an attorney. Served in the New Hampshire legislature. His campaigns were great fun. I'd go with him to hand out fliers. We even did that at the city dump. Being in the legislature wasn't full time then. He continued to practice law and became legal counsel to the governor for two years. After that, he got a judgeship."

"You sound really proud of him."

"He was a terrific dad. He always had time for us kids. He really doted on me. Almost every summer we would go up to Maine and my parents would let me take friends with me. We spent weeks at the seashore. Things haven't been like that for Amy. Oh, we traveled all over, but it wasn't the same." She sounded pained.

"Elizabeth, you're still beating yourself up over not surrounding Amy with hearth-roasted turkeys and clam bakes. This is a different era. You and the likes of your Mount Holyoke sisters made it that."

He silenced her as she started to respond. "If you ask me, it's a better world today. Nice though the Norman Rockwell version is, the difference between a microwaved slice of store bought pie and Grandma's finest is nothing compared to what our mothers were able to contribute to the world and what you've done."

She looked at him, surprised. She'd never seen him so forceful. He was practically yelling at her. "Stop torturing yourself about what could have been. What would you really rather be doing? Rolling out pie crust for one kid or developing microenterprise programs that allow thousands of women to feed children that would otherwise starve to death? Shoot, Elizabeth, figure it out. How many lives have you saved?"

Elizabeth was touched by his earnestness. "So, you're saying that we can't go home again?"

"Don't let yourself be pulled into a past that doesn't exist anymore. You deserve the best. Decide what you really want and go after it. You always have."

"Jack," Elizabeth couldn't stop the words, "will you marry me?"

13

FAIR PLAY

THE SILENCE LENGTHENED between them. Elizabeth felt the tension in her throat as she decided to seize the moment. "Come to New England and live with me."

She steeled herself for his reaction, giving him the chance to respond. Jack's voice jumped up an octave. "You mean give up my career?"

That was the answer then: no. He had jumped straight over the thought of marriage and living together.

"You've told me about your frustrations with the paper. You even mentioned buying a farm and writing."

"I'm not quite ready for the pasture yet."

"I'm not talking about retiring. You'd have a career doing what you want. What I want is more time with you."

Jack was silent. Elizabeth fought back her disappointment. "I guess I thought you were serious when you wanted to write books full time. Will you at least think about it?"

"Is that what this trip was really about?"

"I can't say I didn't have it in mind."

Elizabeth's dream faded into disillusionment, embarrassed for having pushed too hard. Their silence indicated a mutual decision to drop the subject.

A highway sign indicated they had cut across most of Massachusetts and were fast approaching the New Hampshire border. Elizabeth wanted to leave behind any damage her proposal had caused.

"I thought tomorrow we could take a drive on the Kancamagus Highway before heading back to Boston."

"That sounds fine," Jack amicably agreed.

During the hours of sightseeing that took them around the Great Bay, they slowly grew comfortable with each other again.

"There's a quiet place near here called Wagon Hill Farm. It has a trail that goes all the way down to the bay. Shall we try it, Jack?"

"Sounds good."

They pulled into the parking lot of the old farm which the community now operated as a park. Off to the left, atop a hill on the horizon, stood an old wagon. To the right, a long path meandered through an open grass field and disappeared into a row of trees at the water line. They began walking hand-in-hand. For once, "ignore it and it will go away" seemed to work.

Near dusk, they pulled into an overlook above the two-story colonial inn where they planned to stay. A small fishpond shimmered with gold in the sunlight. A wall of piled stones crosscut the farmland surrounding it.

"It's so beautiful," breathed Elizabeth.

"So are you." Jack pulled her to him and kissed her.

From the fullness of his mouth on hers, she was sure any breach she created in their relationship had been transcended.

As she got back into the car, her skirt had slid up. She did not pull it back down. His enjoyment in looking at her legs excited her.

They arrived at the inn just in time for the first seating of dinner. The two had polished off their hot apple pie topped with thick slices of cheddar before most of the other diners had finished their salads. They took the rest of the chilled bottle of Monbazillac Chateau Du Puch dessert wine back to their room to finish it.

The staff already had a fire blazing in the brick fireplace. "Jeez, that makes it hot in here," said Elizabeth.

Grabbing an ice cube from the plastic ice bucket, Jack teased, "I can cool you off." He pulled the front of her sweater up and dropped it into the cleavage between Elizabeth's breasts, laughing, hugging her arms back.

Stepping away from him, she pulled off her sweater and fished the ice out from the lace that edged the silken cups of her bra. "Turn about is fair play."

She pulled up his sweater, wrestling him to the bed. She rubbed the flat side of the ice cube across his nipples and then licked them as they hardened, teasing lightly with the barest edge of her teeth.

"You aren't the only one that can make ice hot, Jack."

"I'm not sure it's the ice that's hot."

She laughed, stepping away. "Politics 101. First rule of public speaking. Always leave them wanting more."

She sucked on the ice as she disappeared into the bathroom. Moments later she emerged swathed in a long, silk, ivory-colored negligee that caressed her every curve. As she moved to him, the gown flowed over her sleek body like cream.

Jack was sitting in front of the fire on the comforter he had moved over from the bed, wearing a terry cloth robe that Elizabeth had sent him for his birthday last month.

"I thought I'd give you a present to unwrap." She took his fingers and led them to the golden laces on her shoulder straps, simultaneously opening the belt on his robe and reaching her hand inside.

They tumbled together. The flames from the crackling fireplace made a play of shadow and light on their bodies.

Each having pleasurably exhausted the other, they climbed into the colonial four-poster. Jack held the thick comforter for her, eased it up under her chin, and slid in beside her. In loving tenderness they fell asleep in each other's arms. The last thing Elizabeth saw as she closed her eyes was the fire still burning in the darkness.

Hours later, in the blackness and quiet of the New England night, Jack awoke to a woman's screams. It was Elizabeth. She was standing in front of the bed by the fireplace screaming for help.

14

SMOLDERING EMBERS

JACK THREW BACK the comforter and went to her side. Elizabeth's anguished scream split open the silence of the night.

"There's plenty of fuel! There's plenty of fuel!"

He realized that she was sleepwalking. Her eyes stared blankly at the smoldering embers.

She woke up with a jerk, her eyes wide. They focused on Jack. She grabbed him, sobbing. She was shaking and soaked with perspiration.

A knock thudded heavily on the door. Jack helped Elizabeth sit down, turned on the light, and went to open it.

The innkeeper stood in the doorway in a robe and slippers. "Want's going on in here?" she demanded.

Elizabeth huddled on the bed. Still panicked, she shouted, "The fire! The fire!"

Jack tried to push the door shut as he spoke, but the innkeeper blocked him. He reassured her, "It's okay. She just had a bad dream."

The innkeeper peered around Jack, looking for signs of upset. Elizabeth screamed again.

"She'll be okay. Just let me get her fully awake. It's only a bad dream." He shut the door.

He took Elizabeth in his arms, rocking her while she cried. When her sobs finally stopped, he continued to hold her and gently urged, "Tell me. Tell me everything."

"I was in the plane. We were going down. I saw — I saw Peter. He was just hanging there. I could feel my legs being crushed. And this pain in my head."

Jack knelt before her, gently massaging her leg, trying to banish the pain. "It's over with, Elizabeth. All these memories you've been dredging up over the last few days must have triggered this."

"The fire. It was something about the fire." Elizabeth looked at the glowing orange embers. "The fire. That's what did it. It was like the flames around the plane. There were lots of fires, small ones."

"That was something I wondered about. In every other similar crash I've heard of, the plane burst into flames. Your Merlin didn't." Jack lifted his head, looking urgently into her eyes. "That's what you said —'There's plenty of fuel!'"

"Fuel?"

Jack lifted her other foot onto his leg as if to protect it. He didn't want her to relive the ordeal of hanging upside down for all those hours with her legs crushed. He placed one hand over her feet, unconsciously shielding her. With the other, he held her hand.

His voice was full of love and concern. "Since you've remembered this much, maybe it would help you to free yourself of the ghosts if you'd talk about it."

"There are no ghosts, Jack."

"Elizabeth, remember who you are talking to. You never come to L.A. to see me, despite my invitations. All your presidential commission work is done in D.C. You take the train to come to New England."

She started to interrupt, but he held up his hand to silence her. "Don't try to tell me you love the scenery. "

Elizabeth stammered, trying to utter a denial that she could not make in good conscience.

"You need to remember what happened."

"I've had therapy from professionals, Jack."

"If you think it would be better to talk with one of them, I'll call anyone you want right now."

"I can't remember anything," she protested.

"You don't want to remember anything. There's a difference. Start with the obvious things you do know."

"Okay." Her voice was sharp. She was angry that he was

pushing her. "I survived. I hung there upside down for hours, seeing those flames and blacking out, then waking up again. I saw Peter. I thought he was alive but he was dead. His legs were ripped off and his guts were hanging out." She screamed at him, "Is that what you want to hear?"

"Yes," he answered calmly, but matching her intensity. "Tell me. Keep talking."

"Peter died!" she shrieked. "Peter died. Will Barton died. And I lived."

"You think you should have died with them."

"Spare me your amateur psychologizing, Jack."

"You're right, Elizabeth, I am an amateur. You know what amateur means? Someone who acts out of love."

"If you loved me, you'd just let me go to sleep." She pulled her hand out of his and swung her legs up on the bed, hugging them tightly.

"Go on, Elizabeth, go to sleep. Have another nightmare." He pushed aside the anger, and softened his tone, pleading with her. "Come on. Don't stop now. Elizabeth, you said once that you felt you survived for a reason. You can't think that and feel guilty about it too. Peter died. Will Barton died. And you lived. Believe there's some purpose to that."

"I lived. And Bud. Bud lived. If you can call it that. His body survived, but his mind was destroyed." She slammed her fist into the bed. "Damn it! Damn the whole fucking world!" She dissolved into tears again.

Jack moved closer to her and cradled her in his arms. She didn't push him away. "You're okay now. You're safe now. You're here with me. Tell me more. Tell me about Bud."

Elizabeth wiped at her nose and sniffled. "Bud Hawley. He was our pilot and our friend. He flew us all the time. We traveled so much that we spent practically as much time with him as we did with each other. Now he's essentially a vegetable. I wanted to see him when I got out of the hospital, but they wouldn't let me. They said I wasn't in any condition for that. I checked up on him later. Frank Shotwell had helped with that too. He set up a trust out of Peter's estate to care for him perpetually. It sounds like a cemetery arrangement. It may as well be."

"Would you still like to see him? I'll find out where he is and go with you."

"Oh, Jack, would you?" The idea captured her enthusiasm. She got up and rummaged through her purse for her address book. Ripping out a blank page, she scribbled across the back of it. "Here's Shotwell's private number."

More memories surfaced. "I saw a man in farmer's bib overalls and a man in a uniform. There was something about top secret papers and army officers. But I think that was a dream. They were in military uniforms. They argued with a local man."

"Peter was working on the Afghanistan investigation then. Would he have had some of those papers with him?"

"Almost certainly."

"And some of those would have required security clearance. They could easily have been scattered in the crash. But how could the NSC have known so soon about the crash?" Jack frowned. "They probably sent someone to recover any papers from the site. They sure wouldn't want to take a chance on that stuff blowing around in the wind."

"Blowing in the wind," Elizabeth repeated, almost as if in a trance. An image formed in her mind of the paper blowing across her face — and a vision of a man in an army uniform bending to pick it up.

She shivered and clutched Jack's arm. "The third man in the pictures — the pictures in Peter's office — he was there. At the crash site. I'm sure of it. And I know what I was saying just before I woke up."

15

EAST OF NOWHERE

"FUEL! THERE'S PLENTY of fuel!" Elizabeth's words kept running through Jack's mind as he taxied to the National Transportation Safety Board in Washington.

He set aside the gravity of that thought and chuckled to himself about the way Farnum had sputtered when he told him he was taking a couple of weeks' vacation. Being a workaholic had its advantages. He'd been banking vacation time for years.

He was happy this morning, even though he was concerned about Elizabeth. He discovered that he enjoyed taking care of her. The difference between his ex-wife and Elizabeth, he was discovering, was that Elizabeth faced her problems, where Joanne had denied them and hid from them. Elizabeth was pleased and grateful for his help and for the love from which it sprang. Joanne would not accept it. He was struggling not to carry his negative feelings about Joanne into his relationship with Elizabeth.

After Elizabeth had stopped crying from her nightmare, he had steered her into the bathroom and drawn a bath for her, encouraging her to relax, happy to be able to help her. Now, as the cab pulled up in front of a utilitarian office building, he was sure that he wanted to go on helping and protecting her.

The NTSB lobby area was drab and unadorned. *There must be some genetic link,* Jack thought, *between bureaucrats and lack of aesthetic taste.*

Toward the end of a hall, he found a door marked "Records Room." In much smaller letters, near the door handle, was the word "Enter."

He knocked and walked into a large, well-lit room that was divided by a counter. As he approached it, a black man emerged from behind the shelves. He was about Jack's age, but smaller and almost bald.

"You must be Jack Bradshaw. I'm Joe Dutton. I've been expecting you. I have the files in a conference room down the hall. Follow me."

Jack looked for a point of personal contact. "You said you were in the navy? My duty was submarines. I was a petty officer on the USS *Daniel Boone*. How 'bout you?"

"Flew Willie Fudds for two tours in Nam."

"Those radar planes sure were slow. I think the subs went faster. What carrier?"

"The *Midway*. Loved that old tub. Lot of history to it."

As they entered the conference room, Jack whistled at the three large storage boxes on the table. "How much of this is the senator's crash files?"

"All of it." Joe chuckled. "First-timers really don't know what they're getting into. Tell me what you want and I'll show you where it is."

"I don't know exactly what I'm looking for."

"Okay. Then the conclusion is the best place to start. If you have questions, you can look through the report for those specific areas that were addressed in the conclusion."

"Okay. Where is the conclusion?"

Joe's smile was too sincere to be patronizing. "The conclusion is the very last portion of this second banker's box. Let me help you out by telling you a bit about the purpose of the investigation and how it's conducted."

He took a breath and plunged into the speech he'd obviously made many times before. "When an accident occurs, NTSB inspectors fly out immediately to secure the wreckage and save any possible evidence. It's like a major criminal investigation. Every piece of information is potentially vital and must be kept in its original state. The first goal of the investigation is to determine if there are any mechanical malfunctions which could have contributed to or caused the accident. The plane's mechanical history is studied. Failure analysis specialists put together the wreckage to see if anything is missing, broken, or ruptured."

"Like a jigsaw puzzle."

"Right. A highly complex 3-D one. We review the weather and the pilots' backgrounds too. But the first effort is directed toward the mechanical errors and malfunctions. Once any possibility of a mechanical malfunction is eliminated, then it automatically becomes a question of pilot error."

"You're telling me that if there is no mechanical malfunction, it's pilot error?"

"Without some extreme weather phenomenon, like a microburst thunderstorm, that's it."

"Isn't there some method for determining whether or not the pilot really was responsible?"

"The investigation of the pilot and his actions is as thorough as humanly possible. We review his background, his flying experience, the state of his health at the time of the accident, any drugs or alcohol in his system, prior accidents or deviations that would indicate some sort of a pattern of poor decision making. We try to find out the actual sequence of actions of the pilot during the accident."

"How do you determine what the pilot did immediately before the accident?"

"We rely on the pilot's testimony regarding his actions as well as witness statements by passengers or people on the ground observing."

"And if he lies or is dead?"

"Our investigation of the mechanical performance is so thorough that we can tell how the controls were set at the time of impact. Say a pilot tells us he was in a right bank. We could tell by things like bends or nicks in the control cables and rods that the pilot was actually in a left turn. Pilots are generally honest when describing the events of an accident because they've been trained to be. We still occasionally get pilots who try to mislead us. If there are no mechanical malfunctions and no weather anomalies, we have no choice but to conclude they are lying."

Jack pondered this. "The physical evidence is that accurate?"

"Like I said, we can tell the exact position of the controls at the time of impact. We can look at throttle controls and linkups and tell you if it was full forward. We can see with the instruments that full power hadn't been reached yet. Knowing how fast a particular engine spools up to that power setting, we can even tell you how many seconds before impact the pilot pushed the throttles forward."

"That's amazing."

"You could do the same thing with a car accident, but it's too expensive. An investigation costs hundreds of thousands or even millions for major mysteries like the TWA 800 crash."

Now that Jack had pressed the play button on this guy, he was wondering how to turn him off. Still, he was an important source of information. Too much talk was better than too little.

"You know the PanAm plane that was bombed by terrorists over Scotland in the '80s?" Joe continued. "That one took a long time to solve, but within hours we knew there was a bomb. Some of the pieces had severe rupture indications with heavy burn marks, all from the inside. They came from areas of the plane where there were no volatile or hydraulic fluids."

"It's that simple?"

"Sometimes. We were lucky that bomb didn't go off over open ocean. Without the pieces, we'd never have known. TWA 800 was close enough to shore that we could recover the pieces."

"So what was the conclusion in the senator's case?"

"I scanned through the conclusions before you came and there is no doubt that this accident was pilot error."

"What was that based on?"

"The evidence clearly showed that both engines were suffering from fuel starvation when the plane crashed. No fuel was getting to them. Investigators dipped the fuel tanks and found only residual, non-usable amounts left in them. There is no doubt the pilot flew the plane out of fuel. The lack of a major fire at the scene of the accident was another clear indication that there was no fuel available."

"Governor Armstrong recalled small fires."

"There were minor fires caused by the burning of some of the aircraft's interior, insulation, and remaining oil, but no major fuel fire — which is expected in a crash of this nature."

"How can a pilot run out of fuel?"

"It's happened in numerous accidents, although it is somewhat unusual for a commercial business plane flown by a professional pilot. Planes that crash due to fuel starvation are usually flown by amateur pilots unaware of fuel consumption and the need for significant reserves. We theorized that Hawley was dodging thunderstorm activity and had to add power. He was consuming fuel at a higher rate than he planned."

"Yeah, but that much extra? They were headed to Texas. They were nowhere near there."

"Experienced pilots flying high performance aircraft like this normally have more than an hour's worth of extra fuel. His destination was still two and a half hours away, so he should have had three and a half hours more fuel on board. We can only conclude that his tanks were only half full when he started."

"How could an experienced pilot make a mistake like that?"

Joe shook his head. "We know from statistics that there's a spike in the curve when pilots reach an experienced level and start taking a lot of things for granted. They ignore safety procedures and become complacent. I have to admit, Hawley didn't seem a likely candidate. He had more than twenty years' experience. Military pilots tend to be sticklers for checklists and following procedures right down the line."

"I understand checklists. We used them on the sub. You just don't skip over things like fuel."

Joe shrugged. "Humans make mistakes, not machines."

"When you are investigating a situation of fuel starvation, what mechanical malfunctions do you look for?"

"We'd dip the tanks and look at the area around the crash site to see if there was any fuel remaining or scattered about. We'd then check the fuel lines to see if there were any clogs or obstructions or a failed valve that locked shut when it should have been opened. We would typically look at the gauges and see how they were operating."

"What did the gauges say?"

Joe looked through the report for a couple of minutes, and then showed a page to Jack. "If you look in this portion of the report, you can see that the gauges were tested and were functioning normally."

He paused for a moment as he continued. "That's odd! There's no indication of what the gauges were reading when they got to the wreckage. Normally that's one of the things they'd look at."

Jack wondered if he'd found a clue. "Do you consider that significant?"

"It's unusual for NTSB investigators. In this case, it turned out they were not on site right away. They took over the investigation from some military personnel who contributed significantly to this investigation. That may explain the gap."

Jack had noted the mention of military personnel, both in the report and from Elizabeth. He was glad he had convinced Elizabeth to wait until after he checked out the NTSB information before he called Shotwell. Even if there was no connection, you could never tell what might muddy the waters. Deciding not to ask Joe about the military involvement, he switched to another issue. "You said the pilot's statement was important. What did he say about what happened?"

"No pilot statement was taken. According to the medical records, the pilot suffered severe brain damage. Although he was alive, he was not coherent."

"So you're telling me that you don't have gauge readings and you don't have a pilot's statement, both of which are key to an investigation."

"The gauge readings aren't all that important. Not when we already know that the tanks were empty. The pilot's statement is merely icing on the cake. Don't forget, in many of the accidents we investigate, the pilot's not alive to give a statement."

Jack had decided it would be best if he could locate Bud without tipping his hand to Shotwell. "Where's the pilot now?"

Joe thumbed through one of the boxes until he came to a section labeled "Medical Investigation - Pilot." He scanned through the documents in it and then laid one of them in front of Jack.

"Here it is. According to this medical report, we last tried to interview him at the VA Hospital in Lincoln County, New Mexico. But that was last year."

Not wanting to waste more time, Jack used a phone in the lobby. He dialed information and tracked down the number of the hospital. Once he got the hospital on the line, he had to run through a layer of bureaucratic staff to get to an orderly who could tell him if Bud was still at the facility. By then he'd concluded that the candid approach would not work. Identifying himself as a reporter was out of the question.

"My name is Jack Bradshaw," he said with authority. "I'm calling regarding a patient named Lt. Col. Bud Hawley."

He got the kind of non-answer he expected. The man sounded almost like a recording. "I'm sorry, we cannot give out information on patients."

Jack was persistent. "This is a matter of extreme importance."

"Can you tell me what business it is of yours and who you are?"

"As I said, I'm Jack Bradshaw. I'm calling on behalf of Colonel Hawley's former employer. We are interested in determining his condition." As an afterthought, Jack added, "There are some worker's compensation problems."

"Identify the name of the employer."

Jack realized the ploy might work. "The employer was Senator Peter Armstrong. The senator's affairs are being handled by his wife, Elizabeth. I'm calling on her behalf."

"All right, Mr. Bradshaw. However, Colonel Hawley is no longer at this institution."

"Where is he?"

"Our records indicate that he was transferred."

Jack decided to assert control over the situation by acting outraged. "Transferred! On whose authority?"

"That's confidential information."

Jack let go with a barrage. "Governor Armstrong was not consulted on this. I demand to know where he went and who authorized this!"

"He was released to his family. This is normal procedure. Let me check the records."

The man was off the line so long, Jack was starting to think he had lost him. He was glad to hear the officious voice again. "Mr. Bradshaw, the records indicate that the patient was released to his cousin, his only living relative, and transferred to the veterans' home in Columbia, South Carolina." The orderly paused. "Oh, shit. This thing's stamped secret."

Jack's voice became friendlier now that he had what he

wanted. "I assure you Governor Armstrong will be both grateful and discrete." He decided to fish a little. "You guys sure are in a tough place to find. Even the phone operator had trouble figuring out what town you're in."

"Yeah, we're east of nowhere and west of someplace else. It's the right spot for patients who somebody wants forgotten."

Jack thanked him and began to sort through what he had learned. Bud Hawley had been stashed from prying eyes. But why?

16

ECHOING THE PAST

"HE SUSTAINED SEVERE brain damage and he's always disoriented. I'll let you look in and see for yourself." The nurse at the veterans' home was deferential, having recognized Elizabeth from the news as a spokeswoman for a UNICEF project.

Jack was concerned about how Elizabeth would take seeing Bud. He wanted her to be prepared. "Governor Armstrong survived the same plane crash as Colonel Hawley. Can you tell us a little more about his condition?"

"He can feed himself and talk occasionally. Not much of it makes sense."

"It there any chance he'll come out of this?" Her voice was hopeful.

The nurse was no believer in false hope. "He'll be like this for the rest of his life." She paused, not knowing if she might be stepping on someone's toes. "It's been a while since anybody has taken an interest in him."

"He hasn't had any visitors? We were told he had a cousin."

"Somebody did drop in after he first got here. Was his cousin in the army? This guy said something about them being buddies in Vietnam, though, so I'd guess it wasn't his cousin."

Jack pulled out the picture he'd brought from Peter's den.

"Could be. It was a long time ago. There wasn't anything that stood out about him."

96

The nurse showed them into Hawley's room. In the chair, a man in a white hospital gown sat rocking back and forth in a vinyl chair next to the bed. He was unshaven and very thin. On one side of his head was a large indentation surrounded by surgical scars. He did not seem to notice that the door to his room had opened or that anyone was there.

Elizabeth took his hand and bent down so that her eyes were even with his. "Bud? Bud, it's me, Elizabeth."

His expression remained vacant, his eyes unmoving.

"Is he always in this kind of a fog?" asked Jack.

"Almost always. Sometimes he seems lucid, but not often. He'll be a permanent resident here."

"You said he talks occasionally. What does he say?"

"Sometimes he has nightmares and yells the same thing over and over. But it's unintelligible. It sounds sort of like 'few gag' or 'hat full.' It's even on the chart because he says it so much. You don't have any idea what his hat would be full of, do you? Sometimes with patients like this, what sounds like nonsense can have real significance. But you have to figure it out in their own terms."

Her beeper sounded and she excused herself, leaving them to sit with Bud. Elizabeth sat on the edge of the bed across from him, holding his hand. Jack settled in beside her, his hand on the small of her back trying to lend her support.

"Bud, it's me. Elizabeth. Can you hear me?" Her voice was gentle.

Jack's mind drifted. The hospital smells evoked memories of Joanne's surgery and the aftermath of her suicide attempt. Jack felt himself pulled into them like falling into quicksand.

He forced himself to concentrate on Elizabeth and Bud. He had read about the therapy a mother used with her autistic child. She put him in an isolated environment and kept his focus tightly on her, so that what she said was the only input he received. Elizabeth was intuitively doing the same thing with Bud. She bent toward him, repeating the same refrain over and over.

After a half hour, Jack's tolerance was wearing thin. "Elizabeth, can't we go get a cup of coffee or something?"

She never took her eyes off Bud. "You can, Jack. I want to stay here."

If he heard, "Bud, it's me. Elizabeth. Can you hear me?" one more time, he thought he'd go nuts. "Let's try something else," he suggested. "What about repeating what the nurse mentioned he says himself?"

"Hat full. Few gag. Hat full. Few gag. . ."

A new litany replaced the old. Jack didn't think it was much of an improvement. An hour dragged by with the refrain dripping away onto his brain like Chinese water torture.

Elizabeth elbowed him. She nodded in Bud's direction. Jack saw that he was mouthing the words.

"Come on," Elizabeth urged. "What is it are you trying to say, Bud?" She stopped and listened.

Was the message getting through? Did Bud know someone was out there who cared?

"His lips moved!" Elizabeth's attention was riveted to him now.

"Hh, hh," he breathed, still not looking at her.

"Hh, hhatful. Hhhafful. FFfewgaj. FFfewgaj."

Elizabeth began echoing the sounds softly. "Hh, hhatful. Hhhafful. FFfewgaj. FFfewgaj."

Elizabeth's attitude had changed now. A half hour into this bizarre chorus, she was still bright and hopeful like a mother adoring the genius of her baby's first babbles.

Jack felt okay about leaving her now — for a few minutes at least. He whispered that he was going to go get some coffee, not wanting to break Elizabeth's pace.

He returned fifteen minutes later with a cup of coffee in each hand and two plastic-entombed vending machine sandwiches wedged under his arm. As he bit into the ham and cheese, something about their odd song caught his ear. He sipped the coffee and really listened this time.

"Hh, hhatful. Hhhafful. FFfewgaj. FFfewgaj."

Jack put the coffee aside and repeated the sounds with them, feeling the words in his mouth. "Hhhafful. FFfewgaj." His tongue and lips did the deciphering for him. "Half full. Fuel gauge. Elizabeth! That's it! That's what he's been trying to say. The tank is half full. Fuel gauge!"

17

PINEWOOD SCARS

Every instinct in his investigative bones told Jack to visit the crash scene near Johnson City, Tennessee. He hustled Elizabeth onto a late-night train to D.C. and let her think Farnum had called him back to L.A.

Jack drove all night, pulling over to a rest stop to get in a brief nap. He hit the Johnson City limits and went straight to the sheriff's office. He could worry about things like food, sleep, and a shave later.

He had the name from NTSB records of the lieutenant from the sheriff's office who had been at the scene. He hadn't had time to make an appointment, since Morris was off-duty when he called, but he did find out the officer would be in first thing in the morning.

It turned out he was a tall, gangly, pleasant-looking fellow. "You came a long way," he offered as Jack introduced himself. "Gonna be a hot one, ain't it?"

He seemed so friendly that Jack knew he'd be cooperative. He knew it for sure when Morris spelled his whole name out three times for him. This was a small enough town that a reporter from L.A. must sound intriguing.

"You're right about the long trip." A plate of greasy eggs, country sausage, grits, and shortbread biscuits beckoned from the desk.

Morris was as hospitable as could be. "Want some? I got plenty to share."

Jack's stomach growled. He started to say, "No, thanks. I'm more of a fruit smoothie guy myself." Despite his good intentions, he found himself thinking of his mother's big hot breakfasts on cold mornings in Colorado. Jack reached out and took the offered biscuit, scooping up an egg and making a sandwich out of it with some sausage.

Seeing Morris smile, he knew he had made the right choice. Nothing established you as someone's friend like the welcomed sharing of their plate.

He munched and then stifled a yawn. "Coffee'd be great." Morris poured Jack a steaming cupful.

Having established good rapport and gotten a second wind, Jack got to the point. "I understand from some of the records that you were the first deputy on the scene of the Armstrong crash and conducted the initial investigation."

"Yes, sir, that's sorta right. I started an investigation, but it was taken over by the military. Right after I got there, all these guys showed up. Some of 'em in military uniforms and some in civilian clothes. Claimed t'be from National Security. The way they handled it still pisses me off."

"As the officer in charge at a fatal accident scene, wouldn't you be responsible for conducting the investigation?"

"I sure thought I oughta be in charge. They quoted me some kinda government regulations. Said they had authority to seal the area off. I didn't agree, but they showed me the federal code and it seemed official."

Morris sopped up some egg with a biscuit and sucked at it before continuing. "As we looked for survivors, the first thing I noticed was there wasn't much fire. Heard a voice and followed it. It was the pilot. He didn't look good, but I thought he'd make it. There was a male passenger. He'd been thrown clear across the field. There was no doubt he was dead. He had multiple compound fractures. We found Governor Armstrong next. Her injuries were real bad. I don't know how she held on so long."

"She's a tough lady." The respect in his voice was considerable.

"You know the condition her husband was in?"

"Yes."

"Good. Describing him's not exactly something I do for shits and grins." He looked as if he was trying to set the thought aside. "We called for a rescue chopper. Before it reached us, a Sea Stallion dropped these army guys in on us. I thought they'd brought medics. But these were security guys. They struck me as goons — the kind that make people disappear. I hope I don't sound like I been watchin' too many movies."

"Not at all. Your impressions are important."

"Would you like to go with me out to the scene? Things have been slow around here."

Jack smiled and accepted. *Maybe I should do more work in small towns,* he thought. In the city, everyone wanted to hide and stay uninvolved.

Later that morning, Morris and Jack parked the car on a dirt road and started climbing through heavy brush. They came to a faint path.

"This leads straight to the crash site. All the investigators going up and down the hill dragging out pieces of the wreckage wore it into the dirt."

"I'm glad the path's here. This is pretty rugged country."

"Yeah, the hills aren't too kindly hereabouts. Even after they radioed the position, it still took us 'til daybreak to find it. My huntin' hounds sniffed it out. They caught the smell from a couple of the small fires that were still smoldering."

Jack was puffing hard by the time they reached the top of the ridge. No wonder it had taken them so long to get into the site.

"That's it," Morris said, pointing down the other side of the ridge.

At first it didn't look like much. Jack noticed a small clearing in the midst of the woods and realized it had been created by the plane. The undergrowth had re-established itself, but he could still see where some of the treetops were sliced off. A large indentation in the dirt indicated where the fuselage had rested. Small paths led away from this scar like spokes from the hub of a wheel. Otherwise, the site was empty.

"Where's the wreckage?"

"The NTSB always takes the wreckage away to look it over. Ain't got the foggiest where it is now. For a while they had it in a hangar at our local airport."

"Can you tell me what you think happened?"

"It looks like the plane came in low over the trees to the east. I'm sure it was tryin' to make it to the Johnson City Airport about ten miles away. Didn't quite make it. See that scar up high on that big pine? It looks like the right wing hit it and ripped off. The NTSB says the plane probably went into a quick roll and hit the ground upside down."

Jack whistled.

"I'm still surprised it didn't explode, because there were fuel lines and hydraulic lines everywhere. Usually there are major sparks. Half these trees woulda burned down if that plane had much fuel on board. Instead, just little pieces of insulation and a couple of small bushes burned. If it weren't for them showin' us the way, we might still be looking for this wreckage up here."

And Elizabeth would have been dead before I could meet her, thought Jack.

Morris became indignant. "These Feds were really high-handed. I did all the right things. I sealed off the site, radioed for the EMS chopper, and took notes. Then these military people showed up and took it all out of my hands. I don't know to this day how they knew about the accident. I didn't quite understand it because it wasn't a military plane, but they insisted the law applied 'cause the senator was a member of the Intelligence Committee and had important national security papers on him."

"Did you see any of these papers?"

"They were scattered all over the accident site, apparently from the senator's briefcase. They spent an awful lot of time and effort looking for all of 'em."

"You mentioned you took notes."

"They insisted on taking my draft report. Said they'd turn it over to the NTSB. I haven't seen it since. They took the papers I found in the area. I could see that some had been marked secret, so I guess they knew what they were talkin' about."

"I don't remember seeing your notes in the NTSB files. But there were boxes of info. Maybe they just didn't get into the summary."

"These guys said they came from the nearest military post, but I don't know. When I called to ask about my report, it turned out they weren't from that post at all. "

"Did you get anybody's name?"

Morris shook his head. "Only one 'cause he was such a SOB. He was in civilian clothes, but he seemed to give all the orders to the military. They addressed him by his last name. Larson was the Bastard in Chief."

A thrill of dread ran up Jack's spine. "Larson? Are you sure it couldn't have been Larkin? Don Larkin?"

"I couldn't say for sure."

"When did the NTSB personnel show up?"

"They didn't come for about forty-eight hours. Man, they were altogether different. They had some military types too, but they were much friendlier. Professional. Really interesting to see 'em work. Showed up with all kinds of tools and kits. Never seen so many clipboards. Those first guys were real assholes. Still frosts me to think about it."

Jack pulled out the picture of the unidentified man with the mole on his chin. "Was he one of them?"

"Yeah — him I remember. He pulled out the senator's body. The condition it was in didn't bother him at all. He patted him down and checked his pockets — what was left of them. Appeared to enjoy it too. He looked like the kind of guy that eats nine gauge sheet metal screws for breakfast and washes it down with a gallon of diesel oil."

18

DESTINY

About halfway down the hall to her office, Elizabeth almost collided with the director of the Red Cross.

"Elizabeth, do you realize who is in your office?"

"I wasn't expecting anyone."

"Charles Harding is waiting for you."

Elizabeth was surprised. She'd worked with Charlie for years in his capacity as chairman of the Democratic National Committee, but she'd made it quite clear last time they talked that she could no longer be active anymore with the DNC. In politics at this level, there was no such thing as being just a little bit involved.

"He's been waiting for you in there for over an hour."

"He should have called first."

"I hope we aren't going to lose you to the Dems' fund raising efforts."

"You won't. I did my rounds in the last election. I told them I wasn't doing it again. They must want to hit me up big if Charlie came himself."

As Elizabeth entered her office, a burly male figure spryly sprang to his feet ,evidently glad to see her. He carried his weight well. With his salt-and-pepper hair and rugged face, he created a distinguished appearance.

He moved toward Elizabeth smiling and hugged her like a comrade in arms. "I'm sorry I came without an appointment,

Elizabeth. I'm in between meetings and thought I could catch you. I really need your help."

She held up her hand. "Stop right there. I told you the last campaign was my last round of fund raising."

"You always cut right to the chase, don't you? But in this case you're achasin' the wrong varmint."

He was turning on the charm full force today. "When you hear what I have to say, I think you'll like it."

"Sounds like we're going to be here for awhile. Would you like a cup of coffee?"

"Yes, I do believe I would. Get me a sweet blonde."

Elizabeth's look cut him cold. "Please," he added, chastened.

Elizabeth looked at him patiently, "A sweet blonde?"

Charlie clarified, "Sugar and cream."

"Charlie, you are as bad as the Texas men I knew who thought it was a compliment to describe a desirable woman as if she were a barrel of oil."

"Light, sweet, crude? Just the way I like 'em."

Deciding he was incorrigible, Elizabeth phoned, placing an order. She knew it would be crowded everywhere at this time of day and this sounded like a conversation that should take place in private.

Harding immediately launched into a monologue. It was a speech Elizabeth had heard delivered many times before.

"There are some of us who think the Democratic Party is in big trouble. Our prospects in the next presidential election against Taylor will not be good. You've said so yourself, Elizabeth. We haven't been able to fulfill our mandate. For the last five decades, since Truman, the party has never had control of both the executive branch and the legislative branch simultaneously, except with one-term presidents. We need to gain and hold the White House."

"I'm in agreement with you there. I'm the one who wrote the speech for you that ran through this, remember?"

"I want to make sure you remember the importance of it. We're becoming more and more concerned about the emergence of a third party. The left wing of the party is well-organized and gets its candidates nominated as representatives of the Democratic Party as a whole. The public perceives them as being too far left and ends up voting Republican."

"I agree. We need a presidential candidate of greater vision and stature. One who doesn't get involved in a scandal."

"Our need for leadership is exactly why I wanted to talk to you. Elizabeth, you've been out of the meetings for over a year now. Many of us have been taking a hard look at these issues and decided that in the next presidential election we need to run a more moderate candidate. We need someone who can appeal to the public as a whole and effectively move our long-term agenda forward — and beat Taylor."

"No matter who we run, Charlie, I can't do the fund raising again. It's too much of a conflict with my work here."

"That's not why I'm here. The National Committee has already surveyed our leading campaign donors. We can get promises of campaign funding only if we commit to promoting a more moderate candidate. Those of us on the DNC want someone more representative of society as a whole — articulate, personable, comes across well on television, and who has credentials and name recognition. We need someone who has distinguished herself in both the national and international political arena."

"'Herself'? Are you saying they are committing to a woman? If you've come to me for names, it's not something I can do off the top of my head. But I can get back to you."

"We have a name. Elizabeth Armstrong."

Elizabeth laughed. "You're joking. I'm out of politics for good."

"We are very serious. We want you." He played his trump card. "You'd be fulfilling Peter's legacy to you."

Elizabeth was silent.

Good, Charlie thought, *I've got her thinking about it.*

He gave her a long enough silence to think, but not to reach a conclusion. Then he quickly added, "Can you think of anyone else who would have the appeal that you have?"

Elizabeth studied the picture of Amy on her desk. She knew the scrutiny they'd be subjected to if she accepted this. It could destroy what little relationship she had left with her daughter and the new one that was just developing with Jack. "Sorry, it's just not in the cards for me, Charlie."

"Get back to my second point for a moment, Elizabeth. Can you tell me of somebody on the horizon who would be a better candidate for the Democratic Party? Anyone who would become as strong a consensus builder and leader as president than Elizabeth Armstrong?"

"I appreciate the confidence. I know I have the credentials. But I have personal concerns. I won't do this."

"If you're talking about Amy, there's not a parent in American who hasn't had some kind of trouble with their kids. Forget what the Christian Coalition will say. People will identify with you. Think about how much you could help other parents who are having similar problems with their children and how Amy will relate to that."

"I don't want to use her like that."

"Maybe Amy won't feel like she's being used. Involving her in the campaign with you could be just what Amy needs. You'd be working together to fulfill her father's legacy. Kids do drugs when they find life meaningless. This would give her a chance to do something meaningful. A way to reach out and touch what was important to her father."

Elizabeth blinked back tears. She tried to hide it, but Charlie knew he had hit the right nerve.

"And if you are worried about Jack Bradshaw, we know you have a personal relationship with him. Nothing pulls in bigger ratings on TV than a wedding. Can you imagine getting married right after announcing your candidacy?"

"Yes. I can imagine that it would turn something deeply personal into a circus. Besides, Jack's not interested in marrying me."

"Maybe he'd be interested in marrying the President." He stopped cold, noting from her reaction that he'd taken the wrong tack. He quickly readjusted. "Elizabeth, we're talking about the direction of our nation. We don't need extreme right-wing Republicans or extreme left-wing Democrats running the affairs of the country. Without you, the two-party system may be destroyed. With you, we have a chance to take control and be a catalyst for consistent, positive change. We know we can form a strong coalition in the middle with you in office."

Charlie tightened in to close the sale. "Your point about a lack of leaders in the party hit the mark. There hasn't been a Democrat on the horizon with strong credentials and appeal since Peter died. Peter was our man. He had the ability, the vision, the appeal. He was a man of integrity. He would have been a great president. Elizabeth Armstrong, you are the only one who can make his name go down in history."

She knew full well what he was doing to manipulate her. It made it no less effective. "Charlie, I'll talk to Amy and Jack. That's all I'm willing to say for now. I am not making any guarantees."

"All I'm asking is that you think carefully. We'll give you all the support in the world to beat Taylor." The tempo of Harding's speech increased as he pressed his case. "Remember Peter's unfinished business. Peter was one of those rare politicians who really believed he could do some good for the nation. He didn't do it for self-aggrandizement. I know your work. You are a lot like Peter. You're not a performer like most of the other politicians. You're a real person who wants to get the job done and do what is right. If Peter were here today, he'd say go for it, Elizabeth."

"Charlie, you were always very persuasive."

Just then the coffee arrived. Charlie insisted on paying for it. He took a sip and continued. "I'm not trying to flatter you, Elizabeth — it's the truth."

"Charlie, I don't want you to misread this. But even looking at it as a theoretical decision, I don't have a body of supporters and I don't have a war chest. Isn't this totally unrealistic?"

"I wouldn't have asked you if I didn't have all that lined up. All we need from you is a yes, and the wheels will go into motion."

Elizabeth drew herself up. "Just be prepared for the fact that my answer may well be no."

"Think of all the other women, and young girls like Amy, who would see you as a role model. You'd be the first woman candidate to ever even be nominated for this office by a major political party. Even if you lose - and you won't - you'll be making history."

"It's my life, Charlie."

"You would be the first woman president of the United States. It's the most powerful office in the world. You'd be President Elizabeth Armstrong."

19

CHOICES

JACK KNEW FROM the moment Elizabeth opened the door to her Watergate apartment that something was afoot. She was wearing the dress she had on the night they first made love. A gardenia was nestled in her hair. Its fragrance touched him.

Elizabeth smiled broadly and moved against him to hug him. With her arms still around his neck and her warm body firmly against his, she whispered into his ear, "I have something important to talk to you about."

Jack's nervous system went on the defensive. What if she proposed again? "Can we have a little of this first?"

He held out a bottle of wine, stalling for time. "I brought a good Merlot this time. You don't even need to chill it. You sit. I'll open it."

Elizabeth liked the fact that Jack knew his way around the apartment now enough to make himself at home. She listened to the comforting sounds of having him there.

Jack retrieved two broad-bowled glasses from the china cabinet. Knowing it was not the connoisseur's way of doing so, he stripped the foil from the neck of the wine bottle. He rolled it into a band, slipping it into his pocket, uncorked the Merlot, and stood there weighing the decision. Was he ready to get married again?

Evidently he had stood there a long time lost in thought because he didn't even hear Elizabeth as she walked in and stood beside him. "Is something wrong, Jack?"

"No, not at all. I was just letting the wine breathe before I poured it."

"Take any longer and it will hyperventilate."

He smiled and poured the ruby fluid. As they lifted the crystal stemware, she paused and proposed a toast. "Here's to wise decisions."

Jack still wasn't sure what she meant by that, but he echoed the sentiment. "To wise decisions, indeed."

No sooner had they clinked glasses and sipped than Elizabeth took his hand. He heard the words she spoke next, but was so startled by them that he wasn't sure he had heard correctly.

Jack was flabbergasted. "They want you to run for president? That's what this is about?"

She nodded. "Harding was the one who spoke to me on behalf of the Democratic National Committee. They want me to run for president of the United States."

"And you told them—"

"That I had to talk with you and Amy."

"I didn't think there'd be any way you'd run for president of the PTA, let alone the USA! You've been pretty clear on how you want to be out of politics." Jack slowly assimilated the news.

"Charlie was pretty convincing. He used all of my old speeches on me. I couldn't come up with another candidate who has both my experience and positions on the issues." She paused, knowing that Peter still cast a long shadow that Jack sometimes resented. "He pointed out that I'd be filling Peter's shoes."

Jack realized that Elizabeth was seriously considering this and that his opinion meant a lot to her. "I think you'd be fabulous, Lizzy. I think he's right. You are the only one who can hold it together."

Elizabeth assessed his response. He had spoken without hesitancy or doubt. "What about us, Jack?"

He slurred into a bad impression of Bogart in *Casablanca,* mangling the line. "When you look at the problems out there in the world, you just gotta know that the problems of two little people like us aren't worth a hill of beans."

He raised his glass, finally getting a line right. "Here's looking at you, kid."

She smiled weakly. "This is serious. You know you'll be investigated and subject to personal attacks. They'll probably even find your wife. She'll end up on *American Journal* and *Geraldo*."

"My former wife. She'd love it. She'd love a chance to dish the dirt on me. Not that there's anything much to dish."

"They'll attack us for living in sin."

"I may have a key to your place, but we aren't living together."

"That's not how they will make it sound."

"You forget. I am one of them. I know exactly how they will make it sound. Don't not do this because of me. I can't tell you what to do. If you decide not to do it, I'll be glad of our relationship remaining private. If you do run, I'll be pleased as a peacock. Proud as punch."

She laughed and kissed him, looking as much for reassurance as affection.

He knew it was dangerous to talk her into this. It had to be her decision. But both the political idealist in him and the man who loved her wanted her to do it.

He couldn't resist putting one more weight into the "yes" side of the balance scale. "Do you remember what Dorothy said when we were in Durham? She told us your mom was the proudest lady on earth when you became governor. When your mom saw your inauguration speech she said, 'Men better take notice of what we women can do!'"

"I'm touched that you remembered. But I'm not running. I don't want the stress on me, or on my relationship with Amy or you."

"But you haven't talked to Amy, have you? Why not ask Amy right now? It's still early enough to call." Jack realized he was now pushing, despite his resolve to let her take her time and reach her own conclusion.

Elizabeth hesitated.

"Go on," he urged. "At least find out what she thinks about it. Want me to dial for you?"

When she didn't say no, he picked up the phone and got Amy on the line.

After hellos and catching up on the trivia of the day, Elizabeth explained the situation to Amy. She paced the floor, the cordless phone in hand, bracing herself for Amy's anger.

Instead, Amy was matter-of-fact, nearly friendly. "I already knew about it, Mom. I just wanted to see how you were going to tell me." Elizabeth was astonished at her daughter's tone. "Charlie Harding came up here and talked to me yesterday. He told me."

Elizabeth was angry Charlie had gone behind her back to talk to Amy. She restrained herself and listened to her daughter. "I think you should do it, Mom. Dad would want you to. I want you to."

Elizabeth was so pleased that Amy nearly sounded like her old self, that she forgave Charlie. If this is what it had led to, maybe he was right. Maybe this would be a way for her to restore their relationship. Elizabeth was thrilled. Amy had actually called her "Mom" twice.

If Jack or Charlie had pushed her for a response just then, Elizabeth still would have put them off. She knew this was the biggest decision she'd ever make in her life.

It was different with Amy asking. "Mom, will you do it?"

"Are you are sure you want me to? You know what things were like before. This will be like that, only tenfold. The press is going to be all over you, Amy."

"Let 'em be. This one's for Dad."

Amy's last words melted Elizabeth's heart. Now she wouldn't be running for the Party, or ideals, or even herself. She'd be running for Peter and Amy.

Her response was swift and sure. She smiled at Jack as she spoke with Amy. "Okay. I'll do it. For Dad. And for you. I love you, Amy."

When she got off the phone, Elizabeth hugged Jack. He knew from what he heard in her voice that she had made a final decision to run.

"Amy sounded so, well — so normal. Next time someone needs to be talked into something, like being their old selves, I'm calling a politician, not a psychiatrist. God bless Charlie Harding."

She kissed Jack again, happier than she could have imagined.

"I've never kissed a presidential candidate before," Jack laughed. "I can't wait until we get to use the Lincoln bedroom. So what's your plan for getting back to Harding?"

"I'll call him tomorrow. I want to get used to this idea myself before going public with it."

Jack reached into his pocket and twirled the band he had made of foil. "Of course if we're going to get to do it in the Oval Office —"

He dropped to one knee and took her hand in both of his. "Elizabeth, I never answered the question you asked me last spring. Yes, I'll marry you, if you'll have me. The only question I have for you is, how soon can we arrange a wedding?"

20

IMAGES

ELIZABETH PACED BACK and forth impatiently in her room at the Savery. Although she knew it was because his flight into Des Moines had been delayed, Jack's tardiness made her furious. It had forced a delay in the strategy meeting with her campaign managers.

Elizabeth took a few deep breaths and tried to calm herself. If her nerves were like this, campaigning in Iowa — the first state in the battle for the nomination — she'd never make it to election day. She'd been in the race less than three months now; there were ten months to go.

Where was Jack? As always when she was tense, she focused on the memory of their wedding last fall. Dorothy and her book club had decorated the Durham Congregational Church with blazing red sumac and white spider mums. Jack's sister Chloe and her kids had come. His mother, now eighty-two, bless her soul, had made the trip from Colorado. Elizabeth had been incredibly happy with them and they with her. It was like having a family again. Peter's parents flew in from Texas, his mother teary but cheerful. Best of all, Amy, in a long maroon dress, had stood smiling by her mother's side during the ceremony. She didn't even try to hit the champagne punch at the reception, let alone the wines or the hard liquor.

Elizabeth mentally surrounded herself with the loved ones who had gathered for the wedding. Within her heart, she repeated a few of the lines from *The Cokesbury Marriage Manual* that she had chosen for the service. The book, dating back to 1888, quoted the even older words of Ian Maclaren. They held great meaning for her. "You are performing an act of utter faith believing in one another to the end. . . . Amid the reality of present imperfection believe in the ideal. You saw it once. It still exists. It is the final truth."

It was a thought she sometimes had to fight to hold onto. She was certain it was the same for Jack. In fact, she knew it was, because what pulled her back to the core of her love for him when she was annoyed was not wedding nostalgia. It was what they had gone through together to be in control of the service. Only a few members of the press corps were allowed — an old friend from the *Manchester Union Leader,* another from the *Boston Globe,* and some of Jack's cronies from California.

As soon as they returned from their honeymoon, Elizabeth announced at a press conference that the rumors were true — she was making a serious bid for the presidency. The media fawned over them for a week and then left them for fresher news. Now she had to struggle to make page one.

The low-key wedding ceremony had been the first of many battles with her campaign managers. The DNC had recommended them — Clint Grossman and Roland Delacruse. Elizabeth didn't know them except by reputation when she agreed to take them on. They were well regarded for getting the job done and getting it done right.

What she hadn't known was that they were from the Fascist School of Management. Delacruse was a tall, imposing man in his early forties. He was simply a martinet. Grossman was short, round, and a decade younger. *No little Napoleon was he,* Elizabeth thought. Though the words would never cross her lips in public, Grossman in her view was quite simply a fat little prick.

He had insisted that not only Elizabeth keep her married name, but that Jack take it too. Elizabeth and Jack both knew that Elizabeth needed the name recognition attached to Armstrong. Jack accepted that, even though it meant she carried another man's name instead of his. Both of them were adamant, however, that Jack remained a Bradshaw. They prevailed despite Grossman. Elizabeth knew they'd be wrong whatever they did. The conservatives would think she should become Mrs. Bradshaw, the feminists that she ought to revert to her maiden name. They did what they knew was right for them.

Then there was the management of Jack's image. Elizabeth had been made over by a publicist when she was governor and again in preparation for Peter's campaign. She was more or less accustomed to tactless people who acted as if she wasn't even there and said things like, "Lose the hairdo. It makes her look like an over-weight Pekinese." She was not ready to hear Jack similarly attacked.

Those who admired the high-gloss images in magazine covers did not know the loss of self that went into establishing the carefully crafted appearances. Elizabeth had to admit she liked Jack looking like he had just stepped off a *GQ* cover. But she loved him wrinkled and rumpled and missed the string of pens in his pocket. She kissed him there occasionally, just to remind him that she remembered who he really was.

A knock sounded at the door. She opened it and there was Jack, bags in hand and perspiring.

"Sorry, Elizabeth. It was the connection from Chicago to Des Moines that was delayed." The words came out in a rush. "After we boarded, they held us for what seemed like an eternity. Boy I'm hot! What's with this weather? It's January, isn't it?"

She motioned him into the room, kissing him on the cheek. "It's okay. I had to delay the meeting, though."

"I figured as much. I saw Grossman and Delacruse in the bar when I came through the lobby. You can't make it through the lobby without being seen. So, I'm sure they know I'm here."

"Take a moment to catch your breath, and I'll call and tell them to come up."

Jack deposited his bags inside the bedroom door and headed for the bathroom. When he emerged, she handed him a tall glass of ice water, saying, "You know, Jack, I really don't like those guys very much."

"That's the understatement of the century. If you were a man you'd have said they frost your balls. But you are not only a woman, you're a lady."

He kissed Elizabeth quickly on the lips. She enjoyed the cool of his ice water-chilled lips, but did not let it distract her from the business at hand.

"By reputation," she continued, "they are arguably the best team of campaign managers in the United States. They've had splendid results. They may be obnoxious, but they got Senator Woolberg elected."

"Charlie thinks they're great." He gulped down more ice water. "You could replace them if you wanted."

"You know what the media and the opposition would make of that. Dissention in the ranks. A woman unable to hold together a team of men. Instability."

Jack went to open the door. Grossman and Delacruse passed Jack without looking at him.

Grossman began speaking without a greeting. "I don't have a lot of time. We have a schedule and list of key events that cover the next few months through the Iowa Caucus and the New Hampshire primary. I want to go over it with you. You'll be meeting with your campaign workers. We've organized an army of them. We also need to talk about the spouses' forum once more before Jack goes out there."

Delacruse opened his briefcase, retrieved some papers, and handed them out. "He's only got two-and-a-half hours before the forum and," he looked at Jack pointedly, "he needs to get cleaned up before he even gets to makeup."

Elizabeth ignored the jibe at Jack, flipping through the pages and frowning. "Just media events. Do I ever get to give any speeches?"

Grossman responded with irritation. That he was her employee seemed to escape him. In fact, he'd have argued that the DNC was his boss, not Elizabeth. They were the ones who paid the bills.

"We've plowed this ground before. You've already differentiated yourself as the moderate candidate. Your strategy should be to let the others chew themselves up. You don't want to be controversial. It's important that you do not make mistakes. That means not getting too specific on the issues."

"I should be articulating more definitive positions. You promised me that my position papers would be ready to print last week. You still haven't even read the drafts that I approved. I'm behind in the polls. I need to take some initiative, strike back and come on strong. What little I do get to say gets eviscerated into meaningless sound bites. I don't want to sacrifice my integrity."

"Integrity, hell! You're a politician trying to get elected, for God's sakes! You can afford integrity after the election!"

There was a long silence as Elizabeth looked directly at Grossman. Her facial expression did not change, but the stare penetrated right through him. He looked away. It was a small victory, but she had won.

Grossman leveled his voice. "Our strategy is for you to make a good showing in Iowa and win New Hampshire. Get some momentum going. The prime consideration is avoiding gaffes, not defining issues."

He dismissed her like a backward child and turned to Delacruse. "Roland, why don't you take Elizabeth and Jack over what we've outlined here, please."

"Okay, guys," Delacruse began. "The next two weeks are in Iowa. Then we'll be hop-scotching back and forth between Iowa and New Hampshire trying to divide our time between the two. Elizabeth, we've agreed for now to your preference to travel by train and scheduled stops for you along the way. We even got Amtrak to put on a special car so you can have photo opportunities staged on the back platform. It's a nice twist. It's a lot friendlier than airport arrivals. The Heartland identifies with trains: Truman's whistle stops, the old-time campaigns, Arlo Guthrie and all that. We'll buy you some time, but you have to get your fear under control. A president who can't set foot on Air Force One is an impossibility."

He paused and turned to Jack. "We'll need you to play an active part in all of this."

"So, how exactly do you see my role?" Jack asked.

"Being the first male spouse in a national campaign is unique. We want to maintain a husband-wife image. Most political husbands have taken the tact of being invisible. You will be prominently featured in the events, although you won't be saying much since it has to be viewed as Elizabeth's show. Any major statements by you would upstage your wife."

The patronizing tone Delacruse used annoyed Jack. As a reporter, he knew the game that was being played. "So you want me clearly visible as a masculine presence, say absolutely nothing that means anything, and simultaneously avoid creating the impression that I'm pussy-whipped."

In the silence that followed, Jack could hear not only Elizabeth's disapproval of the vulgarity, but also the fact that he was further ruffling the feathers. He switched gears, pasting on an amiable smile.

"That's okay by me," Jack said compliantly. "Hey, I'm just here to support her."

Like the political master he was, Delacruse ignored the negative comment and seized the concession to which it had led. "That's the spirit. You're on the team!"

Grossman looked at him with a sternness that caused Delacruse to deflate, but he immediately got back on track. "New Hampshire prides itself on having the first-in-the-nation primary. Since you're a favorite son — so to speak — in the Granite State, you'll be expected to win, and win big. New Hampshire holds the key to unlocking the White House door. But if you aren't clearly out in front, the media may discount it, just like they did Harkin's sweep of the Iowa caucus in '92."

"We both know all this. It isn't as if either of us just got involved in politics yesterday."

"Bear with me," Delacruse replied. "Just follow the whole line of thought. The Iowa caucuses are not an election, but more like mini-conventions conducted at local, regional, and state levels. Groups of Democrats gather locally and declare their preferred candidate. They meet in somewhere like a school auditorium or a home. The groups literally negotiate with each other in an effort to form a majority behind a particular candidate."

Grossman could not resist stating the obvious, "It's our job to make sure that candidate is you."

"In New Hampshire, because you'll be appealing to the electorate in general, we'll be scheduling you for larger media events. It will be far less important for you to speak to individual voters there than it will be here in Iowa. On the other hand, here we're going to focus on seeking out the leaders of each of the caucuses and have you meet them. We'll have you attend events where they'll be present, like coffee hours and political action groups."

Delacruse slowed for a moment and glanced at Grossman for approval. He then turned back to Elizabeth and Jack.

"As you can see, beginning on page one, over the next two weeks you'll be hitting a lot of small towns. With the Iowa caucus on February 10 and the New Hampshire primary on the second Tuesday in March, we put in a variety of train routes swinging through the country. Study the schedule and get right back to me if you see any problems. The last event listed there is in Marshalltown. Then it's off to New Hampshire."

Jack spoke up enthusiastically. "Isn't Marshalltown famous for its quarries and trove of fossils?"

"Who cares?" responded Grossman. "Fossils can't vote."

"Let's go on to the spouse's forum," suggested Delacruse, looking at his watch.

Grossman cracked his knuckles. "Jack, we've reviewed all the materials with you. Do you have any questions?"

Jack shook his head. Elizabeth could see the muscles around his eyes tighten. Did he have something not politically correct in mind?

Grossman continued, "Remember that you're the oddity. Never before has a husband been included. That alone will get extra media attention. Don't do anything controversial. Stick to what we gave you. Work in the stuff about Lake Okoboji, the Hawkeyes, and the great taste of pork. Sound like the home team. No grandstanding. Even something that seems good could have the effect of upstaging Elizabeth."

He stood up. "We'll leave to give you a chance to shower and shave. The car that will take you to Drake should already be waiting downstairs. We'll be back at seven," he said to Elizabeth.

She began regretting that she'd agreed to watch the spouses' forum with Grossman and Delacruse. She was not sure what to expect from Jack. He'd done his share of coffee hours with her and they had written many speeches together, but this was his first time speaking on camera at a major event. It was a hurdle she fervently wanted to get past.

As the time for the forum approached, Elizabeth turned on the television, nervously clicking the remote through the channels while she was waiting for it to start. A knock at the door interrupted her.

When she opened it, she was surprised to find a uniformed hotel employee with a food cart. She signed the receipt and returned to viewing the coverage. The next knock she knew had to be Grossman and Delacruse. They entered, immediately headed for the food cart, loaded up a plate and settled in on the couch near Elizabeth.

"Let's hope Jack learned a thing or two from our briefing,"

mumbled Grossman between bites of pasta salad. Elizabeth would have glared at him to silence him, but she knew he was oblivious to the reactions of those around him.

As the commentator spoke, the television camera moved around the floor of the Drake University auditorium, focusing on each of the six spouses in the audience. Children and grandchildren surrounded most of them. They had a bug-under-the-microscope look about them.

"I knew we should have had Amy there. Maybe you'll listen to me next time." Elizabeth asserted.

Grossman attacked. "While the other candidates' children are hardly the little angels they would have the public believe, none have sunk so low as to have had a judge order them into rehab."

Elizabeth felt as if he had slapped her face. She wanted to fire him on the spot. Delacruse knew that one had hit below the belt. He tried to smooth it over. "Maybe we can find something for her later on. It's like an unwritten law to have any teenaged children of candidates at the MTV Rock the Vote events."

Elizabeth decided not to pursue it now. Amy was happy to be enrolled in Bennington for her freshman year. Charlie Harding stayed in touch with her and kept up the pep talks. She knew that the press would investigate her eventually. If she could build an all-American co-ed image in the meantime, she'd be helping to fulfill her father's dreams.

As the camera zeroed in on Jack, Grossman sniffed in an irritating way. "Thank God we got rid of his old clothes."

Jack's classic tweed sport coat fit him precisely, his shirt was crisply pressed. His smile was easy and natural. There were a number of reporters around him, some of them long-time colleagues, others were rivals who would love to shoot him down.

Grossman moaned. "God only knows what he's saying. I can't imagine him sticking to the briefing."

Eventually, the spouses were herded to the stage. They sat in a row facing the crowd. Jack was assigned to the far end; he would speak last because he was an oddity. People would keep watching to see what he had to say. Elizabeth bit her lip every time the camera caught him.

The host described the procedure: each spouse would speak

for five minutes about their anticipated role as first lady or first man. The audience laughed at that and then applauded.

The women were predictably similar. Delacruse got up to retrieve a second helping and Grossman turned to Elizabeth. "Nothing eventful so far. They sound like they are all just a notch above Miss America contestants. The next speaker will be the main competition."

Their attention focused on the screen. The host began his introduction. "Alison Ellsworth and the governor have been married twenty-one years. She is the mother of three children and has made quite a name for herself in Minnesota working with family support groups and battered children. Please describe what your agenda as first lady would be if the governor is elected president."

Alison rose and walked confidently to the lectern. "Thank you, Will, for your kind introduction. It's a pleasure to be here tonight. As you know, my husband has been quite clear about his agenda for the country. He has many ideas about how the federal government can help those who are less advantaged in our society. I have some priorities which I believe will complement my husband's agenda. In addition to the social programs my husband intends to promote, it is my goal to support the American family. I believe the combination of increased funding for social programs that my husband has outlined, such as Head Start and a federal Aid for Families with Dependent Children, must combine with an emphasis on family structure. Mark and I have had a wonderful relationship for years. We've raised three wonderful children. We hope that our beautiful family will set an example for America."

Delacruse thrust his finger towards his open mouth, as if he were gagging on her sweetness. The audience, however, applauded enthusiastically as Alison returned to her seat.

Grossman got up, plate in hand, and headed for the food. "It makes me sick to hear her talk. So righteous and so full of bullshit. Unfortunately, it's going to play with the electorate."

The moderator began again, "Our last spouse brings a new twist to this event. For the first time in history, a major candidate for the highest office in the land is a woman. Tonight, for the first time, a husband is participating in this event. Let me introduce Jack Bradshaw, husband of Governor Elizabeth Armstrong."

Jack moved up to the lectern amidst scattered applause. He paused for a moment, scanned the audience and made his opening comment. "This is an unusual experience not just for you, but for me. I feel like the illegitimate son at a family reunion." He paused, but the audience remained silent.

Elizabeth winced, steeling herself for Grossman's reaction which was immediately forthcoming. "God damn it! Doesn't that guy know anything?"

She held her breath as Jack tried to recover. His voice cracked a little with nervousness. "Well, after that, I don't guess you want to hear about my cookie recipes, do you?"

She liked that better, especially when she heard laughter from the audience. She knew he could charm them, just as he had her. If — if he would only relax. This forum would establish his image for the rest of the campaign. A serious gaffe now would be difficult, if not impossible, to overcome. She tensed as he began to speak again, more worried about him than about the impact what he said would have on the campaign.

"As many of you know, I have had a long career as a professional writer. If my wife is elected president, I expect to support her career. That means that just as it has for the illustrious women who preceded me, the career I have pursued will have to change. I hope to set an example, showing that men can be effective in a supportive role. I want to provide encouragement for the many families in our society that face the pressures of two working spouses and raising a family. Believe me, I know it's not an easy task to be a working mom. I would like to think that by example, our society could forge new perceptions about spouses' roles in the family."

As Jack continued, Elizabeth could feel the tension subside. She could tell that he was speaking from the heart, and that his message was registering. The lack of any outburst from Grossman confirmed her feeling that Jack had come through okay. That hurdle at least had been surmounted — for the moment.

21

ACTS OF GOD

THE WEATHER SERVICE alert on the radio confirmed Elizabeth's fears. They were on their way to the Hotel Savery, bemoaning that the *Des Moines Register* gave Elizabeth only about nine percent in the polls with the Iowa caucus just two weeks away. Then Elizabeth looked out the car window at some unusual cumulus clouds — very unusual for late January. The last two days had been exceptionally warm, spring-like. Now the clouds were growing faster than white cotton candy spinning off some out-of-control machine, along both sides of the road. Elizabeth had the same sinking feeling as when she was bouncing through the storm clouds in the Merlin.

They were growing higher by the minute and bubbling on top, like a pot of water coming to a rolling boil. Each cloud was turning into a puffy, irregular tower, taller than it was wide, then darkening. Lightning flashed ominously in the distance, cutting jagged slices through the darkest clouds, jumping from cloud to cloud.

"How far are we from the hotel?" she asked Jack.

"We're about twenty minutes outside of town."

A sudden vicious storm of hail descended upon them. Hailstones the size of golf balls. The ground instantly looked as if it were covered with snow. As quickly as it started, it was over.

She switched on the radio. "We aren't going to make it."

Rain suddenly pummeled the windshield. Jack turned the

wipers to high. Within seconds a torrent of rain enveloped them. Day turned to night. Jack could barely see to drive.

The Weather Service alert kept repeating the same advisory. "The approaching tornado is classed as a 3F. Go to the nearest storm cellar immediately. If you do not have a shelter immediately available, take cover in a basement, in a door jamb, or the area of the building with the strongest structural support."

"What's around here?" asked Jack, trying to peer into the darkness through the deluge.

"Nothing close enough," Elizabeth declared in a flat voice. The car rocked violently in a blast of wind and the power lines swayed. Jack flipped on the high beams and slowed to a crawl. Every instinct was telling them to run, but there was no place to hide.

Jack cracked open the window and shut it immediately when the wind drove the rain in sideways. As the wind suddenly subsided and the windshield cleared, they realized that they were under a highway overpass.

"This must be the interstate exchange going into town," Jack observed, pulling the car over slowly to the side.

They could see that they were still in the farm land surrounding the town. A light from a house in the distance glowed in the darkness. "Should we make a run for it?" Jack wondered aloud.

As lightning flashed, they could see a huge black funnel cloud heading their way.

His question was answered when the shingles started popping explosively off the roof of the house. The brush and crops in the field were pulled down flat. They knew they would not be able to walk or even to hold onto the ground enough to crawl.

Lightning lit the stream of debris tearing sideways through the air, making it look as if a strobe light were flashing. One second they could see, the next they couldn't.

"I think we're as well off as we can be if we stay here," Elizabeth suggested.

Jack grimly nodded his agreement.

Seeing the fear in his face, and knowing that for the moment they could do absolutely nothing except wait, Elizabeth said, "Hey, Jack," pointing to her feet and clicking her heels. "There's no place like home."

He smiled, as much to cheer her as himself and joined her in the refrain. "There's no place like home. There's no place like home."

The relief was short-lived. The house exploded from the pressure change as the whirling tunnel descended, dark with the debris it had picked up.

Water flooded through the underpass. Elizabeth shoved the door open. "We've got to get out of here, Jack."

He started to argue, but she was already out of the car. He knew his words would be lost in the wind. He went after her, believing it was a mistake, but not willing to leave her.

He was amazed to find that he had to push the door open against the flood of water. Seeing how high the water had risen, he knew Elizabeth had made the right choice.

He couldn't close the door once he was out of the car. The flood started to push the car forward. He lost his footing and was knocked into the water.

He tried to swim against it, but was helpless against the current. The water smashed him against the side of the underpass. He felt something metallic against his fingers and grabbed reflexively at it. He had seized on a grating.

He felt a hand on his arm pulling him and realized it was Elizabeth. He struggled towards her and found himself clear of the water.

"Come this way," she shouted against the screaming agony of the wind.

She kicked off the business-like pumps that moments ago had served as ruby slippers. She climbed, clawing her way into the arch of the tunnel supports.

Jack followed her and huddled next to her on the bare concrete, trying to shelter her body with his. She ducked her head to protect it from the wind. They had no idea how long they remained crouched there. It might have been three minutes or three hours. Their minds went blank with the horror facing them.

After awhile, the winds died down. The silence was an eerie shadow of the violent noise that had besieged them.

They climbed down and stood in the wet highway, small rivers of water now flooding down the ditches at the sides of the road.

They hugged each other and made their way to the car, which

the flooding had pushed out into the open road.

The keys were still in the ignition. Jack climbed in, his feet in a puddle of water on the floor. He tried to start it, but as he expected, it didn't even sputter. It was waterlogged and dead.

Elizabeth reached for the cell phone. It was still in its case and appeared to have remained dry in the seat-back pocket where she had wedged it.

She dialed the Hotel Savery. The receptionist told her the main part of town hadn't been hit and connected her to Grossman's room.

A half hour later, Grossman pulled up in his black Cadillac with a photographer. Elizabeth was too tired to protest about the idea of them using her bedraggled storm-tossed appearance for publicity. As she climbed gratefully into the car and the shock wore off, she was aware of an excruciating pain in her left arm. She looked horrified at the abnormal bend in her wrist. It was clearly dislocated, if not broken.

She looked back at Jack to see how he was, as Grossman helped him put their wet suitcases in the trunk. His hands were bruised and bloody. Some of the nails had been ripped off when he had seized the grate.

Grossman got them to the hospital. The emergency room was in chaos. Yet anyone who survived to make it there counted themselves lucky. The body count stood at nine. Five of those had been picked up in an open field and dropped down miles away.

It was obvious to Jack that it would be awhile before they were treated. He got one of his shirts out of the car and fashioned a sling for Elizabeth's arm.

A reporter spotted Elizabeth in the mob of people waiting for care. He asked her to comment on the tornado.

Still not quite focused after the trauma of the storm and her own injury, Elizabeth seized upon the facts she could remember. "We are woefully unprepared for disasters like this. There are hundreds of tornadoes a year currently in United States. They are increasing in frequency. Our state of emergency preparedness and response must increase along with them."

Elizabeth's head was just clearing, now that the support of the sling took some of the pain out of her wrist. Her attention was caught by a local special news report.

"This is a highly unusual storm for this time of year," the

announcer reported. "The satellite weather map shows a squall line that stretches diagonally through Iowa, from the northwest corner of Lansing through Waterloo and Des Moines to the southwest corner, where it peters out at Bedford. The line's thunderstorms produced two dozen deadly tornadoes. Most of them struck open farm lands, with damage mainly to livestock. Some destroyed farm homes and other structures. The larger 4F tornado hit Marshalltown here in the center of the state. That's where we have the report of major property damage and loss of life. Behind the front temperatures are dropping rapidly."

Elizabeth turned to Grossman, shifting into a command mode. "I'm calling the Red Cross. They'll have a report on this already, but I can coordinate efforts firsthand."

"No! We haven't time!" Grossman almost shouted. "We're at a critical phase of this campaign. We have every moment scheduled."

"My God!" Elizabeth exclaimed. "These people need help!"

She pulled out the cell phone and called her Washington emergency number. Within minutes, she turned back to the Jack and Grossman.

"The governor has declared martial law. He has already called the Red Cross for help. There are hundreds of people missing. They don't have enough resources for this. I've got to help set rescue efforts."

"What do you mean?" Grossman shouted. "This is a campaign. You don't have time for this."

"I know more about disaster relief and rescue than just about anyone in this state. I have to go."

"Your job is the campaign. You have a responsibility to your supporters in the party."

"Back off, Grossman!" Elizabeth said harshly, in a tone Jack had not heard before. "This is my business! I'm going to Marshalltown to get the Red Cross started. We have to leave now. You," she said with great emphasis, "are driving us."

Turning to Jack, she began issuing orders. "Jack, call the governor and tell him we'll be at Marshalltown in an hour. If he can meet me there tonight, we can coordinate activities with the National Guard, the Red Cross, local relief agencies and rescue teams. Tell him to let me know what he has in the way of blankets, food, water, typhoid and tetanus inoculations, water purification kits, portable heaters, and EMS units that he can call on from other parts of the state."

Jack interrupted her. "I'm all for this, Elizabeth. But I won't let you leave until they treat your wrist."

Elizabeth looked down at her twisted hand. She knew it was going to get worse and possibly incapacitate her if it went untreated. "You're right. Get me in to someone now." She turned to Grossman with disdain. "You're a Doberman. Sic 'em."

Jack saw steel in her. He knew why she had been such a good governor — and would make such a good president.

As Grossman scuttled off to commandeer a doctor, Elizabeth turned back to Jack, his pen at the ready. "It's a good thing Grossman let me keep one pen in my pocket," he joked.

Elizabeth smiled but plunged back into her instructions. "The governor will need a command post — the National Guard will be able to provide him with that, if he hasn't begun that already. Find out how many paramedics the National Guard has and tell him to mobilize all of them. Tell him to contact every hospital in the state and ask them to transfer out their least sick patients, to make room for trauma casualties. And tell him the Red Cross can assist him with this within twelve hours, but he has to give them a nearby airfield capable of handling C-130 transport planes and an Air Force or Air National Guard team of air traffic controllers. The Air National Guard has its own controllers. That will be faster. Otherwise the Air Force will have to fly some in on short notice. There's a good Air Force team at Travis in California. But that will take too long. Aim for the National Guard. Do it now, Jack."

Jack was scribbling notes as fast as he could. He raced to put her instructions in motion. Within minutes, Grossman returned with an intern. He was able to pop her wrist back into place. She was still giving instructions, but the pain that seared through her wrist made her stop just long enough to cry out. She moaned softly just once and then was back to barking out orders. The intern pulled a sling off one of the shelves himself instead of making her wait for a nurse.

Thanking him over her shoulder, she swept out the door, heading for Grossman's car. He had the Cadillac idling at the curb and held the door open for her. Maybe he didn't admire her, maybe he even chafed under it, but at least he had come to accept her authority.

Within twenty-four hours, the governor turned over to Elizabeth most of the responsibility for the relief and rescue operation. He ordered the National Guard commanders to respond to her instructions as if they were orders from him. By then, the death toll was approaching 200, with scores more missing. The event was shaping up as one of the worst series of tornadoes in the nation's history.

Elizabeth appeared on newspapers and magazine covers, rolling up her sleeves and working. Overnight she was a national heroine. The disaster not only sold periodicals, it sold Elizabeth.

Grossman figured that was no reason to refrain from making as much political mileage out of it as possible. As soon as the first cover hit the newsstands, he knew what game to play. He was careful not to let Elizabeth know what was going on, letting her keep her focus on the people in need. *It photographed better that way anyway,* he thought.

A week later, she passed control to the Red Cross Regional Director for the Midwest area and returned to the Hotel Savery in a state of exhaustion. When she finally met with Grossman, the caucuses was a mere three days away.

All three days felt like a blur. She gradually became aware that the campaign had indeed gone on without her. Without any effort on Grossman's part, the media portrayed her as Joan of Arc. Taking advantage of the swell in her popularity, Grossman and Delacruse mounted a campaign: "Elizabeth Armstrong — A leader who is more than talk," with shots of her in action leading the recovery in Iowa.

All the opposition could do was make snippy remarks about her capitalizing on the disaster for publicity. They criticized her for being too hands-on, for getting directly involved in state business. The people she had helped, however, were vocal and enthusiastic about singing her praises.

Late in the afternoon of the day of the caucuses, knowing they had done all that they could do, the entourage boarded a train for a gloomy ride to New Hampshire. Grossman flew ahead, still making dire predictions about Elizabeth's refusal to fly. There was nothing to do now but keep blazing the campaign trail and wait for the results.

22

Turning Point

"IT'S EITHER THE BEGINNING or the end," Elizabeth told Jack as she stepped out of the cab. Biting wind and sleet pelted them as they entered the center of New Hampshire Hotel in Manchester. The treacherous, icy drive from the train station took longer than usual. It seemed interminable to Elizabeth, who was as nervous as a cornered tigress.

Jack grabbed the hotel door for her. She could feel his tension as well.

He spoke as she sped by him. "Grossman said that he and Delacruse would meet us in our room. They're undoubtedly there by now. We'll know how Iowa went in a minute or two."

Jack took giant steps to catch up with Elizabeth as she impatiently headed for the elevators. Finally, the doors opened.

"Jack, you know this week is going to be hell. The voting takes place in seven days."

"Believe me, I know."

"Good thing we didn't check out the last time we were here. I couldn't deal with unpacking right now."

When they arrived at their room, the door was standing slightly ajar. They pushed it further open and entered. The two men were standing in the middle of the room, obviously waiting for them to arrive. Grossman spoke immediately.

"We have the results. It's not great — but it could be worse. Looks like you'll end up tied for second place. Ellsworth came in first as predicted. This showing gives you some viability."

Elizabeth sighed with relief as Grossman continued. "I know the two of you are exhausted, but we've got to spend a few minutes going over the key upcoming events."

"Let us at least take off our coats," said Jack patiently. "We're dripping wet."

Knowing that she was really in the race elevated Elizabeth's spirits, giving her a shot of energy. "Okay, Grossman, shoot."

"First off, I rented a limo. With the intensity of the next few days, the four of us will need the time for strategy discussions between events."

"Sorry, no. Leave the limos to the other candidates. My whole position is supporting the little guy. Rent an American-made mid-line sedan."

Grossman begrudgingly made a note to himself and moved on to the next item. "For tomorrow we set up a photo op with the mayor of Portsmouth outside the Navy Yard. He's giving a speech on employment issues. In the limo — uh, car — on the way back from there, we need to watch *Political Landscape*. I found out they're going to be reviewing the Democratic front-runners."

"Sounds great so far," smiled Elizabeth, trying to make up for Grossman's obvious displeasure about the car.

"On Thursday, I'm including you in a forum on the attorney general's Regional Crime Task Force. The governor will be there. I think you should appear with him. Crime is a big issue in the southern part of the state."

"Even though he's a Republican?"

"I think that will be a plus."

"I support strong law enforcement, so I don't see how it could hurt."

"On Thursday, Ellsworth has an event at an electronics factory in Nashua. I want you to follow him there on Friday. He's after the disenchanted labor vote. We'll upstage him if we can. Saturday you have the dinner speech. Sunday is the last debate at Dartmouth. Those are the big things. We'll fill in around them with smaller media events."

"Clint, I appreciate everything you're doing, but I still don't feel that I'm defining my position on important issues to the voters."

"Elizabeth, you're the moderate candidate. Your position

doesn't need any more definition than that. Don't give me any more grief over this. I got you through Iowa okay, and if you listen to me, we'll do okay here too."

Sensing she was about to take him on, Jack interjected. "We're all tired. Let's get a good night's rest and discuss it in the morning."

After the two men left, Elizabeth and Jack got ready for bed. Jack turned to Elizabeth as she emerged from the bathroom in a long flowing nightgown. "You're gorgeous. I wish I had the energy left to admire you in detail."

She laughed lightly, embracing and kissing him. "And I wish I had the energy to enjoy you doing exactly that."

Jack returned her kiss and they settled onto the bed. He massaged her shoulders, knowing how tense she was about the next step in the campaign. Grossman had been minding his p's and q's since Elizabeth had put him in his place after the storm. Delacruse had basically followed suit. Yet, every time he thought about how Grossman took credit for Elizabeth's success, Jack got mad.

He was hooked into that anger. "Grossman is such a damned egotist. He takes all the credit for what you accomplished in Iowa. Personally, I think your relief work had more to do with it than his maneuverings."

"Grossman should take some credit. Even though I didn't like him mounting the 'she does more than talk' campaign without clearing it, I know why he did. It felt good when I took charge of that relief effort, but I have to admit, I got way too involved."

"Are you buying the opposition's line? Don't let them get to you. Next thing you know, they'll have you wondering if you can handle the job when you have your period."

She laughed. "After President Taylor made that stupid PMS comment, I was practically expecting them to run an ad with my finger on the doomsday button and the caption, 'If a hot flash hits now — It will be a really hot flash.' Cut to a shot of a mushroom cloud."

"It sure backfired on him quick enough. Every woman's group in the country was up in arms."

"I'd bet the first lady gave him some grief over it too."

"No matter what happens, Lizzy, you'll always be my first lady." He pulled her closer to him and she nestled her head on his shoulder.

After a moment or two he pulled back and looked into her face. "I love you so very much. I'm with you, sweetheart. Everything will be all right." Tears filled his eyes.

Elizabeth looked up at him and tenderly wiped the tears from his cheeks. "I love you, too. You make it all worthwhile. Having your support means everything to me."

"Come on, let's go to bed. We both need the sleep."

The next day, they moved from event to event with barely a chance to catch their breaths. In the latter part of the afternoon, they found themselves once again in the car, heading for the hotel and a quick change of clothes. Grossman maintained the demeanor of a Marine sergeant, barking out commands. "We need more ops like that one at the shipyard. That should make the news. Turn on *Political Landscape*, Roland. It's on channel eight."

As Kates started to talk, they scrunched in so everyone could see the small screen. "Today we review the Democratic field. Governor Ellsworth is clearly the front-runner. Will he run away with the nomination? Governor Armstrong seems to have earned a niche in the polls. But is she for real? Can a woman become President? We'll address these and other questions with our favorite syndicated columnists: Jane Rodman and Tom Christian. First, this message."

When the commercial came on, Grossman interjected. "Did you notice what Kates said? As a woman, you're an anomaly, a novelty act. You're going to be scrutinized and judged by a different standard. We need to manage that and carefully craft an image for you that's acceptable to the voters. Most of all, there can't be any gaffes. They'll kill you."

Elizabeth responded, unwilling to keep the sarcasm out of her voice. "So what is it the voters want, Clint? Since you know everything."

He ignored her jibe. "You need to show that you are as competent as a man. You can't be too strident or hysterical. But you can't be a wimp either. You can't be too feminine or you'll be seen as incompetent, but you don't want to come off like a ballbuster."

"Sounds like the ultimate Catch-22. I'm condemned no matter what I do. I think I need to be myself. It's not just a point of avoiding mistakes. It's taking a stand that people can believe in."

"If you take hard line positions on anything, you'll lose."

"You really buy into that, don't you?"

"We've covered this before. My job is to get you elected. After that, my opinions don't matter."

Kates appeared again on the screen. "Tom, why don't you give us your overall assessment of the Democratic race?"

"Clearly, the nomination is Governor Ellsworth's to lose. Governor Armstrong has shaken things up a bit, but only among the also-rans. She seems to have developed a following among older, more conservative Democrats. Somewhat surprisingly, she is not that strong with women. I don't think her appeal is broad enough to win the nomination."

The camera switched quickly to Rodman. "I give her less of a chance than Tom. I think her standing in the polls is an anomaly at this point and that she'll lose ground as her position is clarified. She's been fuzzy on many points, perhaps deliberately so. I think she was aided in Iowa by her work on the disaster. In my opinion, the effect of that will fade."

The comment set Grossman off. "Bullshit!"

Elizabeth's response was almost as quick, but not as vehement. "I agree with her, Clint. I am fuzzy on the issues. That's exactly what I was saying. Because I'm a moderate doesn't mean I don't have views. It's just that a lot of my policies run through common ground."

Grossman cut her off with a gesture, ostensibly to listen to Rodman. "I think women are on the fence because she hasn't been that strong on women's issues, like reproductive freedom and equal pay for equal work. She needs strong backing from women if she expects to have a prayer."

Tom responded, "Then there's the whole leadership issue. Are the voters willing to accept a woman as president?"

Rodman eagerly answered, "I think voters eventually will accept a woman. I just don't think Armstrong is the one."

At that point Kates interjected. "We need to take a commercial break. When we come back, we'll broaden the commentary to the other candidates."

As the car pulled up in front of the hotel, Grossman jumped out. "I want to get upstairs and see the rest of this. Let's all meet for breakfast at the usual time."

Elizabeth overtook him. "You heard what Rodman said about being fuzzy on the issues?"

"You need to satisfy a wide cross-section to get the nomination. You can't just say whatever you want."

The elevator arrived. He stepped in and turned to Elizabeth, who waited outside for the others. "Then there is the leadership issue. Frankly, I think your only prayer is to have a man's perspective guiding this campaign."

The door shut in her face. Elizabeth was fuming. If she were a less controlled person, she'd have followed him and fired him on the spot. She became conscious of Jack and Delacruse. They entered the next elevator and rode in silence. When they reached their floor, Elizabeth and Jack parted company with Delacruse and headed for their room.

Almost before the door was closed, Elizabeth took off her shoes and threw them across the room at the bed. "I can't stand him."

"He's a total jerk. But he knows his business and he works incredibly hard."

"I just feel like a fish out of water. I just don't feel connected to the voters."

"You're the one in charge Elizabeth. More than anyone else, you're going to have to live with the results. If you think you need to do something different than he says, do it."

"You're right. I'll think about it. He can tell me what to say. But once I'm at the microphone, it's all mine."

"The schedule he's laid out is okay. Just bide your time and follow your instincts. You'll know when the time comes to make your move."

Elizabeth made it through the next two highly-orchestrated days according to plan. The pace was intensifying. She decided there would be no further debates with Grossman. When the moment came, she'd simply seize it.

23

BACK ON THE TRAIL

"FROM WHAT YOU SAID yesterday, I know this is urgent," Jack told Lieutenant Morris over the car phone. "I'd estimate I'm maybe forty minutes outside of Johnson City."

The sun was just appearing above the trees as Jack approached Johnson City. He's spent most of the night on planes making connections from New Hampshire to rural Tennessee. He was glad that even though his investigation had dead-ended at about the time Elizabeth accepted the candidacy, he had made it a point to call all of the contacts every month or so, just to keep him on their minds. This time Morris had called him. Elizabeth had resisted, but finally agreed he could go when he promised to keep the trip short.

Morris sounded ominous. "Hold on, Jack, let me shut the door."

There was silence until he came on the line again. "As I explained yesterday, I've located documents from the senator's plane and have to turn them over to the FBI right away. Figure I can delay calling maybe a couple of more hours at most."

"Why the rush?"

"Over the past couple of months I've been visited by federal agents. They said they were from the FBI and had proper ID. I know they're not out of Nashville 'cause I know all those agents. They kept asking about missing documents. Said it was a matter of national security. Really been breathing down my neck. They quote all kinds of laws about secret documents and national security. Now, as far as I know, I turned over everything that I had at the time of the accident and the investigation."

Morris excused himself to sign some papers his assistant brought him. Once the door was closed, he continued. "Night before last, I was takin' some stuff off the top of my roll top desk and, good golly, there they were. They must have been the ones that I picked up and stuffed on my clipboard right before I found out there were people alive in the plane. Somehow they got stuffed in a file folder with some old parking violations."

"Can you describe the papers?"

"They look like bank account information."

"Are they Senator Armstrong's bank statements?"

"I can't tell. It's a numbered account. Must be Swiss. Oodles of caboodle."

"I appreciate you letting me know. I'd like to see them."

"No problem. Had a good feeling about you when we met before. Head on in and I'll show 'em to you when you get here. Just so you know, though, I'm on call."

When Jack arrived at the sheriff's office, he discovered Morris had indeed gone out on a call. He waited nervously in the reception area, praying that the feds didn't get there before Morris got back and he got a look at the papers.

A tall, slim man came through the front door of the sheriff's office.

Jack got up with his hand eagerly out.

"Jack, how are you? Been waitin' long? Sorry I wasn't here. We're pretty short-handed. So I go out on calls whenever everybody else is busy."

He motioned in the direction of his office. "Come on in and I'll show you what I got. I started worrying it wasn't very much. May not even be worth your trip out here. Let me get you a cup of coffee and you can decide for yourself."

They got coffee and headed back into the office. Morris closed the door carefully, unlocked his rolltop desk and shuffled to the bottom of a large stack of papers. Turning back to Jack with three or four papers in his hand, he smiled. "The best place to hide anything is under a stack of administrative papers. Nobody wants to go through those."

He sat down and handed them to Jack. As Jack started looking at them, Morris commented almost shyly, "I hope this is worth your while."

As Jack studied them, he began to realize their significance. "You're right. They do relate to a Swiss bank account. However, from the numbering here it doesn't look like you have all the pages."

"They were scattered around the wreckage. I just picked up what was right in front of me. In fact, I started using the back of one of them for notes about the accident when the feds showed up and took over. I forgot about them because they were still on my clipboard. I clean forgot 'em when I turned over the other notes and the accident report."

Jack made a note of the account number on them. He knew it might provide access to the account.

Morris looked pleased that Jack was taking notes. "As my pappy once said, 'If you want to know the truth about a matter, follow the money.'"

"Is there any chance that I could take these with me?"

"Absolutely not. I've got to turn them over to the feds. If I don't, I could get nailed for obstruction of justice. I'm pissed off enough at those guys to risk showing you this, but that's no reason to go to jail."

He paused and looked down at his watch and studied it for a few seconds. "I've been out on patrol most of the night. I'm goin' for breakfast. It will probably take me about an hour. If I forget that you're in here with these papers and that there's a copier over there, tain't too much that can be done about it. I'll call the FBI when I get back and tell them what I've got."

Jack winked as Morris walked out of the office. Then he sighed. He knew Elizabeth would not be happy with what he was about to do.

24

HALLS OF GOLD

THE ARCHED WINDOWS, stately gray pillars, and a glistening chandelier immediately conveyed to Jack that he was in the hallowed halls of money, old and nouveau.

The Union Suisse Bank in Geneva was the institution indicated on the documents. Jack looked down at the letters of the bank's name inset into the stone floor.

The cavernous room with its floor of white marble was broken into sections by three rows of immense sand-colored pillars. The ceiling was decorated with an ornate, elegant gold leaf design. It was intended to intimidate those who would trespass into the privileged world of the fabulously wealthy.

Accustomed to doing his banking at cash machines in grocery stores or airports, Jack observed a row of teller's windows rimmed with polished brass. He hoped he didn't look like he was casing the joint. He sat on a marble bench with legs sculpted to resemble medieval lions. He resisted the urge to spit on a Kleenex and wipe at the scuff marks on his shoes.

Ultramodern computer equipment glowed faintly at the teller windows and workers' desks. He watched as some of the clerks counted money by weighing stacks of hundred dollar bills. The concept of counting bills by their weight surprised and fascinated Jack.

Straightening his tie, he put on an air of authority appropriate for the husband of a presidential candidate and asked for assistance. He found himself conversing with a clerk who spoke perfect English with a faint accent. Jack placed the documents on the desktop and asked for information about the account.

The clerk keyed the numbers into his computer and peered at Jack. "I'll need to see some form of identification. A passport will do, since you're an American."

"Here it is," Jack responded, handing over his passport.

"Your name is not listed as one of the parties to the account. I'm terribly sorry, but I can't give you any information."

"I thought all you needed was a number to get into these accounts. I have that number."

The clerk smiled patiently. "That's a common misperception the cinema seems to have created. You must have the number to access the account and show that you are the individual listed on the account."

"I didn't know that. This is critical. I need the account information."

"I'm sorry, Mr. Bradshaw. Under Swiss banking laws I cannot do that."

"Let me explain. I am the husband of Governor Elizabeth Armstrong who is currently running for president of the United States."

The clerk was surprised. Jack could tell he had succeeded in arousing the man's curiosity. "I'm well aware of who Governor Armstrong is. We get CNN."

Jack decided his best shot was to tell the truth. "Her former husband, Senator Peter Armstrong, was killed in a plane crash. These papers were found at the accident site. I believe they are related to criminal activity that has to do with the accident."

"That's all very interesting. But I can't possibly help you. These accounts can be accessed when governments come to us with subpoenas regarding criminal investigations. We can't even release them for general information or for tax purposes. Perhaps you can go back to the American government and get a subpoena."

Jack was rapidly concluding that this man had more German than French influence in his background. He clearly would continue to follow the letter of the rules.

Jack gave it one more try anyway. "I can't go to the authorities. Is there anything at all that you can tell me about the account that's not against the law or your policies?"

"I can't tell you a thing," he said, rapidly flicking the keys to close the files.

Jack aggressively leaned forward and swiveled the monitor so that he could see it. The screen showed that the account had been closed the day after the Armstrong's crash.

"I'm sorry," Jack rapidly apologized. "I'll be leaving now."

"Yes, you will," said the clerk, raising his hand to summon the attention of two fierce-looking security guards.

Jack sped across the lobby towards the door, shocked that his hunch had revealed so much.

As he stepped onto the sidewalk, two men shouldered by him. They wore gray suits and had short haircuts that shouted FBI. Just before turning his back to become anonymous in the crowd, Jack looked through the expanse of glass and saw them flashing their badges. He knew they were FBI or Treasury agents.

His hunch about the computer was so on target that he decided to play another one. He hid in a doorway across the street and waited for them. When they got into a taxi, he flagged another one down.

He followed them to a nondescript building and waited out front while they walked in as if they were familiar with the place. Jack wrote down the name on the facade of the building: Afghan Export Company.

25

WIN OR LOSE

JACK ARRIVED AT their hotel room just as the first returns from the New Hampshire primary were about to be broadcast. He had called Elizabeth from the airplane to explain his long absence and told her what he had learned. He didn't want to worry her — God knew she had enough on her shoulders. However, he knew that Elizabeth did best when she knew what she was facing, no matter how challenging.

She met him at the door and embraced him in a matter-of-fact way. He was relieved that she didn't seem more upset. Since Grossman was there to watch the returns, they couldn't talk.

Hardly anyone spoke for over an hour as they watched the numbers come in. At that point, CBS decided to call the election. Elizabeth was the projected winner with thirty-two percent; Governor Ellsworth had come in second with twenty-eight percent. The other candidates pretty evenly split the remainder.

Grossman didn't even congratulate her. "For your home state, it's not a good showing. If it had been under thirty percent, it would have been a disaster. This is a marginal result at best. It's hardly the only reason you didn't do better, but it would have helped if your own husband had cared enough to campaign with you the last few days."

"I told you Jack had urgent personal business. If we didn't

agree it was crucial, he wouldn't have gone."

"I'm afraid you've lost your credibility with me. I've never been involved with such a disorganized effort or a spouse who disappears at the critical moment. The only reason this campaign is afloat at all is because of me. But there's a limit to what even I can do."

Jack despised Grossman as an egotistical asshole, but knew it was not his place to confront him. He glanced at Elizabeth who was staring out the window. She was resisting the temptation to make a comment that could only result in a pissing contest. The phone rang.

Jack answered it, expecting a reporter. Instead, a deep male voice said, "Pay attention, Mr. Bradshaw. Stop investigating Peter Armstrong. If you want to stay alive, drop it."

Before Jack could respond, a click sounded. Jack put the phone down and stood silent for a moment. His stomach and mind were churning. Whoever called had known the secret password needed to reach Elizabeth's room.

"Who was that?" Grossman demanded.

Jack hesitated for a second. "Just something related to the hotel bill. I'll take care of it." Elizabeth could tell by his tone that he was covering something.

There was a knock on the door and Delacruse entered. "The results of the poll we commissioned measuring the Democratic contenders against President Taylor just came in," he said. "The results aren't great, but there is a silver lining. Even though Elizabeth trails President Taylor by about twenty-five points, she still runs better against him than any of the other Democrats, including Governor Ellsworth."

Grossman summarized. "What you're saying is nobody has a prayer."

Jack, however, was reinvigorated. "This confirms what Harding told us. Elizabeth is the only candidate who can win!" The comment went over with a thud.

After Grossman and Delacruse had gone, Elizabeth lit into Jack. "Grossman's right. I need you here with me."

"I'm sorry," was the best he could do as she disappeared into the bedroom and slammed the door.

26

Strange Bedfellows

Attempting to hold her body erect, Elizabeth faced the hotel elevator door. "What city is this?"

"If it's Tuesday, this must be Indianapolis," Jack responded.

Elizabeth was too exhausted to do more than smile vaguely in response. One day of speeches and public appearances had started to blur into the next.

As the doors closed, finally giving them a moment in private, they heard Delacruse shout, "Wait!" His hand stabbed into the door opening to block it.

He practically leapt inside. "CNN just broadcast a press conference with the parents of a teenage girl, a Wisconsin campaign worker, alleging that Ellsworth had sex with her."

"Is he out of the race?"

"Not yet. But I'd bet on it."

There was an awkward moment of silence. As a politician, Elizabeth was thrilled that her opposition was going down in flames. Yet, as an ethical person, she sympathized with the girl and her parents.

Delacruse tried to steer her thoughts. "We need to take the offensive on this. Now is the time to attack Ellsworth. I think you should jump on him with both feet and call for an immediate investigation. That's guaranteed to get you media attention and a spot on the evening news."

"No. I won't do it. That's not the kind of campaign I want to run. Somebody else can have the monopoly on the dirt. I got into this because I represent a point of view. I'm going to rise or fall with that."

"You don't win campaigns on a diet of dishwater and milk toast."

"I said *no*. Now drop it."

As they stepped out of the elevator, a reporter appeared and her cameraman stuck a camera in Elizabeth's face. "What's your comment about the allegations against Governor Ellsworth and his sexual misconduct?"

"No comment. I intend to run based on substantive issues, not allegations."

"Your critics would say that you have yet to take a clear stand on anything."

"This campaign is far from being over. I'm just getting started."

Delacruse tried to wedge his way in, but the reporter held firm. "Governor Armstrong, there have been reports that your campaign is in serious disarray."

"There's an old saying: trying to get a bunch of Democrats to go in the same direction is like having a flock of sheep herded by a cat. Different viewpoints are expressed, but ultimately the decisions on how this campaign will be run are mine. Within our team, we have worked out our differences."

"Is it true, Governor Armstrong, given the primaries which are left and the number of delegates available, that at this point your campaign doesn't have a snowball's chance in hell of making it to the convention?"

"We will be at the convention. I have no doubt about that."

Elizabeth stepped forward assertively, leaving the reporter in her wake. She knew that her last answer was strong enough to make it on the air as a sound bite. If they made it look like it was a response to the situation with Ellsworth, there was nothing she could do about it. She took a couple of deep breaths, knowing Charlie was waiting in her room to see her.

After a brief greeting Elizabeth cut to the chase, "What's the problem, Charlie?"

"Money. Money and votes. The funds are drying up."

"But you promised there would be support through the convention."

"We had backers lined up, but it just isn't going well. You're not establishing yourself with the voters. Super Tuesday and New York were disasters. We've really fallen back."

"Not everything has been bad," Jack offered. "We did well in Pennsylvania."

"Too little, too late. Once the campaign began to falter, they started reneging on their agreements. People just don't want to back a loser. Some of them are trying to shift their money into Mark Harrison's campaign, so that they'll have some juice with him if he gets elected. Face it, Elizabeth, there's no money and if there's no money, there's no more campaign."

"Charlie, you can't do this to me. We only have a few more primaries left. I can't just give up now."

Harding shrugged his arms helplessly. "We've got to pull the plug. There's not enough money to get you through the wind-up primaries. You don't have enough delegates to make any real difference at the convention."

"I know the campaign has had some difficulties, but we're starting to pull it together. And Ellsworth has this sex scandal to deal with. He'll drop out if he has any sense. That will release his delegates."

There had been odd moments when for two cents she'd have thrown in the towel, but now that it was being taken away from her, Elizabeth knew how much she wanted to win. "I'm committed to seeing this thing through. I don't care if there's no money. I'll find a way."

Harding spoke up, "Well, reality is reality. The funds just aren't available and you're going to have to do the best you can without our help. My feeling at this point is that you're going to lose. I think you're making a serious mistake."

Elizabeth was more subdued, but just as resolute. "Whatever happens, I'm not quitting."

As Harding left, the phone rang. Grossman got up to answer it. A gleeful smile crossed his face. "Ellsworth may be indicted for statutory rape. The Wisconsin attorney general just held a press conference. Some other campaign workers came forward."

He clicked on CNN. "There's a press conference on now." A chastened Ellsworth appeared, his weeping wife at his side. "He's dropping out!"

Delacruse jumped up and shouted ecstatically, "It's going to be open! An open convention! No matter what happens in the remaining states! Nobody's going to have enough delegates to carry it on the first ballot."

Elizabeth sat silent and subdued. No sooner had Grossman hung up than the phone rang again. "Elizabeth, it's for you. It's Harding, calling from the lobby."

Elizabeth took the phone. "Yes, Charlie." There was a pause. "I just heard about it. I'm watching it now." She listened calmly. "It's helpful to know you think we're back in business."

Elizabeth hung up, still looking somber. Jack looked at her curiously. "What's the matter, Elizabeth?"

"I was thinking of Ellsworth's family."

Grossman was about to chide her for being sentimental when she shushed all of them and pointed to the TV. CNN had just taken a commercial break. The screen was filled with a close-up of Elizabeth's face. Her eyes were filled with tears. A woman's voice asked, "Is this woman stable enough to command the government of the United States?"

"Damn! They were lucky or prepared for Ellsworth's drop out. They sure targeted you," said Grossman.

The sentence questioning Elizabeth's stability and showing her tearful face, finished over a shot of Air Force One and cut to one of the doomsday plane. It faded into the image and voice of the innkeeper where Jack and Elizabeth had stayed long ago. She was standing in front of the sign marking her inn. "When Elizabeth Armstrong stayed here, she woke me up with her screams."

While the innkeeper spoke, a mushroom cloud from a nuclear explosion filled the screen, "If you ask me, she is unstable."

"You've never cried like that in public," said Jack. "Where did they get the footage?"

"It's from Peter's funeral," Elizabeth said. "They used that shot from his funeral."

27

THE WILD BLUE YONDER

Elizabeth clutched jack's hand as they walked toward the plane. National Airport was swarming with reporters. Jack wasn't sure she could run this gauntlet and make it onto the plane for the flight to the convention in San Francisco. She had flushed an untouched bottle of Valium right after she saw the scurrilous commercial. The last thing she needed was a hotel maid waving the bottle on national television.

The press was only yards away. Grossman had faxed out press releases wholesale. Cameras were aimed at her just the way the hunters in the blinds on Peter's ranch used to target deer.

Somehow she managed to smile. Grossman and Delacruse had wisely positioned Elizabeth's most avid campaigners along the route. They steered her toward the brightest, most smiling faces, each programmed to say something warm and encouraging.

She let go of Jack's hand. They both knew she could not appear to use him for support in any way. He could see the tension in her smile. A really tight close-up would pick it up.

Suddenly their security men moved into action. Something had shifted in the crowd. Something strong enough to move the wall of people aside.

A man pushed his way through the smiling, sign-waving crowd, and placed himself directly in Elizabeth's path. Security people started to move him aside.

Elizabeth asserted, "Let him be." She turned to the man and offered her hand. "What is it?"

"Governor Armstrong, I just got my layoff notice and I want to know what you are going to do for me. There aren't any jobs near me! I've got five kids and a wife who is pregnant! I need my job, and I want to know what you're going to do about it."

Jack watched the man closely. Thank God he didn't do so much as slip his hand in his pocket. Even though the crowd had passed through airport security, crackpots had a way of circumventing even the best of protection systems.

He knew Elizabeth was cognizant of the peril that always stood in the shadows. He had told her about the telephone threat. He hated to, but it was better that she know than not. They had decided not to request an increase in security. If the NSC was involved in this, it might only signal vulnerability.

Elizabeth knew the dangers, but focused on the man's plight. "I'm truly sorry. I wish I could give you immediate help. This isn't something that can be solved overnight. My proposals will stimulate business and create more jobs to help not just you, but those like you. I've proposed tax credits for businesses that invest in America and I'll work towards lowering trade barriers. These programs will stimulate business and bring more money into the United States, which in turn should create more employment."

"Governor, how is that going to help me? I've got lots of mouths to feed and I don't know what I'm gonna do about a job."

Grossman stepped between her and the man, taking her arm and starting to escort her away. He said over his shoulder to the man, "Give your name to my assistant, Roland Delacruse. We'll get back to you and look into your situation."

Camera lights scaled her. She was now facing the unforgiving eyes of a hundred lenses. Jack watched her face shatter for a moment under their pressure. Hoping that they hadn't clicked in that instant, he felt the crowd surge and stretch again. This time it parted to reveal a thin young woman dressed in a loose fitting dress with a high waist and long flowing skirt. Her thick, curly blonde hair hung loosely over her shoulders and cascaded down her back almost to her waist. The only sense of color came from her large gold loop earrings and wine-colored lipstick. Her manner was tentative, her eyes pensive.

It took Jack a moment to recognize her. Amy!

Jack had called her, inviting her to join them. He knew this was a make-it-or-break-it instant. Elizabeth turned and saw her daughter. She hesitated for just a split second waiting to see what Amy would do. Whether joyous or furious, this reunion would be on every front page by tonight unless Elizabeth did something more newsworthy, like fainting dead away on her way up the stairs to the plane.

Amy swooped into her mother's arms. Elizabeth was so over-joyed, she practically skipped on her way to board the jet. The photographer's captured her ebullience. Amy even managed a tiny kiss on the cheek for Jack.

Elizabeth and Amy chattered happily until they had settled into their seats and fastened their seat belts. Jack seated himself in the row ahead of them.

"Thank you, Jack," said Elizabeth. "What a gift!"

"I was really glad he called me, Mom. I've been wanting to help with the campaign. I'd have come anyway because of Dad. But when I saw that commercial showing you crying at his funeral, I was so furious, I threw my shoes at the TV. That ad thing was scuzzy. I got so pissed — uh, sorry — angry, that I just had to come along."

Elizabeth squeezed her hand. "I'm really glad you did, Amykins."

As Grossman and Delacruse boarded, Grossman shot Jack a glaring look. "You're lucky this stunt worked out. Having Amy there could have been a disaster."

"Coulda been," answered Jack amiably. "But it wasn't."

Elizabeth was so absorbed with Amy, she didn't even seem to notice that they were airborne. Jack flipped through some tourist material about San Francisco in the in-flight magazine. He noted that there was an international women's conference at Mills College, thinking that if Elizabeth even had time to breathe on this trip, it was the kind of thing she'd make a point of attending.

He looked around the cabin. Grossman sat diagonally ahead of him, his large body stretched out across two seats. Since take-off, he had been immersed in Airfone conversations, talking to delegates and campaign staff, negotiating plans for the convention. Delacruse was clicking away on a laptop, working on another round of notes to update Elizabeth's speeches. Jack was pleased to see them working hard.

He counted eight campaign workers in the few remaining seats. Some were reading. Some were asleep. They seemed so young — many were working without pay as interns, earning credit from various colleges' political science departments.

He decided to go up to the cockpit and talk to the pilots for a few minutes to stretch his legs. As he got out of the seat, he noticed the emergency briefing card. The plane was a Merlin IIIB turboprop just like Peter's.

The passenger compartment wasn't quite tall enough for a man to stand, so he walked slightly hunched over between the seats. Reaching the cockpit, he squatted down slightly behind and between the two pilots' seats. They both looked at him casually. It was obvious the plane was flying on autopilot.

After a few comments about the pennant race, he got around to the real questions he had. "The emergency card says this is a Merlin IIIB, but I thought it carried fewer passengers than this. I did a lot of reading about the plane because of the crash my wife survived."

"This is a stretch version. Same plane otherwise." The pilot said. "I remember that accident. The senator's plane was the original. Then they built these stretch versions to hold twice as many passengers for use by the airlines in the short-haul commuter market. His was more for business, built for only six or seven passengers."

"Would the controls be the same?" Jack asked.

"Everything's the same," the pilot replied. "The only difference is that the passenger section has been stretched out by adding about ten feet of fuselage."

"Could you show me where the fuel gauge is?"

"If you're talking about the fuel quantity gauge, there are two of them right over here," he said, indicating two gauges on the panel.

Jack leaned forward to see where the pilot was pointing. Then something he had not realized earlier registered. "What do you mean by fuel quantity gauge? Are there other gauges related to fuel?"

"There are fuel flow gauges, fuel pressure gauges, and boost pump gauges. They all give us a slightly different indication of the state of fuel in the airplane."

"What would happen to the gauges if a fuel line were severed or blocked?"

"Depending on where it occurred, the fuel flow gauges would show no fuel flow, while the fuel quantity gauges would show the volume of fuel in the tanks staying constant. There might be an abnormality in the boost pumps, depending on whether it's a severance or a blockage."

Jack thought for a moment. "The NTSB report said both engines quit at the same time. Would it be unusual to have that happen?"

"The odds are millions to one that both engines would fail simultaneously for some mechanical reason. Whenever both engines fail, the first thing to look for is a lack of fuel getting to the engines."

"You mean that the plane would be out of gas or there is a blockage in the lines?"

"That or even a leak. But the odds against something like that happening are astronomical."

"Is it possible to have the tanks on an airplane empty and have the gauges showing that there is fuel?"

The pilot was thoughtful. "I'll have to explain a little about the fuel system. You can see on these gauges that there are numbers showing how many pounds of fuel there are per fuel tank. All that the gauges monitor is a float in each tank. The position of the float tells us whether the tank is half, two-thirds or three-quarters full. Manufacturers simply put marks on the gauges showing how much fuel is available when the float is at that position. A 600 pound tank holds 100 gallons of fuel. There should be 300 pounds of fuel when the float is at the halfway point. So the manufacturer makes the markings on the gauge read '300 pounds' when the float is half way up."

He pointed to the appropriate marks on the gauges to demonstrate that they showed hundreds of pounds in 50 pound increments. "The 300 pound mark was the halfway point for each of the tanks on this plane."

"In other words," Jack clarified, "the gauges are marked to show pounds of fuel remaining, when in fact they are really showing how high up the float sits in the tank itself?"

"Exactly. So to answer your question, I suppose it's possible to reduce the size of the tanks and fool the gauges."

"Have you ever heard of something like that happening? I

mean, where the float is high, but the tanks are really not full or hold less than they were designed to hold?"

"Actually, a friend of mine took a plane out of Fresno, flying to an airport in Los Angeles and he ran out of fuel just short of the runway. The NTSB reported that he was guilty of pilot error for running his fuel tanks dry. He kept insisting that he had topped off the tanks right before he took off. The flight from Fresno to Los Angeles is so short that there was no way he could have had full tanks and still run out of fuel before he got to Los Angeles. So, he did some investigating on his own."

"What did he find out?"

"The plane had been used before he picked it up and was left sitting at the airport with the tanks less than half full. The hot sun in Fresno dried and shrunk the rubberized fuel bladders that line the inside of the tanks. As I said, the float merely measures the level of fuel in the tanks. The volume indications on the gauges are only what we believe the tank will hold. In this case, the tank was reduced to less than a third of its regular capacity. So when my friend topped off the tanks, he was adding very little fuel to tanks that held less than one third of what they should. Of course, the gauges in the cockpit, marked for a larger tank, showed 600 pounds because the float was at the top of the tank. But the tank itself could only hold about 200 pounds."

The pilot paused to make adjustments to the autopilot, as the co-pilot entered in data he was receiving from the navigation systems. Jack maintained a respectful silence as the crew dealt with the changes. The pilot watched carefully for a moment to see the alterations take effect. Satisfied with the result, he turned back to Jack.

"Since my friend didn't know the plane had been flown before, he wasn't aware of how much fuel had been used before he took the plane. When he saw the tanks fill to overflow, he believed that the few gallons needed to fill up the tanks were just topping off already full tanks. He had no way of knowing that he had less than a third of the fuel that the gauges showed."

Jack felt his pulse rate increase. "Have you heard of other times when something like that's happened?"

"Professional pilots constantly read all of the accident and safety reports. I'm familiar with just about every aircraft crash in the United States and every crash of this type of airplane throughout the world. Nothing like what happened to my friend ever happened before."

"Did the NTSB let it stand as pilot error?"

"My friend showed the tanks to the NTSB investigators and proved what happened. The report's conclusions were changed and the black mark was removed from his record. The process took two years and the help of a lawyer to force the bureaucracy to change its official findings. That's as tough a job as getting the IRS to admit a mistake."

"What kind of plane was your friend flying?"

"It was similar to the business version of this plane, although it was made by a different manufacturer."

"I guess I'd better go sit down. I've taken up enough of your time. Thanks very much."

The pilot smiled broadly. "That's okay. Tell your wife that I'm voting for her."

Jack smiled his thanks and went back to his seat, mulling over what he'd heard. Elizabeth was still chatting happily with Amy. This was the most relaxed he had seen her since the campaign started.

28

INDEPENDENCE DAY

"DOES EITHER OF YOU want to speculate on how the convention may go?" Kates asked his two guest commentators on *Capitol Landscape*.

"Let me give it a shot, Sam," began Tom. "Senator Ellsworth had a clear lock on the convention just a few weeks ago because he had won so many delegates in the primaries. But Ellsworth still hasn't released those delegates and we have no idea what will happen when he does. None of the remaining candidates has a surge of momentum in their favor yet. We'll just have to wait and see."

Rodman spoke next. "There are rumors about Elizabeth Armstrong. She's a really hot property as a VP candidate. Over the next few days some powerful deals will be made. But I agree with Tom. I don't think we'll know how this is going to go until after the first ballot."

Grossman leaned back from the TV and looked at Elizabeth for the first time since he entered the hotel room. "Your most formidable opposition may be Senator Harrison, although it's impossible to say for sure. I've talked to his staff and Harrison wants you to see him. I'm expecting him to offer you the VP slot. I think you ought to take it."

"Why?" she asked, hiding feelings that merited a snarl.

"Most of the delegates are liberal. That's why Ellsworth won most of them. Senator Harrison is a strong liberal. You are not."

"I'm not in this to be anybody's vice-president." Elizabeth was calm but firm. "You have no right to put out those kinds of feelers except at my direction."

"Nothing specific has been discussed with anybody. I'm just getting an idea of what will work. I don't think you're strong enough to win. But you have a good shot at getting on the ticket with the person who I think is the strongest candidate."

"I may not be strong enough to win on the first ballot, but neither are any of the others. I'm just as strong as they are. We should be thinking about this ourselves, not discussing it with them. It's a sign of weakness. You're signaling defeat and you know it."

Delacruse joined in. "What do we do about Harrison? We have to give him some kind of an answer."

Grossman agreed. "You need to talk to him."

Elizabeth held firm. "If he wants to talk to me, tell him he can come here."

"You're being unreasonable," Grossman insisted.

If she pointed out that he was being unreasonable, Grossman and Delacruse would take it as feminist rhetoric. Jack said what he knew Elizabeth was thinking. "If she were a man, you'd admire her for defending her territory. You know that. And you know you went too far."

Grossman backed down. "I'll see what I can do."

He immediately picked up the phone. In less than half an hour, Senator Harrison and his entourage knocked at her door.

Elizabeth greeted him. "Mark, it's good to see you again."

"And such a pleasure seeing you, Elizabeth," he said gripping her hand fervently.

She couldn't tell if she felt more like one of two scorpions in a bottle or two Hollywood starlets at a party who were jockeying for the same acting role. Compliments and sweet greetings abounded, none sincere.

Harrison continued in a syrupy voice. "We've certainly seen a lot of each other on the campaign trail lately, haven't we?"

"Yes. And most of it's been pleasant, since until now we've both been chasing the same leading candidate."

"It's a wide-open race at this point. I have a proposition for you that I think you'll like."

"Sit down and tell me," she gestured to the chairs.

Grossman led the group to the dining room table and pulled out a chair for Harrison. Elizabeth took note of that. He was clearly currying favor, looking to jump on the lead bandwagon. Grossman and Delacruse joined them at the table along with Harrison's campaign managers. They pushed the debris toward the center of the table.

Elizabeth spoke first. "What did you have in mind, Mark?"

"This is strictly off the record, right? And that includes everybody here."

Elizabeth nodded her agreement and everyone else acknowledged the point as well.

Harrison leaned back, seeming to relax a little. "We've been doing a lot of analysis that I want to share with you. The party needs a winning ticket. You and I together could take this nomination and sweep the Democratic Party back into power in this country."

Part of Elizabeth wanted to stop him right there. Yet because this could be an opportunity to gain valuable information, she heard him out.

Harrison launched into his speech. "As you know, I come from the left side of the Democratic aisle and so do the other candidates. You're the only one who could be labeled a moderate, or even a conservative Democrat. That's a good balance. A liberal and a moderate, from opposite coasts — New Hampshire and Washington — is good too. Furthermore, if you want the ultimate in balance on this ticket, to state the obvious, I'm a man and you're a woman."

Elizabeth responded lightly. "You have a keen insight for the obvious, Mark."

Jack laughed. Harrison's manager looked around, obviously annoyed, as Harrison continued, "Elizabeth, I have a proposition for you."

"So, Mark," Elizabeth smiled, "you want to be my running mate?"

"Yes, Elizabeth." He realized what she said and stepped right over it. "I want you as my vice-president. We're prepared to offer you the vice-presidency, or any cabinet position you want, if you will throw your delegates my way. We'll also have key positions for your campaign staff," he said, glancing at Grossman.

Elizabeth sat back, looking at Harrison for a while, as

Grossman and Delacruse shifted uneasily. She let them all suffer for a moment, while she took in the scene and the actions of her campaign managers with disgust before responding. "I'm going to need to think about this. I'll get back to you."

"I thought some of this had already been broached. We need to make a decision quickly, before the first ballot. I'll give you about an hour but that's all I can do. Otherwise we'll have to make other plans. I'll be in my room. You know where to reach me."

"I understand. If I didn't know how to reach you, Mr. Grossman certainly does."

Grossman turned to Elizabeth as soon as they left. "You may have offended him. If you want this, you need to make a decision quickly. Being the VP candidate is a significant achievement. I think you ought to take it."

Elizabeth added a bit of drawl to her voice. "As Texas Jack Garner said, the office 'ain't worth a bucket of warm spit.'"

"This is no time to be funny, Elizabeth."

"I'm not being funny, Grossman. I'm being realistic. I'll talk to you in a few minutes." She turned to Jack, "Can I see you in the bedroom?"

Jack followed her into the bedroom and closed the door.

"What do you think, Jack? Is this the best I can do?"

"Being vice-president is mostly prestige. A cabinet post would give you more power, more of a chance to do something meaningful."

"If I go for it, even if we lose, I'd be a front-runner four years from now. But I just don't know."

"What is it that you really want for yourself out of this?" Jack sat down next to her on the bed and held her hand for a few moments.

She had her jaw set in determination, as she turned to him. "I got into this because of Peter and Amy. I also wanted to help the party win a presidency. Now I know I really am the best candidate. But that doesn't mean I can win. With my delegates Harrison can. His is a significant offer."

"You know darn well, if he threw you his delegates you could say the same."

"True. It would be a good ticket, either way. But we know he wouldn't go for it. None of them would let go of their vanity enough to put me in the lead by doing that."

"You've grown a lot since you've been in this race. You've become more of a fighter. Now people are drooling over you for vice-president. You need to realize that you are much stronger and more formidable than you give yourself credit for."

Jack stroked her back as he continued. "When I married you, I knew from what you had been through that you were strong. In this campaign, that inner strength has been tested in ways that would have brought most men to tears. I see steel in you. I think others are beginning to see the same thing. I'm not telling you what to do, but I think you can do whatever you want and be successful. You can go all the way."

Elizabeth kissed him, a long sweet kiss. They both stirred, yet they both knew they'd have to wait. Elizabeth's voice softened. "I'm glad I have you to be the flint for my steel."

After he kissed her again, she took his hand and led him to his feet. "Let's go make some political sparks. Every candidate out there would benefit from me on their ticket. I'm more valuable to each of them than any of them is to the other. And none is as valuable to me."

She smiled devilishly. "I've got a phone call to make."

She passed Grossman and Delacruse without acknowledging them and grabbed the phone. "Mark, this is Elizabeth. I wanted to get back to you as soon as I could. You made a lot of good points. Potentially, we would be a balanced ticket. But after due consideration, I cannot accept your offer. I will, however, extend the same offer to you."

Grossman sputtered and choked. Jack was grinning from ear to ear. Amy, who had been doing her best to fade into the wallpaper, shot her arm up into the air shouting, "Yay, Mom!"

Grossman was apprehensive. "What did he say?"

"He hung up on me." She spoke rapidly, not giving Grossman a chance to launch an argument. "We're in a fight. Get out there and work. You'd better remember your job is to get me enough delegates."

"As far as I'm concerned, you've blown it." Grossman stormed out of the room. Delacruse followed, slamming the door.

"Those must have been some sweet deals Harrison offered," Jack said.

"They'd sell their souls to the highest bidder," Elizabeth agreed.

"What jerks," summed up Amy.

Later that night they settled in to watch the opening speeches on TV. The balloting would begin tomorrow.

Elizabeth evaluated the situation. "It feels like we're stuck. I think it's time to make a move. To do something."

"I'm with you," said Jack.

"Me, too, Mom," offered Amy.

"Didn't you tell me there's a symposium going on at Mills College, across the Bay from here?" Elizabeth asked.

"It's an international women's conference," answered Jack. "There's a big debate about whether the college should become coed. They've had financial problems and may need to do that to increase enrollment."

A flash of fire shinned in Elizabeth's eyes. "I can address the women's caucus there and use them to bring out the press."

Jack guessed her next move. "Want me to get Grossman up here?"

Elizabeth nodded. "He's going to absolutely hate this."

"That's why I am going to love seeing you ordering him to set it," smiled Jack.

"Me, too," echoed Amy.

"Sometimes you two are so cruel," she said, laughing.

The next afternoon, they traveled across the Bay Bridge to Mills College. It was only fifteen miles, but for Elizabeth it was crossing the Rubicon.

Grossman was willing to go along peaceably, because he saw it as a non-issue. He privately said to Delacruse, "Taking on single-gender schools as a significant issue is like taking an ant hill and calling it Mt. Fuji."

"Right," Delacruse had agreed. "Just add the snow and the island of Honshu."

As they traveled on the freeway through urban Oakland and entered the campus, Elizabeth enjoyed the expansive lawns, drooping trees, long brick paths and old buildings. She felt as if she were right at home, back in New England.

No one but Jack knew that she was about to drop the biggest bomb in her campaign.

29

THE BOMBSHELL

ELIZABETH MARCHED ACROSS the campus like a conquering general. When she entered the auditorium, the buzz of anticipation was loud enough to interrupt the speaker, who cut her comments short.

When that speech concluded, the moderator mounted the podium. "Ladies and gentlemen, our special guest has just arrived. Dean Grimes told me to bring her right on, as she has a busy schedule across the Bay. She needs no further introduction. Here she is, America's first woman presidential candidate to make it to a convention for a major political party, Governor Elizabeth Armstrong."

The crowd went wild. Several young women stood on their chairs and cheered. Elizabeth strode briskly to the podium. She felt power course through her body. She hadn't felt anything like this during the campaign. In fact, she hadn't seen such a surge of emotional support since she had campaigned with Peter. Now it was all for her.

With Amy and Jack by her side, Elizabeth stood at the podium and waited for several minutes for the cheering to subside. She tried two or three times to begin speaking, but could not be heard over the crowd. Then, smiling broadly, she raised her arms. Finally, the crowd simmered down and she began.

"Chancellor Wilson, Dean Grimes, gathered guests. It is an honor and a pleasure to appear before you today. Unfortunately,

I only have a few minutes to speak because I do have to get back across the Bay for another previously scheduled function."

The crowd erupted again. "Let me tell you why I am here and why I wanted to speak to you. I know that Mills College is experiencing some difficult times and is debating the issue of whether or not it will become a coed college. I hope that does not happen. I'd like to share with you some of my own personal experiences. As you know, I attended a women's college, Mount Holyoke in Massachusetts. Statistics show that women who attend women's colleges ultimately achieve more in our society. The majority of women Nobel laureates, for example, attended women's schools. If it weren't for my experiences at Mount Holyoke, I would not be standing here now as a candidate for president of the United States. I strongly support the concept of women's colleges. It is my fervent hope that Mills College will find a way to stay all female. As I look out over this crowd, I'm willing to bet that there is some future president out there."

Applause grew into a tumultuous standing ovation. Elizabeth graciously accepted it and continued. "As important as that issue is, however, I wanted to share with you, my sisters, my position on another issue. It has been the cause of conflict in this nation. It potentially affects you and your many sisters who are far too poor and underprivileged to even dream of attending a school like this."

Grossman and Delacruse looked like trapped rats. They sensed Elizabeth was about to cross into forbidden territory.

Confirming their worst fears, Elizabeth continued. "That issue is reproductive choice, especially abortion."

The crowd, which Elizabeth knew was predominantly liberal, cheered again, anticipating her support of abortion rights. Knowing this, Elizabeth firmly continued, "It is my personal belief that abortion is murder."

Abruptly, the crowd turned silent, stunned. Grossman buried his face in his hand. Delacruse was shaking his head and mouthing, no, no. A scattering of booing broke out.

Elizabeth knew she had to get on with what she had to say quickly, before the negative response became as thundering as the support had been. "Just as murder may be justified by governments in such instances as capital punishment, war, and covert assassinations and by individuals in cases of self-defense,

abortion may be justified when it is the best of bad alternatives."

There was a quiet murmuring. She continued, pleased to realize that she had them, and hopefully a large audience at home,
thinking. "Given that the mother must make the choice on the
child's behalf as well as her own, abortion is somewhat like
euthanasia: in certain circumstances living may be worse than
dying. Giving birth to a child in some situations may be worse
than terminating its life."

Grossman was staring at her now, his skin pale. She looked
for Jack and saw him smiling encouragement as she went on.
"The surrounding conditions and emotions, as well as the cul-
tural, ethical and religious values that enter into this decision,
are vast and varied."

Camera operators zoomed their lenses in on her. "The only
proper role of any government concerning abortion is that
which it already has in regard to any surgical procedure: en-
suring that medical standards of safety and professionalism are
met. This applies also in terms of surgical consent. If surgery
requires parental notification, then the same standards should
apply here. If there is concern about the notification placing
the child in jeopardy, then bringing in Child Protective Services
as part of the notification process is in order. This is parallel to
the responsibilities physicians legally bear in reporting gunshot wounds or suspected child abuse."

Elizabeth took a deep breath and headed straight to her conclusion. "I assert that no decision in a woman's life could be as
personal and intimate as the decision whether to bear a child
or abort it. Because of all these factors, I assert that no government has the right to interfere with so private a decision. The
reason this issue has so divided this nation is that both sides
are right."

She paused letting tension descend over her next words. She
could tell by the silence that the audience was waiting expect-
antly.

When she spoke again, she carefully annunciated each word.
"It is a hard decision for women — but one that must be made
by individuals, not government."

She stood still on the podium, her heart pounding. A woman
in a T-shirt and denim coveralls, stood on her chair and
slammed her hands together over her head. A scattering of

applause began immediately. Amy stepped forward and hugged her mother. As if inspired by the warmth in that hug, the applause grew. Women stood and applauded. More students stood on their chairs. The response grew in overwhelming support of Elizabeth.

The girl in the denim coveralls thrust her arm into the air, rhythmically yelling "ARM-STRONG, ARM-STRONG." Soon the chant was deafening. Amy raised her Mom's arm in a victory salute. Jack rushed to her side and lifted the other one.

A few minutes later, they were cocooned in the silence of their car as it sped across the upper deck of the Oakland Bay Bridge toward the skyline of San Francisco. Elizabeth was still exhilarated. Grossman was staring out the window, his face blank.

Jack exclaimed for the fifth time, "Elizabeth, that was great!"

"I've never seen anyone so brilliantly commit political suicide," Grossman jumped in. "It was a stupid grandstand stunt!"

Elizabeth shrugged. "Only time will tell. The audience loved it."

"The Mills College liberals loved it. What middle America will think is another issue."

Grossman nervously studied the portable TV. The lead story on every channel was Elizabeth's speech at Mills College. The head of the National Abortion Rights League was horrified that she had described abortion as murder. The leader of the Christian Coalition was blasting her for supporting abortion rights.

"Congratulations," Grossman sneered. "You've succeeded in turning everyone against you. They'll all kill you with pulling out just the sound bites they want. The talk shows will each run their chosen sentences in a continuous loop. No one will get the full context."

"Maybe they'll put together the two halves and get a total truth for a change," Jack defended.

The next afternoon, as the convention reconvened, reporters were indicating a slight movement in favor of Elizabeth. Commentators noted that most of this shift was coming from women delegates. As the evening's balloting loomed, the commentators started hedging their bets, unwilling to predict what would happen.

On TV, Rodman said what Elizabeth had been thinking. "This thing could go either way. No one has enough committed delegates to have a lock on the nomination. Gender alone is not a clear indicator. Positions on abortion don't divide on gender lines. I think what's happening here is a combination of two factors adding up to more than one plus one.

"First, lots of people think it's time a qualified woman got to take charge. Second, her abortion position was unique in content and because it laid it on the line. People are tired of double-speak. So even if they didn't like what Armstrong said, they liked that she said it."

On *Capitol Landscape* Sam Kates remarked that this was the first convention in which women were making a visible impact. It was even rumored that an ad hoc committee of women had started calling the wives of some of the uncommitted delegates asking them to sway their husband's votes.

"Thank God for quotas," said Elizabeth to Jack, noting that because of the Democrat's affirmative action policies, half of the convention was women. The convention rules dictated that the slots be filled equally by gender.

"Given the importance of the women's caucus, shouldn't you be thanking Goddess?" he replied.

"That would really get them to burn me at the stake," Elizabeth smiled.

30

TEAM PLAYERS

As the voting continued five, ten, fifteen delegates at a time were shifting their votes to Elizabeth. Then the Michigan representative stood up. To thunderous applause and cheering, he announced, "The great state of Michigan is proudly first to cast a unanimous vote for Governor Elizabeth Armstrong, the next president of the United States of America."

When the representative for Ohio stood up, a sudden hush fell over the convention hall. Everyone counting knew that if Ohio announced a unanimous vote for Governor Armstrong, she would win.

"The great state of Ohio, producer of more presidents than any other state, is proud to announce that all its votes go to Governor Armstrong, now the Democratic candidate for president of this great country!"

At that, the convention hall exploded in pandemonium. Confetti and balloons rained down on the delegates. In their hotel suite, Elizabeth and Jack embraced each other and brought Amy into their hug. Campaign workers jumped up and down and cheered. The celebration was almost immediately interrupted by the ringing of the telephone. Grossman took the call, for once smiling happily. On TV, the chair of the convention was calling for another ballot to make the convention vote unanimous.

Grossman called out to Elizabeth, "We need to talk about the VP position."

"I've been thinking about it, Clint. I've decided on Sonoma. I've already discussed it with him. He's ready to come on board."

"You should have consulted me."

"You know if I'm going to win this thing I need California." Elizabeth held her ground. She was certain that from this point on, she needed to call the shots. This unilateral decision was as much about exerting her authority as it was about the issue itself. Political though it was, the vice-presidency was a very personal issue to a presidential candidate.

"You're right," Grossman conceded, without belaboring his desire to review the advantages of the other candidates.

Elizabeth smiled widely. Now she really knew she was a winner. Grossman's attitude had totally shifted. There would be no more jockeying for favor with others who had now become also-rans. Elizabeth continued, "I had a gut feeling about it. I like Sonoma's political positions, his spirit and personality. We make a solid team."

Grossman dutifully ushered her cheerfully through the next days. Now that she was a winner, she was his darling. Let the world think he had masterminded the Oakland speech.

She knew Harrison and the others would be begging at her feet for choice positions. She made dozens of decisions within minutes of the nomination, enjoying her moment in the sun, knowing that when the sun set she would be left with weeks of grueling work that would make the treacherous road to the nomination seem like a single step.

The Republican convention renominated President Taylor and Vice-President Whitaker. It was a bland gathering. The only excitement came when the vice-president suffered a mild heart attack and was hospitalized. It was characterized as mild arrhythmia — a mere anomaly.

Grossman wanted to use it to attack his capability, but Elizabeth refused to hit a man when he was down.

Taylor's campaign led with a well-funded media blitz extolling his record. A series of television commercials followed, criticizing Elizabeth as inconsistent on the issues. The ad pieced together inconsistent statements coming out of her primary campaign. They finished by asking voters to vote for the experienced candidate. Elizabeth knew they would be difficult to counter. Early post-convention polling showed the Republican incumbent with a wide lead that had widened more after the ads were telecast.

The first thing she did was hold an extra strategy session, realizing that the campaign needed some fresh ideas and new energy. She had regular weekly meetings with her whole team, but knew that their decline in the polls required special attention. As the meeting convened, she could feel that everyone present was experiencing the same sense of anxiety over the poll results.

She plunged straight into the agenda. "One of the things that sets me apart from President Taylor is my concern about drugs and drug-related crimes in America. It also continues Senator Armstrong's work."

"It's a good apple pie issue," said Grossman in his new role as cheerleader. "Nobody is going to come out in favor of drugs. Except some leftover hippies who are still touting the miracles of hemp."

"I'd approach it on a two-pronged basis, attacking both supply and demand, instead of one or the other."

"I like that for two reasons. First of all, it allows you to build on the Senator's legacy. He was a popular national figure so that would help your campaign. Secondly, the President is vulnerable on this. Drugs are a huge problem and President Taylor has not articulated a coherent plan to deal with it."

Elizabeth swallowed hard. "Focusing on the drug issue is fairly painful for me because it brings back memories of my husband's work just before he died, as well as the problems I went through with Amy."

"I actually think that could be a plus, in the context of the campaign. Just follow your instincts and be honest about it," Grossman assured her. "That's what made people respond to you so well. Your Democratic opponents in the primaries left Amy alone. The Republicans won't. Your win was solid and unpredictable enough that they haven't a clue how to handle you. They'll attack wherever they smell weakness."

"So how do we take the offensive on this? I'd like to see Amy do something more meaningful for the campaign than make an appearance on MTV's *Rock the Vote*."

Grossman made a note. "I'll see what I can put together."

He motioned to Delacruse to get the phone.

"The campaign desperately needs a solid launch to give it

some upward momentum. The honeymoon effect of the convention coverage wore off fast." Elizabeth turned to Sonoma as she spoke. He had been waiting for them to get to the briefing on the vice-presidential debates. "John's a newcomer to the national scene. We need to establish him fast."

"I agree," Grossman offered amicably. "Fortunately, unless someone is well known already, the public pays little attention to vice-presidential candidates until the debates. We'll get you up to running speed on the national and international issues before then. We've still got time. You're already established with minority groups. Being Hispanic helps."

Sonoma stood, dominating the space between himself and Grossman. "There is one thing I need to make sure we are clear on. You should be careful of labels. It's a common mistake for people to categorize members of ethnic minorities as coming from one political bent or another. I am a third generation Californian and have the same interests as any other American. I use the term Latino rather than Hispanic or Mexican-American because it is a more inclusive term. A Latino name doesn't make me any more a sharer of preconceived beliefs than a candidate with an English, German, or Italian name."

Delacruse obviously had delicious news to share, so Grossman quickly indicated his understanding of the points Sonoma had made. A smile spread across Delacruse's face. "That was my source in the enemy camp. Whitaker's going to resign as VP for health reasons. Rumor has it that Taylor plans to choose General Frank Shotwell."

Jack gave Elizabeth a meaningful look. She knew he had an intuitive dislike of the man, but he never had told her fully how suspicious he was of Shotwell's involvement in the accident. When he got back from Geneva, the campaign was in full swing. He was lucky he even had time to brush his teeth, let alone to continue any investigation.

"That's bizarre," said Elizabeth. "Shotwell's a close friend of mine. He helped me when Peter died. Since he wasn't in an elective office, I never even realized he was a Republican."

Grossman shrugged, "Politics makes strange bedfellows. It makes strange enemies too. He certainly fits the profile they'd use. Arch-conservative military type. He'll bring in the boys from the right for sure. Not that any of them would vote for you anyway."

31

DENUNCIATIONS

THE POLITICAL COMMENTATORS were uniform in their denunciation of Shotwell. They questioned his lack of political experience. Even some Republicans were buzzing with criticism.

There were reports that Taylor had decided to bypass orthodox choices, although no one seemed able to decide why he did. Some saw it as an effort to stress foreign policy expertise. Others saw it as a concession to the ultraconservatives in the party. Whatever the reason had been, within a few weeks the furor subsided with virtually no effect on the electorate. The choice of VP just didn't seem to matter.

Elizabeth had expected this to give her a boost, but as the weeks passed, her position in the polls improved only slightly. She felt that the organization of her campaign had progressed and that her message about drugs was registering well. Despite this, the Republicans always seemed a step ahead.

Whether or not by design, as time passed Shotwell's role as Republican pit bull became clear. While President Taylor attended to his office and remained above the fray, Shotwell spearheaded the attack. The negative campaigning kept Elizabeth's camp on the defensive and generated endless debates.

Exasperated, Grossman cornered her in private after one of their weekly strategy meetings. "Their ads are making a negative impression on the voters that is killing us. You've got to take off the gloves."

Elizabeth remained steadfast. "I have said from the beginning that I'm going to run on the issues."

"The electronic media have no interest in substance. They only want sound bites. The Republicans understand that."

In spite of her flagging fortunes, Elizabeth stuck to her principles. "I told you no mud-slinging."

As Elizabeth held on tight, they worked their way through several more weeks. Polls showed a high degree of disinterest among potential voters. The day of the vice-presidential debate loomed.

32

EXTREME MEASURES

With the vice-presidential debate staring them in their faces, Elizabeth led a meeting with her staff. "I'd like to talk about overall strategy for a few minutes. I think the key issue is how to deal with Shotwell."

Grossman assessed the situation. "You don't get to his position in the military world without being the one in charge, taking control at every opportunity. Typical military man that he is, he's very good at putting people on the defensive. I expect him to continue his negative efforts and to hit John hard."

Elizabeth nodded. "Clint's right. He will try to take charge and will especially try to walk all over John on foreign policy issues. You can't sell him short. He's spent years with the National Security Council and is extremely knowledgeable. For the remainder of the campaign, he and the President will try to slam us with our supposed combined lack of experience in foreign affairs. They'll try to make my Red Cross work sound as if I was a candy striper. Even Taylor will try to ignore the number of commissions he himself appointed me to."

"I think we can handle that," Sonoma replied. "We'll itemize what he had you do. It was only because you are a woman and he never thought of you as competition that he appointed a Democrat like you in the first place. They'll also undoubtedly fall into the trap of emphasizing their military experience. But you and I have far more depth and breadth. As mayor of the largest American port city on the Pacific Rim, I've dealt with major international powers. You have all of your Presidential commission work. We just need to keep steering the debate back to our terms. We know how to successfully deal with other governments. They know how to bomb them."

"You're right," enthused Grossman. "We can emphasize that ninety-nine percent of the business of America is business, not war."

"Actually war is a business," Sonoma asserted. "But they won't dare touch that in a debate. They are the yellow ribbon glory boys and they don't want people to look at the commercial side of their ventures."

Grossman struggled to stay sounding supportive. "I trust you won't come near saying anything like that in public."

"I, Mr. Grossman, am nothing if not a political realist. I am willing to fill the role of vice president as it has always been played — silently, except on rehearsed state occasions."

"I like the business theme you suggested," Elizabeth responded. "So be sure you continue to speak up here. Hitting on commerce steals one of the Republicans' key identities. It shows we are more interested in trade than they are."

"Let me jump in, if I may," interrupted Jack. "Over the years I've written a number of columns about the National Security Council and Shotwell. When you come right down to it, he is an ultra-conservative on certain issues. So much so that with a little push, people might see him as a sort of quasi-fascist. Which, I think, underneath he really is. We may be able to exploit that."

"Jack, I've known Shotwell for years! I don't consider him a fascist, although I agree that his views are pretty rigid in some ways." Elizabeth sounded a little offended.

"You knew the Shotwell who helped you out in a time of need, but I've talked to him on a political basis off the record. Some of his views are ruthless when it comes to dealing with crime, poverty, and the role of the military in these areas."

"I'm listening," Elizabeth said tentatively.

"Having been in the military for several years myself during Vietnam, I realized that there are several types of officers. There are those who follow the rules and believe specifically that the role of the military is to interfere as little as possible in American society. And there are those who feel that the military should directly intervene in domestic issues. Shotwell isn't known for his subtlety. He prefers Plan B."

Elizabeth frowned. "What proof do you have?"

"He clearly said that when it came to drugs he would do away with warrants or probable cause. He'd have the military do house to house searches in problem areas for drugs and guns. It's in total violation of all the principles of the Constitution."

Sonoma voiced his shock in sarcasm. "It only ignores little details like the right to be free from unwarranted search and seizure, to freely own legal property, the right to notice, the right to bear arms, and the right to be secure from the forces of government in one's own home."

"I really find this hard to believe." Elizabeth struggled with her sense of loyalty to the man who had helped her so much. Yet she was troubled about the kind of attitude described. "That sounds pretty frightening."

Jack was firm. "It's more than frightening. Hitler's comments in *Mein Kampf* about violating German laws and standards were less blatant than Shotwell's."

The reference to Hitler reminded both Jack and Elizabeth about Jack's long ago comparison of Peter to Hitler. Hurt flickered in Elizabeth's eyes. "That's a pretty extreme statement."

Jack mellowed his tone, but did not back off from his position. "Don't you think offering to have tanks surround certain neighborhoods while soldiers armed with machine guns do house-to-house searches without warrants is extreme?"

"Particularly when minority neighborhoods will be targeted," Sonoma added.

Jack felt compelled to add more. "Shotwell said he should be put in charge of such military operations against U.S. citizens. As the head of the National Security Council, he thought he was the most appropriate soldier to run it."

Sonoma looked at Elizabeth. "That kind of attitude has got to come out. It will kill Shotwell's candidacy with everyone but extremists. I want to use it."

Jack added, "If John pushes Shotwell on this issue in the debate, one of two things will happen. He will either respond with an even harsher denunciation of drug crimes and confirm his statements or he will deny them. If he denies them, there will be at least ten reporters scrambling to break the story that Shotwell lied. Since off-the-record briefing agreements are void when the official making the statement lies in public, they'll roast him immediately."

Sonoma instantly understood a win-win situation when he heard it. "Then I'll go after him hard."

"Right," Elizabeth pronounced. "Everyone agreed?"

Elizabeth was so used to Grossman arguing for the sake of arguing that she could barely get used to his new attitude since she was crowned with the nomination. Having Sonoma on board too helped tremendously. Grossman sensed they were a team and that Sonoma wouldn't put up with any guff.

"All right, John. I think we are finished here for now," Elizabeth concluded. "Don't take any prisoners tomorrow."

"Yes, commander!" Sonoma saluted her.

"After she's elected, you'd better use her full title — Commander-in-Chief," chuckled Jack.

"Isn't that what every husband calls his wife?" Sonoma asked.

"No, just the smart ones," Jack shot back.

They laughed, easing the tension. For the first time, it felt as if they were a real team. Now, if only Sonoma could hold things together for the debate.

33

SHARKS IN THE WATER

"BE CALM, ELIZABETH, there's nothing you can do to change what's happening," said Jack. Their flight to Denver had been delayed by bad weather. When it finally landed, Elizabeth and her campaign staff rushed from the airport in vans to the Brown Palace Hotel. Along the way, they caught some of the debate on the radio. Sonoma was aggressive and hadn't been put on the defensive.

Within a few minutes of checking in, they had all gathered in the main room of the largest suite.

"We've missed half the debate already, according to my watch," said Elizabeth. Grossman assured her the PR clipping service would have the whole thing on videotape, but that wasn't the point. She wanted to know what was happening while it was in progress.

"We need a win on this one," she said.

The moderator spoke. "This will be the last question, and it will go first to General Shotwell. The questioner will be Beth Chow of the *Washington Post*."

"The Armstrong campaign has been pressing you hard on the issue of drugs. How do you intend to address the illegal drug problem in this country?"

From the word go, Shotwell's tone was pontifical. "Drugs are a serious criminal problem within the United States. We must respond accordingly. We must enable law enforcement to conduct searches. I have numerous ideas on how to do this, all of which are perfectly proper and legal. The problem is that the courts have been too lenient and too concerned about the rights of criminals. We should encourage the appointment of judges who would allow law enforcement officers to conduct searches more liberally, without worrying about some of the technicalities that have thrown out otherwise successful drug cases. We need more effective interdiction."

He continued with the aggressiveness of a prize fighter down on points, looking for a twelfth round knockout. "We've been hesitant to use the vast resources of the United States military in this war on drugs, both outside American borders and within the United States. Make no mistake about it, this is a war on drugs."

He pounded the lectern. "We are at war! We have to use our enormous military resources to rid our own society of drugs and protect our borders from poisonous invasion. We must attack the sanctuaries of drug villains in other countries who are polluting our youth and our future."

"Your time is up, General." The narrator turned. "John Sonoma."

"Elizabeth Armstrong has outlined an effective two-pronged process attacking both the supply of drugs and the demand. It includes punishing drug users if they do not commit themselves for treatment and mandating treatment whenever drug abusers encounter the law. Let me emphasize that without demand, supply is irrelevant. General Shotwell's answer is merely to reduce the supply. That has failed as a policy for the past fifteen years. Furthermore, his plan is frightening. He would have our military become involved in foreign countries. He would patrol our borders with troops, rather than civilian law enforcement personnel. He said here that his ideas on searches are legal. However, in other forums, General Shotwell has suggested a plan to seal off neighborhoods in the United States with select military units. Those units would search house to house to confiscate alleged contraband, including drugs and guns. They would conduct seizures without warrants, including in them firearms legally owned by innocent citizens."

Sonoma leaned on the podium in a classically relaxed and in- charge pose. "Can General Shotwell explain his ideas in the context of the Bill of Rights? How does he explain his proposed violation of the Posse Comitatus Act, which forbids the use of the military in law enforcement in this great land?"

The camera flashed momentarily to General Shotwell. He looked defiant and angry.

The shot shifted back to Sonoma. "The Posse Comitatus Act was passed in 1876 following abuses by the American army in enforcing laws in the United States. The American army became effectually the arm of one political party which tried to use it to control elections in the South during Reconstruction. General Shotwell's answer shows an utter lack of understanding of this vitally important law, a law that all honorable military officers are trained to respect."

"Right on!" Jack exclaimed. "Let's see what Shotwell says about this over the next few days. He can't deny it because too many other reporters heard those off-the-record remarks."

Switching back and forth between channels after the debate, Elizabeth could see that the consensus was that Sonoma had done a much better job than Shotwell. The press picked up on Sonoma's attacks on Shotwell's concept of using the military in violation of federal law.

Elizabeth called Sonoma. "John, you were wonderful."

"I know, my wife tells me that all the time."

Elizabeth found herself laughing. "The commentators are raving about you. I think you gave us a desperately needed win."

"Thanks, Elizabeth. I thought I did pretty well too, but I appreciate your approval. Thank Jack again for his assistance on that last subject."

Over the next several weeks the campaign hopscotched the country, stopping in California twice in deference to its electoral riches. The second trip targeted the famous agricultural horn of plenty of the western United States, the Central Valley. Stops were planned in Sacramento, Fresno and Bakersfield. Elizabeth and her key campaign staff were again on board the stretch Merlin as it winged its way toward California.

Grossman approached Elizabeth. "I have that update you wanted on where we stand in the polls. It appears that Sonoma's victory has given us a little bump. But both the Harris and the Gallup polls show you about fifteen points behind. That's much better than where we were, but we've got a ways to go."

Delacruse threw in his two cents. "John helped, but I think

your style with the voters is also having an effect. The real you is beginning to come through. We need to start building on these little successes and see if we can get some serious momentum."

When the plane landed at the Sacramento airport, it taxied to the privately owned aircraft terminal. A band of local reporters awaited her arrival. As Elizabeth scanned the press corps, she realized there were a number of national media representatives waiting as well. The crowd also seemed larger than usual.

They got off the plane and walked down the tarmac. Reporters shouted questions at her as she walked past, hoping to get a special claim to an exclusive story. She responded to the questions, most of which she had heard before, and gave her usual answers.

Suddenly, one of the national reporters thrust a microphone toward Elizabeth. Her camera operator moved in tight. "Governor Armstrong, we have just received unconfirmed reports from the Shotwell campaign that your daughter is a drug addict. Would you care to comment on that?"

Elizabeth stopped in mid-stride. She tried to gather her wits and think of a response. Her concern about Amy's feelings overtook her thoughts. She knew Grossman had been working on this with Amy, and they seemed to be handling it fine on their own. They planned to come to her for final approval on Amy's statement. Because Amy seemed proud of her independence in working on this, Elizabeth had stayed out of it. Uncertain of the approach to take, she looked at Amy, cleared her throat and tried to speak again.

The reporters closed in like a pack of sharks around a potential victim, responding to her hesitation as if it were blood in the water. She felt momentarily disarmed and helpless.

34

DADDY'S PRIDE

AMY THRUST HERSELF in front of her mother and grabbed the microphone, saying, "Let me answer this, Mother." Amy put on her biggest smile, made sure she looked directly into the bank of cameras facing her, and began bravely. "Yes, I will confirm that I was a drug addict. I emphasize the word 'was.' I was rehabilitated through programs such as those that my mother is advocating in this campaign. I became addicted following the problems that arose from the death of my father, Senator Peter Armstrong. I was only a teenager and I lost my father and saw my mother seriously hurt."

The reporters became silent as she continued. "I felt I couldn't deal with the crisis in my life, so I turned to drugs as an escape. Thanks to the efforts of my mother and stepfather, I was able to stop. I took part in a drug rehabilitation program, which saved my life."

"Are you still an addict?" one reporter asked.

"I'm clean and sober. I'm willing to take a test at anytime — even one without any notice. Since America's corporations use random drug testing on employees in positions of responsibility, it seems logical that it should be used for the candidates and their families. What position could be more sensitive than the presidency?"

A murmur arose from the media as they mulled over the potential scandalous opportunities springing blood tests on candidates and their families would pose. If a reporter could corner a candidate into a drug test, why not one for STDs like AIDS?

Amy asserted the strong crowd presence with which her lineage had endowed her. She continued, "If thousands of others like me had the opportunity that I did to break the habit, there'd be no incentive for smugglers to bring drugs into this country. I am thankful for the help I got. I am extremely proud of my mother for standing by me and for the approach she has taken concerning drugs in this campaign."

Elizabeth was astounded by Amy's declaration. She quickly regained her composure. "Although I am a candidate for president of the United States," she said, "in many ways our family is like any other American family. We've been affected by the tragic loss of a loved one and by the tragedy of drugs. The lesson is that nobody is exempt from these sorts of crises. As I have indicated throughout this campaign, if I am elected president, I will make drug abuse and drug interdiction a high priority. Amy's father, Peter Armstrong, was on the right track, and I plan to encourage the continuation of his interdiction work. It's clear that our daughter, Amy, has gotten the political gene from both sides of the family. I'm very proud of her. I know her Dad would be too."

Grossman stepped between Amy and the reporters, saying, "That's enough for now. You have your evening leads, guys. We've got a schedule to keep."

Once they settled into their car, Elizabeth addressed Grossman. "Thank you for getting Amy started working on that speech. It's a good thing she had it in her back pocket."

"I would have preferred if she had given the whole thing in a controlled situation," Grossman confessed, "But she did a good job of controlling an ambush. So did you."

Elizabeth continued, "I know it's too late to change our minds, but are you sure that this speech at the Vietnam Memorial is a good idea? Wouldn't it be better to stay here? A strategic state like California seems the place to work on getting votes."

"We'll get back to California." Grossman assured her. "We definitely need it. Sonoma's a plus, but he's not enough to count on. Despite that, your D.C. speech on military policy and veterans' benefits is crucial. It will establish more credibility for you in the conservative community. You have to show that you are carving out turf in Shotwell's and Taylor's territories."

Jack made a decision. "I think we need to talk about that crank call you got, Elizabeth."

"As far as I'm concerned, that's all it was. A crank call." She was flashing him unspoken messages to drop it in front of Grossman.

Jack had decided that Grossman had become a team player. It was time for him to know about the added anxiety Elizabeth was carrying. "That caller last night threatened you because of your drug interdiction policy. Remember, I got one like that too. Both times they got through the security system to reach us."

"We've turned it over to the Secret Service. I'm sure they'll take care of it."

Grossman didn't seem terribly interested. "Threats come with the territory. That's why the Secret Service is a whole entity unto itself. I think you are crazy not to accept their protection."

"I can't stand the idea of people following me around," Jack admitted.

"You'd better get used to it. When she wins, you'll be living with it all the time."

Jack knew what Grossman had said was true, but it was not something he was eager to embrace. "I never believed in practice bleeding."

Jack realized that Elizabeth had other things on her mind and decided to drop the issue for the time being. He was feeling increasingly threatened and was glad that Elizabeth had the Secret Service to protect her, but when he was on his own, he didn't like the invasion into his privacy. Having Shotwell in the election increased his uneasiness.

Jack reasoned, neo-Nazis like Shotwell and smugglers will kill you for what you *might* know. They wonder, *How much information does he have? Why has he been doing his own investigation? He poses a risk. Kill him.*

35

THE LONG BLACK WALL

WASHINGTON, D.C. WAS a whole different world when you were among the power elite. Jack barely had time to let that thought graze his consciousness as he hustled to keep up with Elizabeth, Grossman, and a Secret Service agent. They sped through the lobby of the elegant and historic Willard Hotel. Jack thought Peacock Alley, the hotel's main promenade, was well named, considering the vanity that puffed the chests of many of the government officials that had passed there.

He hurried to catch the open door of their waiting limousine. Grossman had finally convinced Elizabeth that people expect a certain aura of power and authority around their leaders. The implications of wealth were part of the expected trappings.

The front seat was already occupied by one Secret Service agent acting as a passenger. The other agent, the driver, was holding the door open. Once the door was closed, the limousine pulled into traffic. A nondescript sport utility vehicle with four other agents followed discretely behind. The limousine wended its way through the traffic and around the White House heading toward the Vietnam Veterans Memorial located on the Mall, not too far from the Lincoln Memorial.

They drove through several construction sites around the Mall, including one just opposite the Vietnam Veterans Memorial. As the Secret Service agents held the door, Elizabeth, Jack and Grossman got out. Other agents — men and women in gray suits wearing Ray-Ban sunglasses and earphones — walked briskly toward the speaker's podium, positioning themselves through the assembled crowd.

They had their hands full just monitoring the huge crowd. The podium was close to the apex of the somber, inverted V-shaped black marble monument. Other Secret Service agents already on the scene had made sure a path was open for Elizabeth to walk directly to it. She stopped several times to shake hands and greet enthusiastic well-wishers, even though the agents tried to keep her moving.

As she reached the podium, the crowd began to applaud. Suddenly a shot rang out and Elizabeth crumpled to the ground.

Oh no! Jack thought. *They've got her!*

His heart in his throat, he tried to get to her. Agents swarming around her stopped him. One agent stood over her, straddling her body, scanning the crowd, an Uzi in his hands.

A man ran out of the panicking crowd, a gun clearly visible in his hand. As several agents shot at him, the crowd scrambled to get out of the way. Police tried to corral the screaming throng. Sirens screamed around them. Helicopters hovered overhead.

Suddenly, another shot was heard. The running man went down.

Jack crawled to Elizabeth's side. She was breathing. An agent was applying direct pressure against the wound.

Jack glanced in the direction of the downed man and noticed a construction vehicle — a six-pack pickup truck — pull away. The rear window slid up. He thought he saw a small metal tube disappearing into a canvas-covered bundle in the back as the truck sped away. He was able to pick up a letter and two numbers from the license plate. It was from Virginia.

He turned back to his wife. Elizabeth was pale but alert. Blood seeped through her blouse over her shoulder. There was no spurting — the wound wasn't too serious.

"Elizabeth, Elizabeth, it's me, Jack!"

"Of course, Jack. I know who you are." She made a feeble attempt to smile.

One of the Secret Service agents elevated her feet, another draped her with his coat. Treating her for shock helped almost immediately. A trace of color returned to her cheeks.

Jack knew it was a good sign. "Elizabeth, don't move!"

"I don't intend to. It's okay. I think I'm all right," she murmured.

"You've been shot! You need to hold still until the ambulance gets here."

"What do I look like? Am I a mess?"

"Don't worry about the blouse. I'll buy you ten. Just hold still."

"You've got a deal. Saks Fifth Avenue?"

"Uh, maybe not!" He was smiling now. "How about J.C. Penney's?"

"You don't look that good yourself, you know. One of your pens is leaking in your pocket again."

Jack looked down reflexively. He knew the pens were gone, but he was humoring her.

"Gotcha," she said, knowing he was less worried now.

Jack held her hand tightly. Sirens continued to sound and the police had now cordoned off the area, keeping the crowd at bay. He was amazed at Elizabeth's calm while hysteria swirled around them.

They made small talk unti the paramedics arrived, pushing their way through the crowd. Within moments, they had a temporary bandage strapped to her arm to stop the bleeding and were preparing a syringe.

Elizabeth looked up at the hypodermic. "What's that? What are you doing?"

"Don't worry, it's just something we're going to give you to take you to the hospital," the paramedic with the syringe replied.

Her voice was calm but tight. "I asked you, what's in it?"

"It's Demerol ma'am."

"I don't need it. I'm not in that much pain. I want my mind clear."

He assessed her as he responded, "Are you sure, ma'am?"

"Absolutely. Let me get up. Don't worry, I'm not in shock anymore. I've survived worse than this." Her determination was evident.

"Wait a minute, Elizabeth," Jack began, but she cut him off.

"It's all right. I know what I'm doing."

Elizabeth struggled to her feet, leaning on Jack for support. Seeing the futility of trying to keep her down, he helped her.

"I want to give my speech to the crowd right now. I won't go to the hospital until I've finished my speech!"

"Don't be crazy! You need medical care," Jack pleaded.

"I can go afterwards. The bleeding's stopped. You can see that. It doesn't feel that bad."

She reached the podium and leaned against it. Jack stayed with her until she began to speak, shrugging him gently away.

A hush fell over the crowd. Their attention was riveted on Elizabeth. "My kindred Americans," she said, "I came here to deliver a campaign speech and I am going to. As Abraham Lincoln once said, 'the ballot is stronger than the bullet.'"

Jack marveled that not only had she summoned the coherence to give this speech, she had the presence of mind to base it around a quotation from a Republican president.

She continued. "Today, I have a new appreciation of Lincoln's words. No bullet is going to stop me from completing this campaign. No bullet is going to deprive the American people of their right to make a choice on election day at the ballot box."

Strong applause rang out, echoing down the black marble walls. "Please do not be concerned, my friends. I'm not as badly hurt as this looks. You all came a long way for this talk on behalf of veterans here at The Wall. This shooting was a terrible act. We should not reward those who are responsible for it by allowing it to deter us from doing our appointed business. I will not let this act of violence prevent me from speaking my mind."

She paused for a moment and continued forcefully. "I intended to speak today about military policy and on behalf of veterans' rights. I support a strong military. More than that, I support all of you out there who have served your country, whether or not you are still active in the military. I especially support the families of those who served and died, so that we all could stand here today."

She paused. There was complete silence. "Behind me, fifty-eight thousand names are listed on this memorial. These courageous men and women gave us far more than anything that I gave today. It would denigrate their memory to let a cowardly assassin prevent me from honoring those who gave so much for this great country. I will never forget their contributions and sacrifices, as well as veterans before and after them, and neither will my administration."

She glanced to the side of the podium and noticed paramedics and Secret Service agents standing next to the platform. "I cannot speak much longer, but I want to say to all veterans and their families that I appreciate from the bottom of my heart what you have done for me, for us, and for America. I am now leaving for medical treatment and would appreciate your prayers. Not for me, but for those whose names appear on the wall behind me and on similar monuments around the world, and for their families and loved ones. Thank you."

She turned from the podium and moved stiffly into Jack's waiting arms. Tears of pride pooled in his eyes.

Cheering followed her to the ambulance, along with the familiar chants of "ARMSTRONG! ARMSTRONG!" Even the reporters and cameramen were applauding her courage.

As they got into the ambulance, Elizabeth asked, "Where are we going?"

A paramedic replied, "We're going to Walter Reed Medical Center, ma'am."

"No, I want to go to D.C. General." She raised herself on the stretcher. "I know they have a good trauma unit there. They handle gunshot wounds on a daily basis."

"Yes, ma'am, we can do that if you want, but as a candidate you are entitled to free medical care at Walter Reed."

"I don't want free medical care. I want the best medical care."

The ambulance, escorted by two motorcycle policemen with sirens wailing and lights blazing, arrived at D.C. General Hospital. It was a scene of unexpected calm. Apparently, every reporter in town was converging on Walter Reed, assuming that she was there. Meanwhile, Elizabeth was rolled into the emergency room.

Once she was in the treatment room, Jack paced the floor like an expectant father outside the maternity ward, or the fearful parent of an injured child. The Secret Service agents who had accompanied them in the ambulance and those who had followed by car posted themselves near the door and in the waiting room.

Jack looked up to see two men in somber suits walking toward him with badges outstretched. The Secret Service agents straightened up as if standing at attention. At the same time, the door to the treatment room opened, and the doctor came out signaling Jack to come in.

Elizabeth was sitting on a gurney, pale but smiling, wearing a hospital gown with her arm in a sling. Jack could see the bulk of the bandages under her gown. Her smile brought a warm sensation of relief to his whole body. All that mattered to him was that Elizabeth was all right.

"Mr. Bradshaw, I have good news for you. Your wife will be fine. The bullet hit her in a fleshy area under the left arm. It passed cleanly through her. There was a fair amount of bleeding but no serious injury. We need to keep her here for observation, but I don't expect any complications."

"Thank God!" Jack's elation was evident.

Elizabeth looked at Jack coyly. "You owe me ten silk blouses. I know exactly where we can shop for them. And I know how much you love to shop!"

Jack was suddenly overcome with a feeling of weakness and steadied himself against the gurney. "Whatever you say, dear," he said in mock exaggeration of a dutiful husband.

She laughed. "That'll be the day."

"Honey, the Secret Service is outside. They seem to want to talk to me pretty bad. Will you be all right if I go?"

"Go ahead, I'm fine. Don't worry. I need to rest a little while."

Opening the door to the hall, Jack was shocked at the mass of humanity packed in that small space, held back by uniformed police officers and Secret Service agents. It was obvious that the press had finally figured out where Elizabeth was. The agents escorted Jack to a side room. One of them locked the door from the inside and all three sat down.

"I'm Special Agent Miklovick," the taller agent said. "This is Special Agent Connolly. We need to know what you observed at the scene of the shooting."

Not one to take things at face value, Jack looked at their badges before saying anything. They were both FBI. "It happened so quickly," he began, "and my real focus was on Elizabeth. I didn't see the shooting itself. But I saw the man running and I saw him go down after he was shot."

"You mean shot by the Secret Service," stated Miklovick.

"I didn't think so at the time. As I was moving toward Elizabeth, I looked over at the man just as he was going down. Directly in my line of vision behind him was a construction site. There was a six-pack truck driving away with the rear window rolling up and what looked like a metal tube or a rifle barrel being pulled back under a canvas tarp."

"Mr. Armstrong—"

"Bradshaw—" Jack corrected.

"I'm quite positive that you're mistaken about that. Secret Service agents shot the assailant."

"If you check, you'll see I turned in reports about threatening phone calls that we received during the campaign. The first one came when I was doing some research into international drug trading."

The two agents looked exasperated. The senior agent worked at being patient. "Look, we don't need any grassy knoll conspiracy theories here. Is there anything else you can add?"

Jack had seen the same reaction when working with other government officials. He recognized a closed mind when he saw one. He decided to keep his mouth shut about the license plate. "I guess not. I was too interested in taking care of my wife to pay much attention to what else was going on."

"Thank you. If we need anything further from you, we'll be in touch. Please don't discuss this with the press while it's under investigation."

As Jack headed towards the door, Miklovick spoke up. "We watched the replay of the shooting and your wife's speech. That was a pretty gutsy thing she did."

Jack glowed with pride. "In my book she's already president."

A towering agent standing guard escorted him back through the throng of reporters to Elizabeth's room. He walked silently through the crowd of reporters, some old friends, who pestering him for information. At the door, he turned back and paused a moment for effect. Reporters jockeyed for position, anticipating a statement. Cameras were rolling. Jack waited until they were all set. He smiled inwardly and stated, "I was instructed not to comment during the investigation. However, I can make one short statement. Elizabeth Armstrong is definitely presidential material. My wife is one tough cookie. You can quote me on that."

Jack immediately slipped through the door, chuckling to himself. He could envision what Grossman would do with that. No doubt he'd have campaign workers handing out bagged cookies with "tough cookie" attached as a slogan. If he thought Elizabeth needed to seem more feminine, he'd enclose a recipe for chocolate chip cookies printed in flowing script.

Jack got a laugh from Elizabeth when he told her what he had said. The peace and solitude inside Elizabeth's room was like a vacuum after the chaos in the hall. He saw she was obviously doing better. "I just wanted to make sure you were all right."

"I'm just a little bit woozy from the pain medication," Elizabeth said with a yawn.

Jack was still worried. "Do you think you'll be okay for a few hours?"

"I'm fine," Elizabeth assured him. "What's up?"

"I want to check out a couple of things about this myself."

"Leave it to the FBI, sweetheart," she urged.

"The agents I talked to sounded like they were just going through the motions."

Elizabeth would have made a stronger case for him staying out of this, but the drugs were making her drift. "Just be careful, Jack."

36

SOLDIER OF FORTUNE

JACK ASKED A FRIEND at the state highway patrol to run the license plate number.

"You're lucky," his friend told him. "Virginia assigns certain numbers to commercial and rental vehicles. The partial number you got was a rental vehicle. That, along with the fact that this was a six-pack allowed us to track it down. There's only one rental company in northern Virginia that handles six-packs. Manassas Commercial Rentals. They rent primarily to construction companies and road builders. Graders, bulldozers, large trucks, backhoes, that kind of thing."

Jack thanked him and took down the address. Forty-five minutes later, he left Washington in a rental car heading for Manassas. He found the rental company on the outskirts of town. He saw a large field surrounded by a cyclone fence topped with coiled razor wire. There were a number of different trucks, including six-packs of the kind he had seen driving away from the Vietnam Veterans Memorial.

Jack strode into the rental office. The clerk sat behind a large counter, reading the latest issue of *Soldier of Fortune* magazine. He stepped up to the counter.

"Hi. I'm looking for some information about a brown six-pack rented a few days ago. Can you help me?"

"Who are you?"

"My name is Jack Bradshaw."

"I'm sorry, Mr. Bradshaw, we don't give out that kind of information. I can't help you."

"Look, I'm an investigative reporter with the *Los Angeles Times*. I'm just trying to track down a story."

"Even if you are a reporter, I can't help you."

Following the tactic used in every B movie and TV show ever written, Jack held up a hundred dollar bill. The clerk knew his role.

"That refreshed my memory a little bit." He swept up the money.

Jack returned his conspiratorial grin. "Now, what can you tell me about any brown six-packs that you rented in the last couple of days?"

"We have about a half dozen. Only one company rented a couple of them in the past week. This guy wanted two that were the same color. It stuck in my mind cause he kept saying he wanted a drab color."

"Can you tell me his name?"

"My memory's not that strong."

Jack dug into his pocket and counted out five twenties. The clerk stuffed the money into his pocket and turned to a file cabinet. He dug up a file folder. "It says here the trucks were rented to a company called D&M Construction. It has an address in Alexandria, Virginia. There's a phone number here in the margin."

Jack noted the information and asked to use the phone. The "202" area code told him it was a D.C. number. A recording said the number had been disconnected. He wasn't surprised.

He decided to drive to Alexandria to see if he could find the address. After searching the area for almost an hour, he realized no such place existed. The discovery made him uneasy, and he knew he would have to pay another call on Lieutenant Morris.

37

JUNKYARD JUNKIE

NOT WANTING TO LEAVE Elizabeth for long, Jack planned this as a quick trip to Tennessee. Morris was as eager to help as ever. He found out that the wreckage was taken to a salvage yard following the investigation and that it was still there. Within minutes of Jack's arrival in town, the two men pulled up in front of a junkyard on its outskirts.

Hundreds of carcasses of wrecked cars and pickup trucks were piled up, looking oddly like a towering sculpture. Here and there odd items were in the stacks including a fragmented aircraft fuselage. Jack turned to the deputy and asked, "Don't they send airplane wreckage to an aircraft junkyard or something?"

"There aren't that many plane crashes. I don't know where we'd send it. Far as I know, it's up to the insurance company," responded Morris amiably. "The owner doesn't cotton to strangers, so let me take the lead. He and I go way back. We see each other just about every time there's a car crash."

Morris exchanged pleasantries with the junkyard owner and introduced Jack as a friend of his who liked airplanes. He walked them further back into the yard, past the fuselage they had already seen.

The owner explained that he bought a couple of wrecked aircraft from the insurance companies in hopes of making more money salvaging instruments. "Just ain't a market for pieces of these planes. I heard after I bought the Merlin IIIB that there weren't many made. Folks who'd buy parts for the IIIB are usually commuter airlines. They want 'em new. The thing's been sitting here for a couple of years."

"Were you able to sell any part of it?" Jack asked.

"Sold a couple of instruments. Altimeters and an ADI — whatever that is."

Jack smiled to himself proud of having learned enough to know that an ADI shows the attitude of the aircraft in relationship to the horizon. He was relieved none of the fuel parts were included in the list of items that had been sold.

The owner continued, "Anything you lookin' for in particular?"

"I'd like to look at the fuel system, gauges, lines, tanks, boost pumps — whatever you've got here."

"No problemo. Those things were separated by the accident investigators over here," he said, pointing to some pieces and boxes lying next to the plane. "They said the fuel lines were in pretty good shape."

The owner helped them sort through some parts. "I kinda enjoyed hearing what they did. Kinda a step above hot rods. They said they pumped fuel through them under pressure to see if there were any leaks or holes and didn't find any. The lines from around the engines are in this box," he said, gesturing.

Just then, a bell rang in the distance. "Oh, shit," the owner exclaimed, "that's my phone. You guys take it easy, hear? Let me know if you want to buy anything."

As the owner scampered off, Jack started rummaging through the box pointed out by the owner. He glanced briefly at the fuel lines. What the owner said matched what he had read in the accident report so many months earlier. Jack kicked himself for not following up on things faster. Maybe if he had, Elizabeth wouldn't have been shot.

He couldn't tell anything from looking at the gauges. He walked over to the fuselage. The wings were tucked up against the side. The heavily damaged one was obviously sheared off by the accident. The other wing showed marks of neat cuts where it had apparently been sawed off and removed from the airplane either by the investigators or in transport.

Jack thought aloud. "The NTSB guy told me that the investigators dipped the tanks. Wonder if it would show us anything."

"I doubt it, but it's easy enough to do." Morris spotted a thin piece of wood, several feet long. "This should work."

Jack unscrewed the gas cap on the surface of the sawed-off wing. Morris stuck in the stick, pulled it out, and showed it to Jack.

"Just like they reported," Jack responded. "Only residual fuel. Might as well do the other one." They repeated the exercise on the damaged wing with the same result.

"I guess those guys at the NTSB know what they're talking about," said Morris, who was clearly enjoying playing detective regardless.

Jack wondered whether or not there was anything else worth inspecting. He noticed the lines leading into the wing. From the outside, he couldn't tell which ones were the hydraulic lines and which ones the fuel lines. He decided to look as far as he could into the wing at the fuel tanks to see which piping originated directly from the tanks.

As he peered in, he saw something that looked unusual, but couldn't quite make it out. "Do you by any chance have a small flashlight?"

"Sure do."

Jack took the small light and shined it on the fuel tank in the damaged wing. "Boy, this tank really took some heavy damage in the accident. It's all dented in."

The deputy leaned over Jack's shoulder, looking where the flashlight beam was shining. "It sure did. It's real compressed."

"Let's take another look at the other wing. I'm trying to figure out where the fuel piping comes from."

They bent over the other wing and Jack looked for a long moment without saying anything.

"What's the matter?" asked Morris.

"I don't know. This is real odd."

The deputy leaned in again. "Yeah, the tank looks damaged too. It's compressed just like the other one. You'd think it'd be uneven. They look like they were crushed in exactly the same way."

Curious, they went back to the first wing and compared again. There was no doubt about it. Both tanks showed the same type of indentations which resulted in the compression of both tanks.

Jack reached in and felt the side of the tank in the right wing. "I'm no expert, but I think these feel like hammer marks. Why would there be hammer marks on a gas tank? There wouldn't be any reason to hammer in a tank. I know that much."

"Let's take a look," Morris said.

Jack produced a Swiss Army knife and pulled out a tiny Phillips head screwdriver.

Morris chuckled. "What you use that for? Taking the back off your computer? You need a bigger tool for this. A man-sized one."

He laughed as he walked over to the office. He returned with a set of tools and began unscrewing the fasteners holding the exterior aluminum panels around the tank. In a few minutes, the skeleton of the wing was exposed. Now they both could see clearly. The tank on that wing was pounded into nearly a "V" shape.

"You know, if I ain't as dumb as my father said I was, I'd swear those marks look the same size as a number ten sledge."

"You sound like a pretty sharp police investigator to me."

Morris was pleased with the compliment. "If you want a comparison, let's go to that other aircraft fuselage. I'm telling you right now, there'd be no reason for anybody to do that kind of work on a car. Why do it on a million dollar airplane?"

"If you had a tank that big and you pounded in the tank this way, how much fuel capacity do you think you'd lose?"

"I don't know. If I remember high school geometry, it looks like you've got less than half a tank there."

"This looks like where the float valve goes. See here how it's right in the middle of this tank area? If the pounding didn't hit the float valve, the gauge would show a full tank — six hundred pounds of fuel. When in fact there would be less than three hundred." Jack felt a rush of sickening certainty move through him. "The crash was planned."

Morris nodded, convinced by the evidence in front of him. He remembered only too well the condition of all of the crash victims. "I do believe we've the beginnin' of a murder investigation here."

Jack was glad someone else finally shared his opinion and that it was now more than a hunch. "I think you're right. What do we do now?"

"I'll have my office start on it," Morris assured him.

"Can I give you a piece of advice? Be careful and keep it quiet. Whatever you do, don't tell the FBI."

Morris nodded. "Sounds like a good idea to me. I never trust the Fee Bees anyway."

After Morris warned the junkyard owner to leave the wreckage alone and not let anyone near it, they headed towards his office. Jack was deep in thought. Finally he asked, "Can you run a check on the National Aviation Maintenance and Transport Company. I think they have offices in Alexandria, Virginia."

"Anything I should know about?"

"According to the accident report published by the NTSB, they did the last maintenance done on that plane a day or two before the accident. They gave it a clean bill of health."

"Sounds like a good place for us to start." Morris seemed a little uncomfortable. "I have to inform you the things we've discussed must be kept confidential while our investigation is pending."

"I understand completely. I have other reasons for pursuing this."

Jack spent the next few hours at the sheriff's office telling Morris what he could remember about the NTSB report. He promised he'd fax the important parts as soon he got back.

Morris' secretary, enthusiastically chewing gum, surfed the Internet and made a few calls while the men talked. She reported the results of her effort, "We can't find D&M Construction anywhere. It's probably a fictitious name. We had a little more luck with the disconnected phone number you gave us. We were able to trace it to an address in Washington, D.C. It's an office building. 1152 K Street Northwest."

"Thanks, I'll check that out. Anything on the National Aviation Maintenance and Transport Company?"

She snapped her Juicy Fruit. "All we can figure out so far is that they're incorporated in Delaware and that it's the subsidiary of a company called NAHGFA."

"NAHGFA, that's a strange name. Is this D&M company mixed in with all this somehow?" asked Morris.

"I don't know." Jack was hesitant to share his ideas, but he trusted Morris. "I think it has something to do with Elizabeth being shot."

Morris raised his eyebrows. "Do you think they're connected?"

"I have my suspicions. We've had a couple of death threats and I've felt someone following me more than once. This started right after you and I started poking around. "

He paused, frowning. "I'm sure of it. Someone's after us."

38

Corporate Entities

Jack stared at the notes on the desk in front of him, pushing the phone away. The words of his stock broker still echoed in his ears. "The NAHGFA Corporation was incorporated in Delaware in 1984. The CEO is a Donald Larkin." He could believe what he had heard only too well. It confirmed his worst fears.

Jack called Morris and filled him in on it. "I know they have at least one subsidiary, but find out if there are other subsidiaries out there. If you can come up with a list and some additional information, anything at all, let me know."

"We'll get you what we can." Morris might have taken exception to Jack telling him what to do, but he liked Jack and figured any man whose wife was lying in a hospital bed deserved a little leeway. "I saw your wife's speech at The Wall. She's one tough lady. She's got my vote — and I'm a registered Republican."

"Thanks. I'll talk to you soon," Jack assured him. "And I think we'd better start being more circumspect on the phone."

Jack caught a cab and pulled up in front of 1152 K Street, NW. It was a three-story office building in one of the busier business districts of Washington. Jack had to dig deep to find enough money to pay the cab driver. He figured he'd better find an ATM soon, but he wanted to check out the office building first.

As he approached the entrance to the building, Jack was blocked by moving men who were carrying out furniture. At least two desks went by before Jack was able to make his way through the entrance. Straight ahead was a counter with a security officer behind it. He was a portly, aging black man. As Jack approached, he could see the shoulder insignia of Ajax Protective Services.

"How's it going today?" Jack began, sounding as cheerful as he could.

"About as well as can be expected. How's it with you?"

"Not bad, not bad. Say listen, I was looking for a tenant in this building called the D&M Construction Company."

"You sure you've got the right address?"

"Yes. Would you mind checking your records to see if there's ever been one here?"

"I don't have to check any records," he said with a confident air. "I've been here nineteen years and I know every company in this building. There's no D&M Construction Company and there never was."

Another desk hit a wall with a loud bang. "God damn, that was loud! Those damn movers are so careless," the guard complained. "I don't know where they find these boys who work for these moving companies. Not like when I was younger. You took pride and care with other people's possessions."

Jack fished a little. "So what's going on? Who's moving out?"

"Oh, some big international trade organization. They've been one of our oldest tenants. Been around almost fifteen years."

"Listen, are you sure about that D&M Construction? This is really important. I've got important work for them to do."

"This old body of mine may be going, but my mind's still sharp as a whip. I know the names of every firm in this building. That's not hard to do considering there's only five of them. D&M Construction was never one of those five."

Jack had a sudden brainstorm that he hoped would pay off. "NAHGFA Corporation isn't one of them, is it?"

"Nope. Sorry. Nothing remotely like it."

Jack's shoulders sagged. He realized that he'd better call Elizabeth since he'd called her at least once an hour since he'd left her bedside.

When he reached her, her voice was cheery. She had gotten more rest in the hospital than at any point since deciding to run. Her enthusiasm was renewed. "I've been busy answering the mail and telegrams that have flooded in. Amy's been helping me. And Clint and I have been mapping out our new strategy. It's actually been kind of nice. But I'm ready to get out of here. We expect the doctor to release me soon. Don't forget my suitcases when you come to get me."

"I won't. Thanks for the reminder." Jack wanted to wait until they were home to tell her about the murder investigation. Even private rooms in hospitals were not very private places.

"Amy just came back from giving away some of the flowers and candy to other patients." Jack could tell by Elizabeth's tone that she was smiling. He realized that at least one card and bouquet had better be from him.

Jack found a florist and picked out an arrangement of lavender roses. He was tempted by the red ones, but figured Elizabeth could use a break from red, white, and blue. He had them waiting on her bedside table when he brought her home.

He gave her a hug and a kiss, carefully avoiding her arm in the sling, as he tucked her into bed. Jack re-evaluated. Maybe this wasn't a good time. The ride home had been exhausting for her.

Regardless, her mind was still on the go. "I've got so much to tell you about the campaign. I want to discuss our strategy and get your input."

Jack was feeling tense. "We do need to talk."

She sensed the gravity of his feelings. "What's more important than the campaign?"

"I've pieced together more details of the plane crash. Your nightmares about the crash, what the pilot said, coupled with the findings of the NTSB investigation, confirm that the plane was out of fuel when it crashed."

"I know that," she responded, frowning.

"I have proof that the fuel tanks were altered so that the gauges were showing full when there was almost no fuel. The tanks could only be filled to less than half their capacity."

She reached for his hand, visibly shaken.

"Elizabeth, I have proof now that it was sabotage. I think someone wanted to get rid of Peter. Lieutenant Morris has started a homicide investigation." He paused, pained by the distress in her face, but knowing that she had to face the truth. "I no longer know who we can trust. You can't say anything about this to anyone."

"Jack, how much danger could we possibly be in? They've tripled my Secret Service protection."

"You were supposed to have adequate protection at the time of the shooting. You know if an assassin doesn't care about dying, there's no way to stop him."

"If the press gets hold of this, they'll make you sound like a nut. The shock jocks will say you are teaming with Oliver Stone for his next film. Why didn't the NTSB find what you found?"

"They had no reason to compare the two tanks. They analyze what they find. I was starting out with a theory." Feeling an urgency about convincing her, Jack laid out the evidence. "Peter was investigating illegal links between drug smuggling and support for resistance movements like those in Afghanistan when he was killed. There is no doubt that the crash was caused by sabotage to the plane's fuel tanks."

Her grim face caused him to pause, but after a moment he forged ahead. "As you know, some of the documents from the accident scene led me to Swiss bank accounts that seem to indicate a major money laundering scheme. The accounts were closed the day after the accident. While I was at the bank, men who appeared to be federal agents also showed up. I followed them to an office housing the Afghan Trading Company, which I suspect is a front organization.

"Just before that, Lieutenant Morris, the officer who showed me the documents in Johnson City, said he was being pressured by federal agents. Think about the death threats we got before the attempt on your life. I'm sure I saw a gun barrel pulled back into a truck. I traced the truck to a non-existent company. I'm convinced that the FBI ballistics reports will confirm that the assassin was killed by a different type of bullet than the Secret Service uses."

"Your reporter's instincts may be jumping the gun on this — or at least the ballistics reports. They should already have the results. I'll have Grossman follow up."

"They won't release it. I already tried. There's more here than meets the eye." He braced himself, knowing he was about to step into even more dangerous territory. "I think Frank Shotwell is behind all of this."

"Now, I know you're crazy. I still count Frank as my friend, even though he's opposing me in the campaign."

"Don't forget his aide, Larkin, showed up at the scene of the accident shortly after the plane was discovered and lied about who he was. He's an officer of a company that has direct links to the National Aviation Maintenance and Transport Company. They did the maintenance on the plane just before its last flight."

"Frank specifically recommended National to take care of Peter's plane."

"Exactly."

"Jack, everything you're saying is circumstantial. You can't have any connection to this. If it gets out, it will look like the worst kind of political ploy."

He nodded his agreement. "Now that Morris and his office are officially investigating, I can let go. He has no love for any federal agency and no reason to cover up anything."

39

ENEMY ACTION

JACK KNEW THE DICTATES of investigative reporters and intelligence operatives were the same. As James Bond said, "Once is coincidence. Twice is enemy action." The more he thought about it, the more convinced he was of Shotwell's direct involvement, even though he knew, as Elizabeth had said, that much of the evidence was circumstantial and some of the events potentially coincidental.

Despite his suspicions, they quickly got into the swing of campaigning again. They had no choice. The rallies were large. The crowds enthusiastic. Elizabeth's brave stand at The Wall had made her a folk heroine. She had the highest Q rating in the nation. Even the least-informed members of the general public could link her face and name. The press had affectionately dubbed her the "Iron Lady."

A few days after she left the hospital, Elizabeth sequestered herself with her campaign aides to prepare for the next presidential debate. They went over the briefing book until she nearly had it memorized, but they were still grilling her. It was not simple material. A team of top domestic and foreign policy experts had formulated educated responses to the most likely questions. Now it was up to Elizabeth to assimilate it all. Committing it to memory wouldn't do. She had to be able to shift it accurately from one context to another.

Elizabeth was so absorbed in the debate preparation that Jack found himself alone in the hotel room with nothing to do but worry. Unbidden, his mind focused on the investigation that seemed to be going nowhere. On an impulse, he took a gamble, picking up the phone and calling Shotwell. Using his position as Elizabeth's husband, in a few minutes he was connected.

"Frank, this is Jack Bradshaw," he said levelly.

"This is a bit of a surprise right in the middle of the campaign. What can I do for you? Maybe you are calling to give me advance notice on the concession?" He laughed at his own joke.

Jack did not. "It's not about the campaign. I have this little problem, Frank. You see, I know about your scheme."

"Scheme?" Shotwell's voice crackled with irritation.

"I know now about the drug operation. Furthermore, I have proof that Senator Armstrong was murdered. I know you were involved."

"Jack, I don't have time for this kind of bullshit. Is this some kind of a joke?"

"It's no joke. Unless you think that the sabotaging of the Senator's fuel tanks by the National Aviation Maintenance and Transport Company is a joke. I saw the tanks with my own eyes."

There was a pause and then a response. "Frankly, I didn't think Elizabeth's campaign would stoop this low. Or maybe it's just you. I've known Elizabeth for many years. A lot longer than you have. I know she wouldn't do anything like this."

The conversation wasn't going the way Jack wanted. He decided to bull through and take it all the way, adding a lot more bluster to his bluff.

"I know about the Swiss bank accounts, the Afghan Trading Company, NAHGFA, the Aviation Maintenance and Transport Company. Frank, I even know about D&M Construction. I have a tape with Larkin's voice on it that links you to this."

"There isn't any such tape. You're bluffing. I'm not going to listen to anymore of this shit."

There was a click. Shotwell had hung up.

Jack realized he was sweating. He sat and stared at the wall for almost an hour, wondering if he had just done something incredibly stupid.

40

CRISIS

"ELIZABETH! CLINT! Turn on CNN quick!" The voice at the door was urgent.

Grossman lunged for the remote. A face came into focus. A reporter was describing the takeover of the American Embassy in Caracas, Venezuela. A U.S. Marine guard had been killed. Over 100 hostages had been taken. Venezuelan sources claimed that narco-terrorists were behind the assault. Terrorists had sent death threats against the hostages to the Venezuelan government.

Grossman and Elizabeth looked at each other. Both of them knew what a fast-moving crisis could mean for the campaign.

Grossman exploded, "Shit. This is going to help Taylor. He's going to get away with just sitting there and looking presidential. Voters stick with the known in a crisis."

"You may be right, Clint, but all we can do is to continue doing the best job we can."

Grossman ducked out to get another briefing paper for the upcoming debate. Jack and Elizabeth sat mesmerized in front of the TV. Someone on camera suggested possible links to a South American drug cartel.

Jack had the sinking feeling that his call to Shotwell could have some something to do with the crisis. The drug cartel reference spurred him to review everything he knew about Afghanistan.

Suddenly a revelation clicked into place in Jack's mind. "NAHGFA! That's it! Nahgfa spelled backwards is Afghan!"

Elizabeth was startled. "You think there's some kind of an Afghanistan connection with the situation in Venezuela?"

"NAHGFA is a holding company. It controls a number of subsidiaries including the National Aviation Maintenance and Transport Company and the Afghan Trading Company located in Switzerland, with an office in the United States."

"National Aviation and Afghan Trading are owned by the same people! Why didn't you tell me?"

"I just found out. I was going to tell you after you finished your preparation for the debate."

"I think you'd better tell me now," Elizabeth declared. "If it relates to this crisis, it could be vital."

"Let me backtrack a step. I got suspicious because holding companies are normally formed to hold different companies relating to the same type of business. Here we have a foreign trading company in Switzerland and an aviation company in the United States. It's similar to what the CIA used to do in the old days when they put together corporate fronts. In this case, these companies could smuggle drugs and then launder the money earned from it."

Elizabeth paused and then returned to her original question. "So, what's the connection?"

"Right now I'm not sure." Jack responded. "Let me do a little more research. If I come up with anything solid, I'll let you know."

"No, Jack. This hits too close to home. We approach this as partners."

Jack stared at the floor, unable to meet her eyes. When she saw that, Elizabeth knew there was something he had held back from her.

The weight of the silence told him that she was aware of this. With all the guilt of a spouse in a melodrama admitting to an affair, Jack confessed he had made a call to Shotwell.

Elizabeth was stunned. "You shouldn't have done that without consulting me."

"I know. I'm sorry. I could say I was trying to allow you to keep plausible deniability."

Elizabeth answered with a stare.

"Okay, no, I can't say that. Evidently." Jack finally met her eyes, "I'm sorry." He paused for an instant and tried a faint smile. "I will submit my resignation as secretary of state right after the election."

"That's not funny."

"I know."

"As your wife I accept that. Even with love. As the next president of the United States, I have to tell you that you don't dare do anything remotely like that again without us having a full discussion first."

Jack fished an ice cube out of his Diet Coke and traced it along Elizabeth's wrist. "Maybe someday we can make ice hot again."

Elizabeth jerked her wrist back. "Don't try to use sex to get around me on this, Jack. What you did could have caused a catastrophe. It was impulsive, childish, and immature."

"Hey, I'm an American male. What do you expect?" He realized the second he had said it that humor was also a mistake.

"Better," Elizabeth flatly. "From you I expect better."

"I'm sorry," he repeated, contrite.

"Apology accepted. Now then, you think the call and the crisis are related. How do we find out? Let's consider our next step — together."

Jack thought out loud. "Remember when I first came to see you in Washington? We sat in on a Senate Intelligence Committee hearing. General Teufer testified. He seemed to have integrity and he knew what he was talking about."

"Right. And he's on the board of directors of the American Association of Retired Intelligence Officers."

"Okay if I call him?"

Elizabeth nodded.

Jack got him on the first ring. "General Teufer, my name is Jack Bradshaw. I'm a reporter for the *Los Angeles Times*." Jack omitted saying "former." He could certainly file a story with Farnum anytime.

"Jack Bradshaw? Well now, I read the papers. I know who you are."

"I'm gathering information on the Venezuelan crisis. It appears as if it is connected to international drug trafficking. I know you're knowledgeable about that. I saw you testify a while back before the Senate Intelligence Committee. I was hoping I could ask you a few questions."

Teufer was cautious. "I didn't know you were still working as a reporter."

"To be honest, this is more personal."

"Well now, the folks on Capitol Hill didn't listen very closely, so I'd be happy to talk with anyone who is interested enough. But only if it is kept strictly off the record."

"Understood. Does what CNN is saying about the Venezuelan terrorists having links to the narco-terrorists of the 1980s seem likely to you?"

"Realistically, no. In the '80s, narco-terrorists were primarily hit men and assassins working on behalf of the Colombian drug lords who supplied drugs to dealers in the United States. The information that I have about this bunch down in Venezuela right now is that they're connected to the international drug rings that operate outside of the Colombia-United States venue. In particular, it seems that they're getting most of their drugs from southwest Asia through routes that were established by resistance movements during the Russian occupation of that area."

"Was this matter actively investigated?"

"Yes and no. As you may recall from my testimony on Capitol Hill, I was by then retired and a private citizen, working actively to support freedom fighters in both Nicaragua and in Afghanistan. In Afghanistan, I uncovered evidence of a growing smuggling ring, some of which involved supply links set up by the United States government to assist rebel movements. As soon as I started to report this, my official contacts dried up. I was told to leave Pakistan where I was conducting support operations for Afghan refugees. Senator Armstrong shared my concerns. Then he was killed. Since then, nobody'll give me the time of day."

"What about General Shotwell? Wasn't he involved in establishing supply lines at that time?"

"Hell, yes! I never liked that guy or his aide, Larkin. Shotwell was responsible for funneling supplies to various resistance groups and setting up the routes and air strips. He handled the logistics of flying the supplies in and made sure they got to the right group. It was basically an officially sponsored smuggling operation. Shotwell was superb at that."

"What bothered you about him?"

"I was concerned about the groups he was involved with.

There were literally dozens of different Afghan resistance groups and fronts that were set up during that period. Most of those were legitimate and several of the largest of those groups did the greatest damage to the Russians. However, a few of the groups were heavily involved in smuggling drugs out of Afghanistan and in making themselves wealthy. That shit, Shotwell, was funneling a significant percentage of arms and equipment to those groups. Yet we were getting nothing back from them in terms of doing damage to the Russians."

"Wasn't Senator Armstrong working closely with General Shotwell?"

"Yes, in the beginning. In fact, we owe a great deal of gratitude to Senator Armstrong for convincing Capitol Hill to support the Afghan resistance movement against the Russians. I credit that particular war with helping bring down the Soviet empire. However, as the years went on, it became apparent to me that Shotwell was using his connections with Armstrong for his own agenda. Or maybe Shotwell changed after being out there for years working with these groups. I don't know. But just before Armstrong's death, when he started looking into this, I told him about some of the resistance groups that Shotwell was funding. In his last conversation with me before he died, Armstrong indicated that he now had reason to share my suspicions. He also said he was maintaining appearances with Shotwell. It sounded like he was being extremely careful with him." Teufer paused and switched gears. "Well now, seems like I've been doing a lot of talking. Mind telling me what you know about all of this?"

Jack weighed everything, including Elizabeth's cautions, and decided to trust him. "I have information about the Afghan Trading Company, a trade organization in Geneva, Switzerland. I suspect that it's a money laundering operation for the drug cartel. Could it be tied in with all of this somehow?"

"Yes. I had reason to believe that it was one of the money laundering operations for the National Islamic Resistance Movement and other resistance groups to which Shotwell had provided aid. It's a Swiss company, but it had offices here in Washington, D.C., right over here on K Street."

"K Street! Where on K Street?"

Teufer grabbed a phone book. "Here it is, Jack. 1152 K Street."

"Holy shit! D&M Construction Company!"

41

PIECE OF CAKE

GROSSMAN WAS SO NERVOUS that he was talking non-stop in what was supposed to be an attempt to calm Elizabeth down. The second and final presidential debate was only minutes away.

"I think they wanted the debate held in Baltimore in order to stay close to Washington," he said. "As far as timing, everyone assumed that a woman candidate would be strongest on domestic issues and weakest on foreign policy. Now we've got only these last ten days left before the election. That doesn't give us much time to deal with damage control if there's a problem."

"Still, this debate creates an opportunity for us," Elizabeth replied. "Since the president is expected to win it, if we do well, it will be a real plus."

"Talking about yourself in the royal 'we' now, Mom?" Amy asked. They were waiting nervously in an anteroom at the auditorium.

"She's right," Jack said. "Much as you are a team player, there's no 'we' about this. You're the one on the line out there."

"I'm not sure I want to be reminded of that right now," said Elizabeth, pulling her suit jacket into place.

Grossman continued, "You're correct. Low expectations are not necessarily a liability. But, like I say, they probably didn't see much risk, because they don't perceive you as strong in foreign policy."

"Right," said Elizabeth. "In 1984 Marvin Kalb asked Geraldine Ferraro if she thought that the Soviets might be tempted to take advantage of her just because she was a woman."

Amy spoke up. "Women who achieve anything are still viewed as the exception. I saw a headline reading, 'Woman Appointed to Circuit Court of Appeals.'"

Grossman seemed to take note what Amy had said. "Personally, I think they may have been selling you short, Elizabeth. You've been pretty effective"

"'Pretty effective.' Thanks, Clint. Coming from you that's high praise indeed. I know that I've become more sophisticated and streetwise as the campaign has progressed. But we've still have an awful lot of ground to make up."

Grossman sipped a cup of decaf. Jack had substituted it for the high-octane variety, not knowing if he could tolerate it if Grossman got any more wired than he already was. Grossman refilled his cup as he continued. "In every poll we get a little closer. You got a significant bump after the shooting and you've been able to hold onto that. Over the last couple of months the economy has slowed a bit. That may hurt the president. I expect their media blitz to begin any day now. We'll be pummeled by negative ads during the closing days of the campaign."

Amy was still angry over the use of footage of her mother crying at her father's funeral. "That last ad was really rotten. We just have to give it our all for the next ten days. There's always hope."

"That may not have been the royal 'we,' Amy, but it sure made me feel like a queen." Elizabeth hugged her.

A production assistant knocked on the door. "One minute, Governor Armstrong."

"Good luck, Mom." Amy hugged her mother again. "Oh, and you know that trip to Europe you promised me? Let's schedule it for eight years from now, when you'll be retired."

Elizabeth kissed her forehead. "That's the best good luck I could possibly have gotten. Thanks, Amykins."

Jack walked her to the door and kissed her on the cheek. She looked into his eyes with a smile and said, "Make sure you fill the ice bucket in the room tonight."

Jack clicked his heels and bowed from the waist, "Yes, Commander. So let it be done."

She laughed and readied herself for the cameras.

Amy and Jack took their places in the front row near Sonoma and his wife, readying their reaction shot faces. Elizabeth stood confidently at the podium. President Taylor, standing at the other podium, nervously wiped his brow with a handkerchief and checked his watch.

"Piece of cake," Jack mouthed to Elizabeth.

The debate began with Elizabeth on the offensive. Taylor acted as if he knew she was besting him. Now he was waiting for Elizabeth to finish her attack on his last answer.

"The president's solution to maintaining credibility in foreign policy is to keep the production line for the B-2 stealth bomber going at $2.2 billion per copy. We can't afford it. Every B-2 bomber purchased means fewer troops and less training to meet the crises like that which this country successfully met in Iraq. B-2 bombers were available then and were not used because they are so expensive that we couldn't afford to lose one. Yet we used every tank and soldier we could mobilize. For a secure future, we need a credible army of well-trained soldiers, not a stealth bomber designed for a war with a crumbled empire that no longer exists."

The moderator indicated that the next question was for her. A panelist asked, "What are your views on how we should handle the crisis in Venezuela?"

Elizabeth straightened her shoulders and began speaking in measured tones. "I am surprised by that question. Not because it is not important, but because of the sensitivity of what is going on in Venezuela. There are lives at stake. You're asking me and the president in the midst of a political debate to make public statements about an ongoing international crisis. In my opinion, the question is inappropriate and I will not comment on it. I, like all Americans, will support the commander-in-chief in his decisions on this issue. If the crisis goes beyond the election and I am elected, policies will not change regarding any negotiations. I want the terrorists to know that. They cannot get us to play political games with this. This is an American issue, not a Republican or a Democratic issue."

She folded her hands on the podium, indicating that her answer was complete, two minutes before her time was up. Surprised, the moderator turned to Taylor. "Under the rules you still have your three minutes to respond if you so desire, Mr. President."

The cameras shifted to Taylor. Perspiration was now visible on his brow and he nervously twisted his hands on the podium. "Yes, thank you. Let me just say that our administration is closely watching the situation in Panama — uh, Venezuela. I do appreciate Governor Armstrong's comments. This is a highly sensitive matter. Because it is a matter of national security, I cannot comment on the strategies we may be employing. Governor Armstrong has referenced the continuity of effort that would take place if she is elected. Let me just say that my administration is making every effort to solve this crisis quickly, without any further loss of life."

The moderator concluded the debate by requesting that all Americans exercise their right to vote. The stage lights and cameras went off. Jack noted Taylor still looked distraught.

The president approached Elizabeth and took her hand. She jumped slightly at his touch. He looked into her eyes for what seemed to be a long time. Then he turned to Jack, studied him for a moment and walked away without saying a word.

"That was odd," said Jack. Elizabeth didn't respond, but seemed to be behaving somewhat strangely herself, looking around the room as if hoping to see someone.

She turned to Jack. "Let's head for the limo. I'd like to catch the coverage."

Jack, puzzled by what he had witnessed, followed her out. As they entered the limousine, a special session of *Capitol Landscape* was just beginning. As usual, Don Kates was moderating. "Well, pundits, what are your opinions about what we just saw? Tom, you lead off."

"It's obvious that Governor Armstrong won this debate hands down. She came across as highly knowledgeable in foreign policy. She gave good, crisp answers. She was strong, confident and vigorous. The president, on the other hand, seemed nervous and shallow. Inexplicably so. And his blunders, particularly on the answer to the question about the crisis in Venezuela, are going to hurt him."

"Jane, what are your views?"

"For once, I agree with Tom. Governor Armstrong took that one hands down. She showed a depth in foreign policy that I wouldn't have expected. Her answers on how to handle nuclear inspections around the world showed a great deal of thought. Her grasp of military affairs was simply astounding for someone not considered experienced in that field."

The camera flashed back to Kates. "Let's talk about the president a little bit. I noticed his nervousness. Tom, what do you think was going on there?"

"Quite clearly he did not come across well. It's probably due to the severity of this crisis that's going on in Venezuela. The two mistakes that he made in that answer certainly cannot help him. He confused the country when he said Panama instead of Venezuela. It reminded me of Gerald Ford's blunder about Poland in his debate. A really stupid blunder."

Rodman jumped in. "Frankly, the president seemed stunned by Governor Armstrong's response to the question. I don't think he expected such a strong statement of support. At the same time she subtly undercut whatever policy distinction he might have made between himself and her. He came into this debate overconfident and underprepared. It would seem by his answers that he didn't take her as seriously as he should have."

Jack quickly interjected. "Good going! You did good!"

"Thanks. It felt good," admitted Elizabeth.

Kates continued. "Obviously, the crisis in Venezuela overshadows everything here. How do you think this is going to affect the election? You first, Tom."

"The latest polling data, which is a day or two old now, still shows Governor Armstrong somewhere between six and ten points behind. And there's probably a margin of error of roughly two percent. That's too much ground to be made up in the next ten days. Her performance tonight is going to help her and hurt him. But I still think the president will be re-elected."

Rodman responded with a grin. "Again we agree! This is incredible! However, I will remind my friend Tom that in the Kentucky Derby, one should remember to bet on the filly." They both laughed as she continued. "In all seriousness, however, I agree that there's a lot of ground for her to make up. On top of that, a crisis like this always helps the incumbent. Also, at risk of making Tom say nay, many voters will feel that they don't want to switch horses in midstream."

Kates smiled. "I won't be a naysayer about that one. That will be a big factor here."

Elizabeth clicked off the set. She had insisted that the campaign staffers ride in another car so she could be alone with Jack. He again tried to congratulate her on her performance, but her demeanor hushed him. He had expected much more euphoria after the stunning victory.

She pulled a small scrap of paper from her pocket. "Taylor gave me this note when we shook hands."

"I wondered what was going on. What does it say?"

"It just says to call this number," she said.

He handed her the cell phone. She punched in the numbers, listened for a moment, then hung up. "It was a recording. It said to watch CNN tomorrow morning at eight."

42

A MAN OF INTEGRITY

ELIZABETH STRUGGLED THROUGH a fitful night. She awoke early and couldn't go back to sleep. What was President Taylor planning to do?

At a few minutes before eight, Elizabeth, Jack and the entire campaign staff assembled in front of the television set in Elizabeth's suite. The broadcast opened with a news account of the status of the crisis in Venezuela. The terrorists had permitted the recovery of the body of the Marine guard and negotiations were continuing.

Abruptly the news broadcast was interrupted with a special bulletin. The picture switched to the White House press room. The CNN White House correspondent intoned that a significant announcement related to the crisis in Venezuela was expected momentarily.

CNN cameras focused on the empty podium in the briefing room. In a moment a balding, portly man strode up to the podium. No one needed to be told that this was White House Press Secretary Hanley Stassen. He shuffled through a sheaf of papers for a few seconds. Flashbulbs popped.

He cleared his throat and the room fell silent. "Ladies and gentlemen, I have called this meeting to make a brief announcement on behalf of the president of the United States. Due to the seriousness of events occurring in Venezuela, the president has become concerned that there may be an effort by the terrorists holding American citizens hostage to manipulate this presidential campaign. This point was also noted by Governor Armstrong last night in the debate. Therefore, the president is calling for a private briefing between himself and Governor Armstrong. The focus of this meeting will be to prepare a joint approach, so that American strategy can remain consistent, regardless of the outcome of the election. The president wants to make it clear that the terrorists will gain nothing by continuing this hostage situation until the election or inauguration. The president expects that this unusual action taken in the middle of the campaign will send a message that the United States is fully united against this terrorist act. We will not allow the American democratic process to be influenced in any way by terrorists. This concludes my prepared statement."

Stassen looked up from his notes and stared into the assembled cameras. "I will take only one or two questions. I cannot respond with any details regarding the meeting between Governor Armstrong and the president other than to indicate that it will occur within the next twenty-four to forty-eight hours. We are in the process of making arrangements with Governor Armstrong at this time."

Immediately, there was a clamor as reporters jumped to their feet, raising their hands and voices, demanding attention. As Stassen pointed to one, the others quieted down, allowing her to ask a question. "Mr. Press Secretary, will you tell us where the meeting is going to take place?"

"I can only respond that the meeting will be in the White House briefing room at a mutually convenient time, which hasn't yet been established."

The clamor rose again. Stassen's voice rose above it. "I'll take one more question." He pointed his finger to another reporter on the other side of the room.

"Mr. Press Secretary, is there a plan underway to use military force in order to solve this crisis?

"Dick, you know I can't respond to a question like that. If there were ever military plans underway, we would never divulge them at a press conference. All options are open and will be considered by both the President and Governor Armstrong at their meeting. That's all the questions I can take. You'll be briefed on any further developments. Thank you very much."

With that, Stassen walked off the stage. In Elizabeth's suite,

Grossman turned to Elizabeth, his face red with anger. "You didn't tell me anything about this."

"That's because I didn't know anything about it. This is all news to me."

"You told us to watch CNN today for an important message. You must have known something."

"I only knew there would be some form of announcement, but I had no ideas about the content. The White House has not contacted us as far as I know."

The phone rang. Grossman picked it up and looked up at Elizabeth. "It's the president."

Elizabeth took the phone. "Hello, Mr. President."

"Hello, Governor. Did you watch the announcement?"

"Yes, I did. And frankly, Mr. President, I'm a bit confused. The announcement seemed to imply that I had been consulted about this, when I knew nothing about it."

"I'm sorry, Governor. This is a matter of highest national security and urgency. I had to do it in a manner that you couldn't refuse. It is absolutely imperative that I speak to you. How soon within the next day or so can you clear a space on your calendar for me?"

"Well, Mr. President, we're still in the Washington area. We were intending to leave Baltimore later today, but our departure could be pushed back until tomorrow. Obviously, the sooner we have the meeting the better. Say this afternoon?"

"Agreed. Make it two o'clock. I'm asking you not to bring your campaign manager. But I'm specifically asking you to bring Jack. It's important that I speak to the two of you together."

"We'll see you at two o'clock, then. Goodbye."

Elizabeth hung up the phone and looked around the room. Grossman spoke first. "So, Elizabeth, are we heading down to Washington at two o'clock?"

"Clint, we need to spend a lot of effort analyzing how to reorganize the rest of the campaign schedule in light of this development. I'd like you to stay here and work on that. Jack will go with me to the White House. I think that's the most efficient use of our resources."

Grossman was leery. "This could be some kind of a campaign trick, or a plot to gain the advantage."

"I understand your concern, but I don't believe that's the case. First of all, I can't conceive what advantage the president could gain by putting me essentially on the same level with him. Second, even though I am in a tough political contest with President Taylor, I've always respected him as a man of high integrity. I wouldn't expect him to pull a stunt like this for political gain."

Jack entered into the conversation. "I tend to agree with you, Elizabeth. Although it seems to me that there's more to this than just a briefing."

A few hours later, Elizabeth and Jack sat alone in the back seat of a limousine on their way from Baltimore to Washington. A carload of Secret Service agents followed behind.

Elizabeth felt decidedly somber. The hostages' fate weighed heavily on her. Although the privacy screen was up, she spoke to Jack in a hushed tone. "I agree there's more to this than a briefing on coordinating policy. I didn't want to discuss it in front of the rest of the staff."

His expression became serious. "I still wonder whether or not I did the right thing. If this business down in Venezuela turned out to involve Shotwell, I may have put many lives in jeopardy."

She reached over and placed her hand consolingly on his forearm. She knew the possibility was weighing heavily on him.

"I'm sure you did what you thought was right at the time. I'm beginning to understand how difficult the office of president would be. I'd be making decisions that place lives in jeopardy all the time. The main thing I'm concerned about is that we operate as a team. There's nothing that can be done about it now. Let's just see what Taylor has to say."

"I'm beginning to appreciate the responsibilities of the office too." He squeezed her hand. "We are a team. But I won't forget that you're the president."

She placed her other hand on top of his. "Thanks, partner," she responded.

Within minutes after the limousine arrived at the White House, Elizabeth and Jack were being ushered through the stately mansion in the direction of a door which led into the briefing room. Their Secret Service guards quietly disappeared.

They sat down in overstuffed chairs around a large table and waited nervously. Elizabeth was struck with a slight sense of awe, even though she had visited the White House many times as a senator's wife and as governor of New Hampshire.

They arose as the president entered the room, flanked by several members of his staff. He greeted them, shook their hands, and introduced them to the others.

Then, turning to the staff, he announced, "Now, if you folks don't mind, I'd like a few moments alone with the Armstrongs."

The staff immediately left and the door closed behind them. As soon as they were gone, Taylor began. "Governor Armstrong, Mr. Bradshaw, this room is secure. You have my personal guarantee that nothing is being recorded here. I want your guarantee that nothing we say leaves this room. This is totally off the record. Forgive me, Jack, if after half a century of public life, I don't quite trust the press. So, if you can't live with that, I'll have to ask you to leave."

Elizabeth and Jack looked at each other. She spoke first. "That's fine with me, Mr. President. Jack?"

"Of course."

Taylor smiled. "Good. Now please join me for a cup of coffee." Elizabeth and Jack followed his lead. As they were pouring coffee from the silver service on the table, Taylor seemed to lighten up a bit. "Now that we're in private and off the record, let's use first names. That President stuff all the time makes you pretty lonely after a while. Elizabeth, I want to compliment you on your campaign. I would have expected such a strong campaign from someone like your late husband, but not from you. Frankly, my staff and I didn't expect you to be as aggressive as you have been."

"What's the matter, Gordon? Haven't you run against any women with *cojones* before?" asked Jack.

"Touché. You have to at least admit, however, that your campaign was in a bit of disarray in the beginning."

"Yes, but that was when I was relying on others who claimed to have experience in the field. Once I started following my own political instincts I did a lot better."

"Your instincts are certainly a match for Peter's. You have done an extremely effective job in the last couple of months. I'm impressed."

Elizabeth smiled. "Thank you, Gordon. I've always had a great deal of respect for you. The way you handled the Korean nuclear crisis was brilliant — a delicate balance between waving the stick and offering the carrot. It shouldn't have surprised anyone that it came out the way you wanted. I've always been impressed by the way you handle foreign policy."

"Too bad I can't quote you on that." He smiled, but it faded into a sigh. "What I'm about to tell you may shake your confidence somewhat in my foreign policy abilities."

"What is it, Gordon?"

"This isn't easy to admit." He looked like a deer caught in the headlights. "I guess there's no way to say it, but to say it. Frank Shotwell is involved in a master drug ring and is apparently behind the crisis in Venezuela."

His voice was heavy with tension. "It wasn't entirely clear at first. The terrorists were making strange demands which related to Shotwell. So, I decided to initiate an investigation. The problem was that all of my information from security and intelligence agencies is filtered through the National Security Council and thus through Shotwell himself. I had to initiate a private investigation. The results are still coming in, but what we have clearly shows that Shotwell is dirty."

"Go on, Gordon."

Taylor stared levelly at Elizabeth for a few seconds. "You don't seem very surprised by this."

Jack interjected, "We already had our own suspicions. In fact, just a day or so before the crisis I confronted him with information that I had uncovered about drug activities."

Taylor seemed a bit surprised and then recovered. "That explains something that he said. When he finally admitted some involvement, he talked about the efforts to expose him."

Jack felt he had to speak. "Mr. President — Gordon, it goes far beyond just drugs. I believe that Shotwell is responsible for Senator Armstrong's death and the attempt on Elizabeth's life."

"The imminent danger to Elizabeth's life is another reason why I called you here and did it so publicly." He spoke with gravity. "I have the classified results of the Secret Service investigation of Elizabeth's shooting. It concludes that the bullet that shot the assassin was from a different weapon. It does not match the chambering or characteristics of any of the firearms carried by the Secret Service agents who were on duty that day."

"I was right!" Jack exclaimed. "I told the investigators I saw another gun there!"

Taylor continued after nodding to acknowledge Jack's statement. "Elizabeth, it's clear that the shooter was supposed to assassinate you and then be shot down himself. Shotwell is a desperate man. From what our investigation put together, he precipitated the Venezuelan crisis to provide him with an avenue to negotiate himself out of the country. I don't know if he plans to change his identity or go underground in some country that has no extradition treaties with us, such as Libya. I don't even know whether he can hide, but he's made demands and we need to discuss them."

"Absolutely," Elizabeth agreed.

"The initial demand was that the investigation be quashed and every piece of evidence leading to him be destroyed. On that basis, the hostages would be released alive. You know there's no way the government could make a deal like that and just let him go free. Obviously, I had to turn that down."

"Obviously. There's no other choice when you're dealing with a terrorist."

"He's demanding that he be given safe conduct out of the country and sufficient time for a head start. After forty-eight hours, he promises that the hostages will be released alive and unharmed. I told him I'd have to think it over. I was stalling for time."

Taylor looked gravely at Elizabeth. "Actually, I wanted to talk to you about it because I want this to be a joint effort. He's making death threats against the hostages. We hold the lives of over a hundred people in our hands."

"Mr. President, what are you asking of me? It seems to me that at this point, it's your decision."

"You're right, Elizabeth. But this impacts on both of us and the election. If I agree to allow him out of the country in exchange for the hostages' lives, it means we will both have to keep quiet about what we know."

"You don't sound like you are asking for my opinion as a means to creating a solution. I suspect you just want my consent about something you plan to do anyway."

He paused, obviously contemplating what he was going to say. "I will make you an offer. We won't take any action ending the crisis in these few days before the election, unless there's some way to guarantee getting the hostages out safely during that period. If they are safely released through our negotiations, I will offer to include you in a press conference in which we both share responsibility for gaining the release. That way, there would be no political gain for either of us in ending the hostage crisis. In return, I ask you not to go public with this. I would like to have the option of letting him make a run for it, if it will guarantee the hostages' safe release."

Jack was suspicious. "Wait a minute, Gordon, if this broke now and the public knew that your vice-presidential candidate was involved in this thing, it would ensure Elizabeth's election. You're basically asking her to give up being president of the United States."

"I'm asking her if gaining the presidency is worth a hundred innocent lives."

Elizabeth forcefully interjected. "First of all, Gordon, whichever of us is president, this man must be pursued."

"I think you know my reputation. I am a man of my word. If I'm elected, once the hostages are freed, I will turn loose every agency of the government to track him down. We will use our allies around the world, some of whose methods are — shall we say, less civilized than our own. He and the drug ring will not survive."

"Then what you're asking for is my concurrence in remaining silent in order to secure the release of the hostages. Once they are released, you guarantee that you will use every resource at your disposal to turn the world upside down and bring him and the other terrorists to justice. Is that correct?"

"That is correct. And if you are elected, I would expect you to do the same. You may be giving up the presidency by doing this, but you'll have saved over a hundred lives. My presidency will not be pleasant by any stretch of the imagination. Once this is over, and especially if Shotwell leaves the country, I'll face a major investigation and possible impeachment for allowing a terrorist to go free. At the least, having had Shotwell as my chief of National Security and as my running mate will be considered extremely bad judgment. That, coupled with the fact that I let him go, should be enough to have Congress screaming for my impeachment. The United States will not exchange hostages for terrorists, but this is an extremely unusual situation. I am willing to face the prospect of impeachment if it guarantees the safety of the hostages. I don't know if I need this option, but I'd like to have it available. In reality, I don't think there is any place this man can hide."

"I understand what you're saying. It's a burdensome decision. One hundred innocent lives are in the balance."

Taylor balled his fists. "I passed over a number of highly qualified people to make him my running mate. It's a shock to find out that somebody I had given so much authority is worse than a common murderer."

Elizabeth was equally devastated. "I considered him one of Peter's and my closest friends. I trusted him implicitly."

She stood and walked around the room, intuitively sitting where the president usually sat. "It seems to me that we only have one other thing to talk about — the rest of the campaign. I will agree not to discuss this, but as far as the rest goes, I'm going flat out to win this thing."

"I wouldn't have it any other way. I've always said that if it ain't worth fighting for, it ain't worth having. May the best man — best person — win."

43

Silver Lining

OVERWHELMED BY THE importance of the decision she had made, Elizabeth and Jack did not talk during the ride back to the hotel. Finally, she broke the silence. "You were right about Shotwell. I'm sorry I didn't believe you at the very beginning."

"I'm sorry it turned out this way. But I am so proud of you."

"Thank you. I didn't have much choice."

"You've probably given up the opportunity to be president."

"I know. But Taylor is in a tough position on this. I couldn't take office with blood on my hands. The presidency isn't worth killing a hundred people." She sighed. "Maybe I just don't have enough fire in the belly for this kind of job."

"Christ, Elizabeth! With how hard you've fought and everything you went through, how can you think that for an instant? If Taylor had been in your shoes, he'd have made the same decision. In fact, it seems to me that you two are alike. You're both people of high integrity who place a high value on human life. Both of you are presidential timber."

"Thank you." She paused barely a heartbeat. "Based on my standings in the polls, it looks like I've lost my shot anyway. I don't think we can strategize a way to beat the hit that their media blitz is going to lay on us. That wave of negative publicity Grossman anticipates could well knock me out."

"You're right. It will be hard to overcome a last minute blitz. You know that if either of us revealed the scandal, you'd be

227

handed the win on a silver platter."

Elizabeth was appalled at the thought. "You aren't being tempted by this as a story, are you?"

"Of course. But it's not a temptation that I have to work to overcome. Not with lives in the balance. If Taylor were corrupt, if I felt he would damage the country irreparably, I'd break my word."

"I'd be shocked if I didn't feel the same way. It would be a hideous decision to sacrifice the hostages. But in some circumstances it would be justified. This isn't that kind of situation."

"You did great capitalizing on events as they played out. You turned around what could have been disaster and made it a viable contest. So much in this game depends on factors beyond control. You may have missed the brass ring, kid, but we both know you made the right choice. Besides, there's always four years from now."

"I don't know about that. Four years seems like an eternity. I'm not sure I'd ever want to go through all this again. You know, you are sitting on the biggest story of your life."

"I suppose so. Someday it will be written. Since I know more about it than anybody else, I'll still essentially have an exclusive."

"But you've given up the scoop of a lifetime. It would have guaranteed you a Pulitzer. I'm proud of you."

"Thanks. And I respect you for what you've done. You've handled every decision with grace. You've certainly shown that your principles are even more important than being president of the United States." He smiled warmly.

She looked at him lovingly. "It's certainly been an interesting two years."

"I wouldn't trade these years with you for anything. No matter what happens with the election, the future will be ours and it will be great." He put his arm around her and kissed her. Their kiss grew from affectionate to passionate.

"You know, if I lose this thing, we'll have more time for each other," she said, her kisses deepening.

"A definite silver lining. But there's no law that says presidents can't play those games. Enough men before you have certainly exercised their libidos while in office."

She smiled at the thought. "I wonder how many presidents have done it in the Oval Office?"

"Power is a potent aphrodisiac," said Jack with a knowing smile. They both laughed.

"I think we'd better focus on giving them a run for their money for the next few days," said Elizabeth. "Now you've given me some real incentive."

"You're right. It's time for you to start thinking about how you can still win this thing."

"All kinds of things can happen between now and the election. In politics, an hour can be an eternity. We need to get together with Clint as soon as possible. If we're going to have any chance at all of winning, we're going to have to do some brainstorming."

44

PERSEVERANCE

ELIZABETH EMERGED FROM the polling booth in her home-town of Durham, New Hampshire, at 8:10 on the morning of election day. In spite of the hostage situation, her mood was upbeat. She was pleased with how well the campaign had gone in the last few weeks. She might not win the election, but she had put on a credible performance. At 8:11 the barrage by well-wishers and reporters began.

"Governor Armstrong," shouted one of the eager reporters, thrusting a microphone at her face, "the polls published yes-terday showed you were four points behind President Taylor in the popular vote. Even with an error factor of two to three percent factored in, that still means you're losing."

Elizabeth spoke into the microphone with a smile. "Your grasp of statistics is excellent."

The reporter continued, "Republicans and conservatives vote in larger percentages than Democrats and liberals. Do you think you have any chance at this point?"

"I have a great deal of confidence in the voters. As you know, the polls have been tightening dramatically over the last couple of weeks. Just a few weeks ago, I was almost fifteen points be-hind. The momentum is in our favor and I expect that we will close the gap. The election is the only poll that really counts."

Another reporter jockeyed for position in front of her, using her elbows as deftly as an NBA forward. "When women are alone in the voting booth they may be more inclined to vote for you regardless of their party. Is that a factor you're counting on today?"

"There are many people in this country, both men and women, who think it is time for our country to have a woman president. People will vote for me because they think I am the best candidate."

"What are your plans for the rest of today?" asked another reporter.

She was glad to hear a question that didn't require careful consideration. "I'm immediately taking a plane for California. I'll be covering most of that state today."

Knowing he had to keep today's schedule to the minute, Grossman stepped forward, using his body as a shield from the reporters to stop further questions. "Thank you very much, ladies and gentlemen. We have to leave now."

Elizabeth made her way through the crowd to a waiting limousine. A few minutes later she, Jack and Grossman boarded a small chartered plane and winged their way to Boston's Logan Airport. In less than an hour, they were escorted through the departure area of the main terminal to a waiting aircraft. They had taken over the entire first class section of a scheduled non-stop flight to San Francisco. Once in the air, Grossman opened his briefing books and began preparing for the upcoming events.

"Let me go over again what I've got planned. I think it's a suicidal schedule, but I gave you what you wanted. We expect to arrive in San Francisco first. We have a rally planned right there at the airport. Then we'll pick up the Merlin and whistle stop our way through the state. I've coordinated it carefully with the pilots and air traffic control." Reading from his notes, he continued. "We have rallies scheduled in Sacramento — if we arrive in San Francisco on time — San Jose, then on to Fresno, Bakersfield, San Diego, and back up to L.A. What we're looking for is live press coverage at each location. I know I agreed to let you do this, but it must have been in a very weak moment." He was only half-joking.

"You know this will get my name before the voters while they're thinking about going to the polls."

"I know, but it's still a ridiculous schedule."

Jack held Elizabeth's hand. "The day I met her she set the

pace, jogging at a breakneck speed, and she hasn't stopped since."

Elizabeth squeezed his hand, but spoke to Grossman. "Did you reconfirm the hotel?"

"Everything's set the way you wanted. In L.A., we'll meet up with Sonoma and Amy to watch the election returns. Sonoma's been working the hell out of the state for the last two weeks and we've been getting some good results at his rallies. Amy's also been doing a fantastic job. We're making some inroads."

"You didn't have to drop anything off?"

"We've got it extremely well organized and, unless something goes wrong, we should be able to do the next to impossible and cover the whole state."

"Thanks, Clint. I'd like to go talk to Jack for a few minutes."

"Don't take too long. We've got lots of work to do," he said impatiently. Elizabeth noted his tension, realizing that his career was on the line here too. "I've got a list of numbers of campaign offices," he continued. "If we divide them up, we can call most of them before we land. It's really important. And we need to talk about what you're going to say."

She nodded her understanding and Grossman left to get on the telephone. She turned to Jack. "I'm nervous about the last couple of days. I'm not sure that the decisions we've made have been the correct ones."

"It's too late now. It's not like you to Monday morning quarterback. This isn't the time to start."

"That's true. While you're into sports talk, why don't you throw in 'it ain't over 'til it's over.'"

"Nope. I got culture, kid. I was going to say, 'It ain't over 'til the fat lady sings.'" He paused, "Take it easy on yourself, Elizabeth. It was a big decision for you."

"In terms of affecting me winning the presidency, I am comfortable with the decision I made."

Thirteen hours later, Elizabeth, Jack, and their troops reached L.A. and straggled wearily into the Biltmore. Once they had made their way through the storm of camera flashes, they relaxed.

In the elevator Elizabeth commented, "My face actually hurts from smiling so much."

All of them were too tired to smile anymore. They headed for the suite, drawing on their final reserves of energy to even walk through the door. Amy was waiting for them with Sonoma and his wife.

Exhausted, everyone collapsed onto the couch and over-stuffed chairs. Elizabeth kicked her shoes off and nudged Jack to the side of the couch so she could stretch out with her head in his lap. Sprawled out, she gave a deep sigh.

Jack stroked her hair. "The polls are closed. It's all over. We don't have to do anything but wait."

"At least I gave it my best shot."

"Your speeches today were some of the best I have ever heard," Grossman said, giving her the first real compliment of the campaign.

She responded jokingly, "What do you mean speeches? There was just one speech. I gave the same speech at every stop."

Jack laughed. "I know, Elizabeth, but they all sounded good, and kept getting better."

"Yeah, and you didn't leave anything out," added Grossman with a chuckle.

Elizabeth sat up and looked over in Sonoma's direction. "John, I want to thank you for all your effort. You've really helped this campaign. Regardless of the result, I am deeply in-debted to you."

Sonoma bowed his head. "It's been an honor to share the ticket with you."

"Thanks, John. And Clint, Roland, we had a rough begin-ning, but we moved through that. You can't imagine how grate-ful I am. You've made a great effort."

"It has been my pleasure," said Delacruse.

"I just hope we're successful," added Grossman.

Amy hugged Elizabeth, then sat on the floor leaning against the sofa.

"Having you back means the world to me," said Elizabeth. "Thank you, honey, for all your support."

"I wish I had done it sooner. I love you, Mom."

Elizabeth looked at Jack. She reached out and took his hand. "Thanks for just being in my life." Tears welled up in her eyes. Jack smiled but didn't speak.

Elizabeth took a deep breath, then looked toward Grossman. "So, how does it look?"

"You know everything I do," Grossman responded. "The polls have been closed in the East for three hours. The initial indications are not good. Most of the voting in the East has gone pretty much as we predicted. You're behind in both the popular vote and the electoral college."

He turned up the volume on the TV as the election logo was broadcast. They had been watching CNN with the sound off during other coverage.

Kates was doing special election coverage. "Things do not bode well for Elizabeth Armstrong. Her strength was primarily in the East and she has not done well there. It would take a miracle upset in a number of large states for Armstrong to have any chance at all."

As the evening wore on, the news did not improve. The popular vote count continued to tighten some. Elizabeth won a couple of states that she had not counted on, but also lost a few she hoped to win. The suite was littered with the debris of room service meals. Elizabeth's meal remained untouched in front of her as she dozed on the couch. Exhausted and with nothing to do but wait, sleep was doubly welcome.

Kates was back on CNN. "Within the past few minutes, two of the major networks have called the election in President Taylor's favor. But Governor Armstrong is making a respectable showing, so we're not quite prepared to go along and call the result yet."

Jack nudged Elizabeth. "Honey, it's not looking very good."

"Is it over?" she asked groggily.

"Not quite yet. Two of the networks have called it, but CNN hasn't."

"Clint, are you working on some kind of a concession speech?"

"I did one to vent some hostility early on in the campaign. I'd be sorry to have to use it."

"You've got to get some rest," Jack insisted, touching her cheek gently with his fingertips.

"No, I want to see this to the end," she insisted.

"Okay. All of us are taking little catnaps. I'll check on you in a couple of minutes."

Elizabeth closed her eyes, but could not tune out the voices of the commentators. One way or another she would have to take action soon. She nodded off, believing she had lost and trying to adjust to that fact. A little later, not knowing how much time had passed, she snapped to alertness as she heard the words "surprise turn of events in the election." CNN cut to a commercial.

Grossman raised his eyebrows but said nothing. Delacruse sighed. Elizabeth jiggled Amy's shoulder and woke Jack. They roused each other. Gulping some coffee, they waited for the commercials to end.

Kates talked over graphics showing the voting breakdown. Finally he concluded, "Elizabeth Armstrong is the next president of the United States."

A shout of victory went up in the room drowning out the rest of Kates' statistical analysis. No one here cared how narrow the win had been — it was a win!

"Madame President," said Jack with a smile. "You sure are a mess. Your mascara is more on your cheeks than your eyes. And your hair looks like it's been through a tornado — believe me, I know what that's like!" Elizabeth was elated.

"You're the next president! I'm the United States' first first gentleman!" Jack was laughing and shouting, but her expression remained suspicious.

They calmed down a bit and listened to Kates' recap. "Armstrong eked it out in the electoral college. She won both California and Texas. Those states put her over the top. She won both states by less than a combined total of 100,000 votes. Her husband's memory helped in Texas. Sonoma bolstered California. Despite ending up slightly behind in the popular vote, Armstrong has won."

"We expect the president to make his concession speech any minute."

Elizabeth was now wide awake.

"Well, what are we waiting for? Let's get organized." She started thinking quickly.

"The press is still camped out at your campaign headquarters," Grossman told her. "The count took so long, it's pretty dead down there."

"Well, call out the troops," said Elizabeth. "Just give me five minutes to straighten up."

"Yes, Madame President," said Grossman and Jack in unison.

45

TO THE VICTOR

N O SOONER HAD Elizabeth closed the bathroom door than Jack burst in. "You better get out here, pronto! There's an important story breaking."

The pipes squealed as she shut the water down. She rushed out and they watched together.

The news anchor read off the monitor. "We have a late breaking story. There has been an automobile accident just outside the beltway that has taken the life of the vice-presidential candidate, General Frank Shotwell. For live coverage, let's go now to the scene."

The cameras switched to a Virginia state trooper. He stood near an overpass surrounded by rolling wooded country. Off to the side was a broken guard rail.

"That looks like the George Washington Parkway," Elizabeth commented.

The reporter asked the obvious. "Officer, can you tell us what has happened here?"

"It appears General Shotwell's car went through the guard rail, rolled down an embankment and came to rest near the edge of the Potomac River."

"Can you tell us anything about the cause of the accident?"

"It's still under investigation, but I can tell you that the car was apparently traveling at an extremely high rate of speed. There are no skid marks."

"What are your conclusions then about the cause of the accident?"

"I can't speculate while the investigation is continuing. There will be an autopsy and toxicology reports."

"Does there being no skid marks imply this was a suicide?"

"You know I can't answer a question like that."

Jack turned to Elizabeth. There was a lot they wanted to say to each other, but couldn't with others around.

The phone rang. Grossman answered immediately. Taking the phone away from his ear, he cupped the receiver, "Governor Armstrong, it's the president."

Amy quipped, "That's President-elect Armstrong. And it's the soon-to-be former president."

Taylor's voice was weary and resigned. "Congratulations, Elizabeth."

"Thank you, Mr. President."

"I'll be delivering my concession speech in about fifteen minutes, but I wanted to call and congratulate you personally. You ran a hell of a campaign. Frankly, I think the better person won. This may well be the best result for the country."

"Thank you. The comments I made the other day about you and my respect for you were sincere. I still feel that way."

"Thank you. That's nice of you to say. You heard about Shotwell."

"We just saw it on the news."

"I know the possibility of this being less than coincidental crossed your mind. I want you to know our government was not involved in his death. Even more importantly, we're getting some preliminary indications that the hostages may be released. We'll set up a communication link to ensure that you are constantly informed."

"I appreciate that, Mr. President. I also wanted to talk to you about Larkin."

"He's already in custody."

"In custody?"

"Yes. Now that the race is over and I've lost, I decided to do your new administration a favor. I'm initiating an investigation of General Shotwell's activities. I expect that within the next couple of months, well before the inauguration, we'll get to the bottom of this. Your administration will start with a clean slate. This will solve a problem for both of our parties. My party will be perceived as cleaning its own house before leaving office. Yours will avoid being perceived as engaging in vindictive investigations of the prior administration. I think that would be the best approach for the country. Don't you agree?"

"Mr. President, I appreciate your efforts. I'd like to make sure that I'm constantly advised on the progress of the investigation."

"Without question."

"Gordon, I don't suppose you had anything to do with the media blitz being pulled."

His silence answered her question.

She thanked him again adding, "You're an even better man than I thought."

As she hung up, Elizabeth heard a knock at the door. Grossman opened it, revealing a young woman escorted by a female Secret Service Agent. She was carrying a shallow basket containing shampoo, scissors, combs, brushes, hair spray and other paraphernalia.

"My present, Elizabeth," said Jack. "A president should have an expert to comb her hair!"

Minutes later Elizabeth was dressed and prepared to meet the press. Delacruse practically bowed as he showed her to the door. *Power changes everything,* she thought.

"Amy and Jack, I want you next to me. We're meeting the others at the elevator door and we are likely to be ambushed before we ever get to campaign headquarters."

"Mom, don't you think that you should say this was a great day for women? After all, you're America's first woman president. Your position in history is guaranteed."

"I don't know, Amy. That really had very little to do with why I ran."

"I know, but it's still a significant milestone in American history. People will want to know how you feel about it."

As they walked down the hall, Elizabeth continued. "In four years, it's not going to make any difference whether I was a man or a woman. I just need to do a good job."

Jack took her hand. "You shouldn't downplay what you've accomplished. Every election is bigger than the individual candidates and involves events they can't control. The most important factor above all is who you are. You can't forget that."

"Thanks, Jack."

Excitement charged the air as the group arrived at their head-quarters. The troops had returned jubilant.

The group strode up onto the stage and into the brilliance of the camera lights. Elizabeth waved at the assembled throng, her face radiant. She spent several minutes reaching down to shake the hands of well-wishers. The room continued to fill with people. When she approached the podium, cheering and applause broke out. She stood silently until her presence commanded the crowd to quiet down.

When she could hear the banners wave, she began. "There are many, many people to thank for this great victory. First, let me thank the campaign workers here and across the country whose tireless efforts made this possible." As she gestured to the audience, the campaign workers mixed into the crowd cheered and applauded.

"I also wish to offer special thanks to my running mate, John Sonoma and his wife and family for all the support that they've lent to this campaign." Again, applause broke out. "Finally, special thanks to my friends and family, and especially to my daughter Amy and to my dear husband Jack, without whose support this effort would have been utterly impossible. There is another person whom I wish to mention and that is my former husband, Peter Armstrong, whose legacy is with me." She smiled at Jack, no longer needing to fight back tears.

Cheering and clapping again filled the room until she began again. "I have spoken to President Taylor. He has been extremely gracious. He offered his full cooperation with regard to the hostage situation in Venezuela and the transition of power."

The crowd grew quiet, as if everyone knew that the next words would be significant. "This was a great victory. I see a victory of progressive ideas, of integrity, and of the unification of the American people. I see a strong America moving into a new century. But I have no feeling of triumph today. Rather, I have a feeling of solemn responsibility about leading this nation well. The great objective of this administration will be bringing the American people together. This will be an open administration. Open to new ideas, open to men and women of both parties, open to critics as well as those who support us. I want to bring America together."

The crowd rose to its feet in a thunderous ovation. Out of the corner of her eye, Elizabeth caught a glimpse of Jack and

Amy. He had his arm around her, and both were smiling from ear to ear. She was swept with emotion.

As the tumult began to subside, she again focused on the crowd. "At face value, my election is a milestone in American politics. The world has produced some great women leaders. Now the people of the United States have elected a woman president. But this presidency will not be only about women. It will be about stability and peace in the world. It will be about a stronger domestic economy. It will be about compassion and opportunity for all of our citizens, regardless of their gender, race, or political affiliation. The significance of my election will be that in future presidential elections, a candidate's gender will no longer be considered remarkable or unusual. I intend that as my legacy."

The audience rose to its feet, cheering and applauding. The new president of the United States had taken charge — President Elizabeth Armstrong.

CORINTHIAN
BOOKS

Write your own book review!

We love to hear from our readers, and we pass along all the reviews to the authors. Tell us what you liked. Tell us what moved you. Tell us what you found most provocative!

Send your reviews to Corinthian Books, P.O. Box 1898, Mt. Pleasant, SC 29465 USA or e-mail them to:

reviews@corinthianbooks.com

Thank you!